MAGGIE DOVE
AND
THE LOST BRIDES

SUSAN BREEN

Maggie Dove and the Lost Brides

Copyright © 2021 by Susan Breen. All Rights Reserved.

For information about this title or to order other books and/or electronic media, contact the publisher:

Under the Oak Press
Irvington, NY

Paperback ISBN: 978-1-7373172-5-8
eBook ISBN: 978-1-7373172-7-2

Publisher's Cataloging-In-Publication Data
(Prepared by The Donohue Group, Inc.)

Names: Breen, Susan (Susan Jean), author.
Title: Maggie Dove and the lost brides / Susan Breen.
Description: Irvington, NY : Under the Oak Press, [2021] |
Series: Maggie Dove ; [3]
Identifiers: ISBN 9781737317258 (paperback) |
ISBN 9781737317272 (ebook)
Subjects: LCSH: Women detectives--New York (State)--Westchester
County--Fiction. | Brides--New York (State)--Westchester
County--Fiction. | Missing persons--New York (State)--Westchester
County--Fiction. | Murder--Investigation--Fiction. | LCGFT: Cozy
mysteries.
Classification: LCC PS3552.R36466 M343 2021 (print) | LCC PS3552.
R36466 (ebook) | DDC 813/.6--dc23

For my Savannah Rose

Chapter One

Maggie Dove had never believed that a wedding was the happiest day of a woman's life. Happiness, she thought, like grief, could not be scheduled. Her husband's touch one long-ago night when they danced under a full moon. The sound of her daughter's bat when she slammed her first home run out of the park and into the Hudson River. A friend's whispered confidence. A cat's soft fur brushing against her cheek. An oak tree's sudden burst into leaf. These were the memories that popped into her head far more frequently than the details of her wedding day.

However, even from that philosophical vantage point, Bethany Coleman's wedding was shaping up to be a disaster.

Everything that could have gone wrong had done so, and the bride hadn't even walked down the aisle yet. First of all was the snowstorm that slammed down the Hudson Valley early that January morning. The sanctuary reverberated with the sound of plows. The organist couldn't make it down to church, so Bethany had to scramble for a substitute, and came up with a gentleman who played at a funeral pace. To cap it all off, the Rolls Royce that was supposed to carry the bride and groom to the reception came whistling to a stop at the front of the church and immediately broke down. Smoke filled the sanctuary, mixing unpleasantly with the floral aromas, causing everyone to cough.

The most patient person in the world would have been sorely tried by the events of the day, but Bethany Coleman was famous for her lack of patience. She was both hot-tempered and oversensitive, a toxic combination. Years ago, when she'd been one of Maggie's Sunday School students, more than one class had ended with Bethany in tears.

She would not take this well, Maggie felt confident.

That must be why the wedding was delayed in starting. Somewhere, Bethany was festering, even as her groom, Graham Lockwood, stood patiently at the front of the church, and Maggie sat in the front row, waiting to be called up to read the Scriptures. Another unexpected twist to the wedding, the honor of being asked to read.

Well, on the bright side, Maggie was pleased with the way she looked. She'd found a stunning lavender dress at the last Attic sale and she'd paired that with a sheer pink shawl. She probably should have waited until Easter to wear the outfit, but she was so tired of the snow and slush and dreariness of winter, and she wanted to glow. She wanted color.

"There she is," she heard a voice boom behind her. She turned to smile. Her fellow detectives had arrived, and were making their way into the pew.

First came Helen Blake, dressed in a simple black tunic, her attention focused on a message on her phone, though she did look up quickly and grin at Maggie. "Very fetch," she whispered.

"Thank you," Maggie said, just as Helen's seven-year-old son, Edgar, vaulted past his mother and onto Maggie's lap.

He was going through a cat phase and licking everything. It was not as bad, nor as painful, as his rattlesnake phase, but it didn't feel exactly sanitary. Then came Agnes Jorgenson, dressed in white, for whatever reason. She so loved to be a spectacle. Thank heavens, Maggie thought, she hadn't put on a veil.

Agnes perched herself at the end of the pew to block anyone else from sitting with them. Maggie noticed a bit of grease on her hem, which meant she must have stopped to help with the Rolls Royce. A kind act. Funny how Agnes liked to keep her good deeds to herself. Why would it be so embarrassing to be considered a good person?

"Is the car fixed?" Maggie asked her, but before Agnes could reply, the sound of Bethany yelling seeped into the church.

"I told you that you should hire something first rate. You've always got to be so cheap about everything."

Someone buzzed a reply, most likely Bethany's father. Meanwhile everyone in the church began to shift around awkwardly.

"I don't care how much it cost," Bethany yelled back. "I told you to get the deluxe model. Now we have this cheap piece of junk and how am I going to get to the reception? I'm not driving there in a Subaru, I can tell you that."

The gentle groom began to shift back and forth. He'd been standing at the front of the church for the last twenty minutes. He couldn't go back and help his bride because he couldn't risk seeing her in her gown, but Maggie doubted anyone but Graham could calm down Bethany. In fact, Graham Lockwood was probably the one person in the world who would marry Bethany. He was one of those gentle down-trodden souls, a walking Eeyore, the youngest of five rough-and-tumble sons. He was the bookkeeper for the family landscaping business. Maggie's main recollection of him as a Sunday School student was the time his brothers tossed him into the church trash bin and she'd had to go fish him out. They were a tumultuous bunch, those Lockwoods.

"This is my special day," Bethany shouted. "And you've ruined it."

Maggie had a sort of elemental desire to restore order. That was why, she supposed, her private detective business was thriving. Probably also why church rules never bothered her. But she couldn't think of anything to do to restore order in this situation. She'd learned the hard way that when Bethany was upset, the only recourse was to let her shout it out. But the tumult disturbed her. She could feel the sound waves battering her, creating waves of anxiety. It was the same feeling as when a plane hit turbulence, the sudden understanding that things can go terribly wrong. The memory of a phone call. *"I'm sorry Mrs. Dove. Your daughter's been in an accident."*

She exhaled sharply.

"You okay, Maggie Dove?" Edgar whispered.

She looked down into his little pinched face. "Yes, my lamb" she whispered.

He tucked his hand into her's, but then Helen snapped at him. "Sit down, Edgar, and get off Maggie Dove's lap. You'll muss her up."

"Really, Helen. It's all right."

"No, it's not. He's got to learn how to behave," she said, and snapped Edgar off Maggie's lap onto the seat alongside her. He hunched over slightly, began chewing on his lip. Maggie knew she was right. Edgar was out of control, but there was an edge to Helen's anger that was running sharper.

Fortunately, at that moment, the Reverend Sunday came striding down the aisle. She walked up to Graham and patted him on the back, whispered something to him. He flushed and smiled.

Then the Reverend Sunday turned toward the congregation and lifted her arms. She wore an embroidered wedding stole which she'd brought from her home country of Ghana. "We're ready to begin," she called out. "Yes?"

"Yes!" the congregation called back, and so the organist began to play, a little less slowly, and the ceremony began.

First the ring bearer vaulted out from the back of the church, as though kicked, followed by the flower girl, who tossed rose petals in all directions. Then came the bridal party, dressed in maroon velvet, carrying bouquets of ivory rose and baby's breath. Each of the bridesmaids was married to one of the Lockwood brothers. No friends as bridesmaids, Maggie noticed. But then came the maid of honor, Eleanor Hunt, a local celebrity. Her father was a prominent New York politician. She and Bethany had been in the same Sunday School class and must have stayed friends.

The father of the bride walked down the aisle clutching his wife's hand. They looked, Maggie thought, more in love than the bride and groom.

Then came a column of Coleman police officers. Three generations of Bethany's family had served in the Darby police department and most of the Coleman cousins were in some form of law-enforcement, from the FBI to the Coast Guard. They strode down the aisle, regal in bearing, all of them with the red Coleman complexion and the jutting Coleman chin. Maggie'd always been surprised that Bethany hadn't become a police officer herself, but instead she chose to become a loan officer at the local bank.

Lastly came Bethany, who burst out the doors like a bull at a rodeo. Her face was a little red from hollering, but she had the pleased expression of a woman who knows she's the center of attention. She wore a gorgeous ruffled gown that she had the height to carry off. Her thick brown hair was twisted up into an elaborate style. Her eyes were stunning. She must have gone to the new cosmetician who'd just opened a store on Main Street. She looked like a cat with her eyes outlined in brown.

Automatically Maggie turned to Graham to see his reaction. She loved to watch a groom's face when he saw a bride for the first time. She remembered the gaze on her own husband's face when she walked down this very aisle more than four decades ago. Graham did not disappoint. He teared up.

Then Bethany got to the front of the aisle. Her father moved forward to kiss her, but she brushed him off. Not a woman who wanted to be given away. Instead, she grabbed onto Graham's waiting hand, which she raised victoriously. As though she'd won a wrestling match.

Reverend Sunday beamed at them both and began to speak and Maggie began preparing herself to stand up and read. She wasn't a nervous public speaker. Once she got to the lectern, she knew she'd be fine, but it was anticipation that made her anxious. She looked over toward the stained-glass windows. It was only 4:00 in the afternoon, but the sun was starting to set. The Tiffany windows that adorned the church began to shimmer with light. She breathed in deeply, trying to find the calm she knew was somewhere inside her. Somewhere.

Then the reverend beckoned her forward.

Maggie walked toward the lectern, flipped on the microphone. The large church Bible was open to the appropriate page from First Corinthians.

Maggie paused for a moment to smile at Bethany and Graham, and then to look out at the congregation. The sanctuary was full. There, in front of her, were so many of the people she loved: Sunday School students, neighbors, friends. The chief of police, Walter Campbell, was sitting without his wife, which was interesting. He cocked his head and smiled at her. Victoria Spencer was there. The biopsy must have gone well. The Finnigans were entwined with each other. There had been complaints that they were too affectionate in church. Reverend Sunday had laughed over that. Maggie wondered where Walter's wife had gone. Only a few weeks ago she'd been sitting next to him.

Maggie turned her attention back to the Bible and began to read the well-loved words.

"Love is patient," she read. "Love is kind."

From the back of the church, she heard a sound. Maggie looked up, surprised. It sounded like laughter.

"It does not envy," she continued. "It does not boast."

Now Maggie was certain she heard laughter, but couldn't see where it was coming from. People started rustling around nervously. A few people giggled. Maggie looked over to Reverend Sunday, who motioned for her to keep going.

"It is not proud. It does not dishonor others."

She could hear the laughter growing, didn't know what to do. She glared toward the back of the church, thinking if she caught the perpetrator's eye, she could put a stop to this, but before she could go further, Bethany turned to the congregation and yelled. "How dare you?" she shouted. "How dare you pack of losers mock me?"

Then she flung aside her bouquet, charged down the aisle and out the door.

Chapter Two

Maggie felt sure Bethany would return. In her experience of life, brides did not go stalking into the snow in full wedding regalia and disappear. Yet, an hour passed and she didn't come back.

Graham had chased her, of course. He'd gone tearing down the aisle as soon as Bethany slammed open the door to the street. But she had a car waiting. The Rolls Royce was warmed up and ready to go, whereas Graham's Subaru was snowed into the parking lot behind the church. By the time he got his car cleared off, Bethany had a ten minute head start.

They'd all sat there, in the sanctuary, waiting for Graham to return with Bethany. Confident that Graham would find her and soothe her and marry her and go to St. Lucia on their honeymoon and probably get a divorce two years later. It was just hard to imagine Bethany walking away from all that planning. All that money. But an hour into the wait, one of the Lockwood brothers got a call that Graham had driven into a snow drift. He needed help.

His brothers, laughing, went out to retrieve him. It would all be a great joke to them, Maggie suspected. He'd always been the family joke. "Too Slow," they called him. Or, "The Mistake." Seven years younger than his next oldest brother. He'd tried to leave Darby. He'd signed up for the Army, but had vertigo. He signed up to work as a park ranger, but got bit by a rabid squirrel. He'd signed up to work on a cruise ship, but the company went bankrupt. Finally, Graham surrendered and came back to Darby.

Poor Graham would never get over this, Maggie thought. He had just inadvertently entered the Darby Screw-up Hall of Fame.

Not long after the Lockwood brothers departed, Bethany's parents walked, hand in hand, to the front of the church. Unlike everyone else in the sanctuary, they looked calm. They thanked everyone for coming, but suggested that, under the circumstances, it would be best for everyone to go home. "I apologize for my daughter's behavior," Ben Coleman said. "I'm sorry to have wasted your time."

Then he put his arm around his wife and the two of them walked down the aisle and out the front door, which Maggie found, in its own way, just as shocking as Bethany's more vigorous departure. What happened to seeing things through to the end? Only an hour had gone by since the wedding was scheduled to start. They were ready to write off the whole thing so quickly?

Agnes thought they should all go out drinking, as long as they were all dressed up. Disaster excited her. One of her happiest memories was of getting stuck in an earthquake in San Francisco and narrowly missing getting hit by a falling beam. She thrived on tumult, but Maggie didn't share her enthusiasm. She liked things to go forward in an orderly fashion. She liked for things that started to come to an end. For weddings to end happily. For children to grow up strong. For the world to get along. For no telephone calls in the night, for no sudden implosions of life. She also didn't like the idea of staggering around drunk in the middle of a snow storm.

So she excused herself and started to walk home, but then suddenly Walter Campbell was at her side. For a large man, he had a way of appearing out of nowhere. He didn't offer an explanation. Didn't ask if she wanted company. He just walked alongside her for the five blocks back to her house. His legs were much longer than hers, but he matched her pace, and his large presence blocked the wind. She actually felt a little warmer with him beside her.

They trudged over the slippery sidewalks, him reaching out to grab her at one point when she might have slipped forward, and then they were at her house. Climbing up the steps to her porch, which were deep with snow. Joe Mangione would be by later to shovel. Her cats were silhouetted in the window, their dark shapes against her lace curtains.

"Would you like to come inside?" she said. "I could make some tea. Or something stronger."

"I'd love to," he said. "But I can't. Have to get back to the police station. Just in case."

"You think Bethany's in trouble?"

He grinned. "She's definitely in trouble, but I imagine she's checked into a hotel somewhere. If she'd crashed, I would have heard."

"I guess that's comforting."

"You okay?" he asked. He wasn't a handsome man, and yet he had the gift of focusing, which was very appealing. When he asked you a question, you sensed that he would wait a good long time for you to answer.

"Yes," she said, because it was pointless to say that she felt numb with anxiety. That she was convinced that Bethany had come to some great harm because in her experience the worst thing that could happen generally did. That that awful laughter really bothered her. It menaced. It was out of proportion, forced, angry. Ominous.

"Everything's fine," she said, but she didn't feel that that was true. Not for herself and definitely not for Bethany Coleman.

Chapter Three

It was not yet 6:00 by the time Maggie walked into her house. Way too early to go to bed, but her eyes felt so heavy. Her body felt like it was still moving through snow. She hung up her coat and kicked off her shoes, and then she went up the steps, the cats following her. She didn't even bother to wash up or change. She just lay down in bed and pulled the comforter over her. Kosi nestled in alongside of her, grabbing the premium spot by her stomach, and Shadow lay toward the tip of the bed. He was a rescue and even though he'd lived with her for months, he was still skittish. Wouldn't let her pet him. Did not like to be confined in any way. He lay like a sphinx, head raised, front paws stretched in front of him, and he was in that position when she woke up at 1:30 in the morning.

Immediately Maggie looked at her phone, but there were no missed calls. So Bethany had not reappeared. Pellets of snow shattered against the window. The airports must be closed down. The roads impassable. Where could she be?

Maggie thought of how carefully the details for the wedding had been arranged. The ivory rose and baby's breath bouquets hanging from the end of each pew. The candles flickering at the front of the church, the waterfall of roses. The printed program for each guest, the baskets of mints for those who might cough. How horrible to pin such hopes to the day, and then to be so disappointed, and then to make such a fool of yourself, and then to have those parents so quick to throw in the towel. She whispered a prayer for her. Dear Lord, please protect that foolish girl.

Snow swirled against her window. There was no way she would get back to sleep. Instead, Maggie got up and took a long, hot shower. When she was done, she smoothed lotion all over her; she could feel her dry skin sucking it in. She put on her warmest pajamas and a new pair of socks she'd bought that had aloe in them, and then she went downstairs, the cats darting in front of her as she walked. They were hungry, and so she put out some dry food for them, and some water, which they immediately began to bat at, sprinkling puddles onto the kitchen floor. Maggie wasn't particularly hungry herself, and yet she hadn't had dinner.

The prospect that she might feel hungry in the future bothered her. She had some banana bread in the freezer and she figured she could warm that up and put some butter on it. Boil up some tea, and then, when she had done that, and had settled down at her kitchen table, she looked over to the clock on the wall and saw that it was 2:00.

The Insomnia Club!

Leona Faraday had just been telling her about it. They were a group of friends from the village who congregated on Facebook every night at 2:00, and watched Jeopardy. They'd started it up to help Polly Nathan, whose baby had colic and was causing her no end of stress. But others had joined in. The Faraday sisters, who would join anything. Members of the ambulance corps, who were often up at night. Some random person named Adele. Joe Mangione, who never seemed to sleep. And Maggie had been invited. She hadn't tried it yet but it seemed like a better plan than lying awake all night and worrying about death.

She picked up her plate and went into her den, which had once been her husband's study. She'd put the TV in there, which she knew he would dislike, but one could have only so many arguments with a man who'd been gone for twenty years. She'd kept all his books, anyway, so it still had quite a bit of his vibe. Plus, she was certain she could smell his pipe when she sat there. Then she went over to the TV and turned it on to the Game Show Network. Fortunately, it was a commercial and they were showing a woman who'd fallen in the bathtub. Then she logged onto Facebook and into the private Insomnia Club group.

She saw the gang was all there, and immediately welcomes began bubbling up.

"What do I do?" Maggie typed in.

"Put your TV on pause," Leona typed back. "NOW."

It turned out that the rules of the game were to hit pause on the TV every time Alex Trebek asked a question. It was an episode from several years ago and you could probably google the answers, but it didn't really matter. It wasn't about the competition.

They would then type in their answers, then unpause the TV and see the correct response. Whoever had posted the right answer first, won. Then they would unpause the TV again. Maggie suspected it would take an hour and a half to watch a half hour show.

"Why do I feel like there's an easier way to do this?" Maggie said, though there was no one to hear her except for two cats who clearly disapproved of game shows, though they did seem interested in Alex Trebek. Part cat, she suspected.

She felt much better by the time the game ended, especially because she knew the Final Jeopardy answer. It was in the category of Ancient Egyptian Customs. *When a pharaoh died, his heart was carved out and replaced with a stone rendering of this little creature.* "What is the dung beetle?" Maggie shouted out, accessing that tidbit from some deep part of her mind, and everyone was so amazed with her they clapped, and she felt encouraged for the first time in a while.

This time when she went to bed, she slept until 8:00 a.m., only waking up when Agnes called.

"I'm not going into the office today," Agnes said. "Don't even try. The roads are treacherous."

"Any word about Bethany?"

"No, nothing. No sign of her. Disappeared into thin air. But the Colemans donated all the dinners from the reception to a homeless shelter."

"That's thoughtful," Maggie said.

"Smart," Agnes said. "I bet they can declare it as a tax deduction. Fifty filet mignons, forty chicken breasts, fifteen salmons and one special plate. Which did you order?"

"Salmon," Maggie said. Out of principle. She really wanted the steak, but figured the salmon was healthier. Somehow, she'd put on two pounds and she couldn't seem to lose it, though it would probably help if she cut down on calories and increased exercise and stopped eating Swedish pancakes. "How about you?"

"A special plate. I told them I had allergies. They have to make the food up special if you tell them you have allergies."

"I didn't know you had allergies," Maggie said.

"I don't, but why should I get warmed-over food when I can get it made up fresh."

"What if everyone did that?"

"Then everyone would get fresh food."

Maggie noticed Mr. Cavanaugh making his way down her street, his little dog tugging him forward. He seemed such a solitary figure, making his way through the unplowed street. Ten inches must have fallen during the night. She knocked at the window and waved and he waved back. They were the only two people living on the street right now. Her neighbors had gone to Orlando for winter break, and her other neighbors, the van Dorns, had divorced and left their house empty. It seemed remarkable to Maggie that a house in one of the most beautiful neighborhoods in one of the most beautiful villages in the Hudson Valley was sitting empty. But her friend Sibyl, a real estate agent, had explained to her that the divorce was nasty and neither side would pay taxes. Now there was a lien on the house and no one wanted to buy it. It was a living monument to anger, Maggie thought. An empty hollowed-out space.

"Did you see who laughed?" Maggie asked. She could still hear it, could see the rigid bright hue of Bethany's anger.

"It came from behind me," Agnes said. "I would have thought you'd be able to see it though, standing up front."

"That's what I thought too, but I didn't. I heard it, but I didn't see it."

"You were too busy looking at Walter."

"I was looking at the Bible, Agnes. I was reading Scripture."

"Ha."

Maggie pictured Agnes leaning into the phone, grinning. The woman had no sense of personal space, even over the phone.

"*He* was looking at you."

"Now how could you know that? Walter was sitting four rows behind you."

"Ha," Agnes cried out in triumph. "I told you so. You were paying attention to him. Anyway, his wife's gone. For good this time."

"She's left him before."

"But this time it's for good. I hear there's a neurosurgeon involved. With a Central Park practice. No, our police chief is yours for the taking."

"Honestly, Agnes, he's not low-hanging fruit."

That unfortunate image set Agnes off, and Maggie knew there was no point to pursuing the conversation. It could only go downhill.

"Call me if you hear anything," she said.

"You'll be the first."

It was just 9:00. Already shaping into the world's longest day. Maggie could simply not believe that Bethany had driven off into a storm and that she was perfectly fine, but if she wasn't fine, surely someone would have discovered her.

Anyway, Maggie had work she needed to do. She was in the midst of a big project for Darby Savings & Loan. They were hiring two new tellers and they wanted Maggie to check out the applicants' resumes, find out if they had criminal records, whether they'd actually graduated from where they said they had, and whether they had good post-employment records. It wasn't exciting work, but it was a bit like doing a jigsaw puzzle, putting together all the pieces of who a person was.

She supposed they'd be hiring a new loan officer too, if Bethany didn't come back. Maggie'd actually spent a lot of time at the bank lately, sitting in the empty office alongside Bethany's. There was always so much noise coming out of Bethany's office. So different than the rest of the bank, which had a library's hush. Bethany never spoke when she could yell. No handshakes for Bethany. Her greetings were more like body wrestling. She bellowed questions. Maggie loved listening to the new customers, who always sounded a little terrified when they entered her office. Bethany's walls were covered with old maps of Darby, pictures of the Colemans, awards for most loans issued. She couldn't picture her walking away from that.

Unless, she planned to reemerge victorious. With a handsome new lover by her side? Or more likely with some form of pay-back against the people who'd wounded her.

But a wedding seemed like an awfully elaborate form of pay-back.

Pointless to just sit worrying. There were things she could do to check up on her. She checked into Facebook, but Bethany hadn't posted anything new since right before the wedding. "Getting my eyes done!!!"

The most likely thing was that she was at a hotel, and it happened that one of Maggie's former Sunday School students worked at a hotel directly on the route. So she called her, but she had no record of Bethany checking in. She called the two other hotels in the neighborhood, but she'd not checked in there either. Just a bunch of people from Con Ed who were there to do repair work. She also called the local hospitals, even though she assumed Walter would do that. Good to be sure. Then she called the morgue, but no one answered. Finally, she logged onto the local traffic web cam. Maggie looked for a bit, but saw no shot of a Rolls Royce heading north. Maybe it had gone south. She'd assumed it was going north because that was the direction in which it was pointed, but she supposed she could have turned around and then head south, toward New York City. She looked out the window at her little oak tree, which seemed to have flung its branches up in surrender.

That was when Maggie noticed Cecily Embers wading through the snow, mail pouch slung around her neck.

Maggie opened her front door. A blast of wind almost knocked her off her feet.

"Cecily," she called out. "Come on in out of the cold and have some coffee."

"I can't, Mrs. D.," she called back. "I'm behind on my rounds. But you could fill my mug if you like."

"Of course," Maggie said, beckoning Cecily inside while she went and brewed a fresh pot of coffee.

Cecily stood in the entry way, stomping her feet. She'd wound a scarf round and round her face so that only her brown eyes were visible. Her hands were encased in gloves that looked appropriate for a logger. She wore heavy boots. She smelled of gum, always snapping bubbles. Maggie poured the hot coffee into her mug, and Cecily handed her a stack of letters.

"You got one of your blue notes," she said. "And this one's marked urgent."

Then she waved good bye and went back into the snow, leaving Maggie holding a bomb. Or the epistolary equivalent of it.

Chapter Four

Every month Maggie's brother-in-law, Linus Dove, wrote her a note on blue stationery, though he didn't generally mark the letter urgent. He was not an urgent sort of person. He lived according to the centuries, not the minutes. His entire family, his wife and daughter, did not approve of the 21st century and were not convinced by the 20th. Maggie believed that Linus Dove felt time stopped somewhere around Thomas Jefferson. He taught ancient languages at a small college in Indiana.

What could urgent possibly mean in that context?

Nothing good. She felt confident of that. Someone had died, or was about to. Could it be Livy? She thought of that pale spindly girl who she'd last seen when she was ten. Maggie'd dragged Linus and Livy and his wife around Manhattan, taking them to the Metropolitan Museum and the Empire State building and the Statue of Liberty, and the whole time they'd spoken to each other in ancient Greek or occasionally in some made-up language that their immediate family used. She took Livy to the M&M center, just to see the look on Linus's face when they told her what flavor of M&M she was.

Red. She could only take so much ancient Greek, and when they'd left, she'd settled on the couch and watched TV for days. That was in her dark period. Before the detective agency, before much of anything, when all she did was mourn the loss of her husband and daughter, and teach Sunday School.

What if something was wrong with Livy?

Livy hooked up to a respirator. Livy in a car accident. Livy needing a kidney transplant. Good grief, did everyone's mind go in such directions?

Of course, she could just rip up the letter. Letters did disappear, and at the rate Linus wrote, he wouldn't even realize she hadn't answered until February and by then whatever was so urgent would have resolved itself. But that seemed cowardly, and she really preferred not to be a coward.

All right, she would read the letter, but first she wanted to have something to eat. Something tasty. She decided to make some German pancakes. She cracked three eggs into a bowl, then microwaved some butter. Poured that into the bowl, whipped in some flour, then placed the whole molten mess into the oven. Then she clicked on the light and watched it cook.

The batter began to bubble and rise. The house filled with the aroma of butter. When the pancake had risen as high as it could, she carefully lifted the pan out of the oven and then she shook confectioners' sugar all over it. Then she put the whole thing on a plate and ate it. This was no time for half measures, and when the whole thing was gone, and her fingers sweet with sugar, and she felt warm and full, she picked up the letter and went into the living room, which was her favorite room in the house.

The couch was upholstered in a floral pattern that Agnes dismissed as 1950s British knock-off, but Maggie embraced as 1950s British knock-off. She loved those pink and violet swirls. Sometimes she fancied she could smell them.

The backs of the sofa were covered with doilies her great-grandmother tatted. In a silver frame was a picture of her daughter dressed as Princess Anastasia and Maggie's husband dressed as Tsar Nicholas. Maggie'd dressed up as Rasputin that Halloween and made huge batches of hot dogs for the trick or treaters. At the far end of the room was a china cabinet filled with cups and saucers. Everything in the room rattled slightly. By each window was a perch for the cats. They loved to curl up there and stare out the window.

Now, finally, she was ready to open the letter.

The gum stuck tightly. He must have licked it a lot. She tore it open and withdrew a blue linen notecard.

My dear Maggie Dove,

I regret causing you worry, but I'm sorry to tell you that Livy has been abandoned by her fiancé. She's in some distress, and, remembering how much fun she had with you during our last visit, Nora and I hoped you would be amenable to hosting her over mid-winter break. If possible, we would like to send her this Sunday. Please let me know if that would be convenient.

Fondly, Linus Dove

Maggie read the letter three times, but didn't get anything more out of it the third time than the first.

Who knew Livy was engaged, for one thing? Who knew she'd had fun with Maggie? And was he suggesting he'd already bought the ticket. It seemed so cavalier to buy a ticket without checking, and the Doves were not at all cavalier people. They were doting, serious people and they revered Livy. She was the center of their world. So the notion that they would pack up their daughter and send her to New York was unfathomable. She must be in bad shape. This *was* an urgent situation, Maggie thought.

She found Linus's number in her address book, written in her husband's hand. She pushed in the number and almost jumped when Linus answered on the second ring.

"Oh Maggie," he said. "Thank you for getting back to me so quickly. This is a great relief, a great relief."

She sank down into the cushions of her couch. She pressed her legs together tightly. Across from her grinned her husband and daughter dressed in their Russian attire. The photograph was so old they might actually have been real Russian monarchs.

"We've been in such desperate shape and then Nora suggested your name and I thought, and please forgive the cliché, you were an answer to a prayer. Or perhaps it's not a cliché to you?"

"What's happening?"

"I don't know. Livy won't talk to me. She won't discuss with me why they separated. It's as though she no longer trusts me. I feel as though a wall has risen up between us. I can't help her and I blame myself. I'm the one who introduced her to Shiv. I thought they were perfect for each other. An outstanding young man. Star of my department. A great future in front of him, and his research tied in so perfectly with Livy's. Now it's all fallen apart. She's devastated. She can't work. Her career is crumbling and then we thought, well. Maggie Dove. She could bring some fun back into Livy's life."

"Linus, I can say in all honestly that you are the first person in decades to look to me for fun."

"You'll be perfect," he said. "You were always so good with Juliet."

That brought Maggie up short. Had it been anyone else she would have thought he was trying to manipulate her, but the Doves were not that way. They were proud and arrogant. They loved Scavenger games and lost languages. They actually did argue over how many angels were on the head of a pin. But they were not manipulative. He would not bring up her late daughter's name to guilt her into doing him a favor.

"Juliet," she said. She so loved to hear her daughter's name said out loud. It happened so rarely now.

"I always envied you your relationship with Juliet," Linus said. "I always loved the way you two could laugh together. Remember the time you and she went bowling and you got the ball stuck on your finger and she kept trying to put ketchup on it to get it out and then the police came because they thought you were bleeding."

Maggie'd completely forgotten.

"I don't think I've laughed so hard in my life. Livy was only three years old at the time, but she kept talking about it. She always said you were the only member of our family who knew how to enjoy yourself. Bring some laughter into my daughter's life. Please Maggie."

She felt insanely touched.

"Just for two weeks," he went on.

How could she possibly say no? "What time is the flight?" she asked.

"Five o'clock," he answered. "Coming into LaGuardia. Thank you so much."

"No trouble," she replied.

"Wait just a minute, Linus," she said, but it was too late. He'd hung up. There was no escape.

The magnitude of what she'd just agreed to do staggered Maggie. It felt like an awesome responsibility. Plus, there was the matter of Bethany. There was a missing young woman in Darby. All right, she'd made herself go missing, but it was odd she hadn't reappeared yet. She could have come to harm. It was strange, it was worrisome. What if she was exposing Livy to danger?

Just then one of her cats went flying by, landing right on top of a tea cup that fell to the floor, breaking into shards. Impossible to fix. Hopeless.

Chapter Five

Maggie spent Monday night worrying about Livy's arrival, Juliet's death, whether she should buy new linens for the guest bed, what she'd done with the coupon for Bed, Bath & Beyond, if the headache that burst behind her skull was a brain tumor, and whether Bethany Coleman was trapped somewhere in the snow. Poor Bethany! Maggie slept just long enough to miss the Insomnia Club. Finally fell back asleep ten minutes before the alarm went off. So by the time she got to the detective agency on Tuesday morning, she felt hung over.

She bypassed Agnes, who was yelling something into her phone about an alien abduction, and tiptoed over to the quiet part of the office, at the far end of the cherry-wood table that served as their command center. There Helen sat scanning through her phone.

"How you?" Helen asked.

"Would you say I'm fun?" Maggie asked.

Helen looked away from her phone. "Is this a test?"

"Never mind," Maggie said.

"No, no, no. Of course, you're fun. Are you planning a party? Did Edgar say something?"

Maggie wanted to tell her that Livy was coming, and yet the words lodged in her throat. She couldn't get them out. She felt embarrassed, which was so odd because Helen was the perfect person to talk to about the whole situation. She might well be a good friend to Livy. They were reasonably close in age.

And yet she hesitated. She worried, although she knew she was being ridiculous, that Helen might think she wasn't up to the job. That she might feel Maggie should turn Livy away. That she might think that Maggie was the last person in the world to offer comfort to a troubled young woman, having done such a profoundly bad job with her own daughter. Maggie knew she was being ridiculous and yet anxiety made her shy.

What if something happens to Livy on my watch? she wanted to scream.

"I'm not saying aliens abducted Bethany," Agnes yelled into the phone. "It's just that she did disappear into the blue. And no one's seen her since. You can't argue with that."

"Would you like some tea?" Helen asked.

"That would be nice."

"And I'll bring over the heater for your feet."

On the wall across from Maggie was a huge TV screen. Agnes's latest donation. She kept it always on the local news, which was primarily car crashes and the occasional fire. Now it was all about the weather and the snow clean-up. She wondered if they'd have anything about Bethany.

"Here you go," Helen said, handing Maggie a cup of tea and then sitting down next to her. She wore a T-shirt and jeans, although it was freezing out. Her arms were muscular. Surprisingly strong for such a thin young woman. On her hand she'd written a word with marker.

"Nuclear code?" Maggie asked, nodding toward Helen's hand. Helen worked for the CIA, when she wasn't working for the detective agency.

"No," she said. "Lunch. I wanted to make sure I made a sandwich for Edgar. He does keep eating."

"Children do. Though I thought they served lunch at the school."

"The teacher wants to spend some extra time with Edgar, so she asked me to pack a lunch. He always seems to need extra time and attention. And he has this big project coming up."

"He's in first grade. How big can it be?"

Helen ran her hand through her hair. "He has to write a report about what Darby was like in 1934. Every kid got a year, though of course he's not happy. He wanted 1942, and I guess he had a bit of a snit about it. He can't ever just let anything be."

Maggie put her hand on Helen's arm. "The library has a whole section of old newspapers. I'll take him to do the research. I'm sure he will grow to love 1934."

Helen smiled softly. "Is he allowed into the library? I thought they'd put him on a watch list."

"No, the library forgives all. It's Stop & Shop that won't let him in."

Helen laughed softly. Then her eyes closed briefly, as though she were so exhausted it was impossible to stay awake.

"He went after one of his classmates with a scissor. It was a children's scissor, but still. My father would have got out his belt. Obviously, I'm not going to do that, but some nights, after he goes to bed, I just count the days until he'll be grown up."

Maggie looked at her haggard face. She knew Edgar's father had been someone Helen feared. The pregnancy wasn't wanted. She was a young woman who took her responsibilities seriously, but that didn't mean she had to enjoy them.

Maggie sought to find words of comfort, but before she could say anything, Sibyl the real estate agent came into the office. She was one of Maggie's favorites. A good-natured girl with a hearty laugh and a triple chin.

"Have you heard?" Sibyl cried out.

"What?"

"Bethany cleared out her honeymoon fund. Emptied everything out on Saturday. There's nothing there."

"But she was going on her honeymoon," Maggie said. "Isn't that what the honeymoon fund is for?"

"She took it all in cash. And it's with her, wherever she is. She must have stowed it in the Rolls Royce and driven away with it. She must have planned it all out in advance."

"How much money was there?" Agnes asked.

"Twenty thousand dollars."

"There goes my two hundred," Helen said.

"Mine too," Agnes said.

"Me too," Sibyl said. "How about you Lady Dove. How much did you give?"

"I didn't give her money," Maggie said. "I never like to give money for a wedding. I gave her a cake pan. But it was a really nice one. From Williams Sonoma. It cost $200."

"So somewhere Bethany's roaming around with $20,000 in cash and an expensive cake pan," Agnes said.

"You think she meant to walk away with the money?" Maggie asked, trying to take it in.

Was it possible? Could Bethany have arranged an entire wedding just so that she could disrupt it and run off with $20,000? It seemed ridiculous. The wedding itself must have cost $50,000. But that money came from Bethany's parents, and the Colemans were notoriously cheap. The sort of people who turned off all their lights on Halloween so they wouldn't have to spend money on candy for the trick-or-treaters.

"It would explain why no one's found her," Helen said. "If she planned all this out beforehand, she probably arranged for a place to stay."

"But what about the chauffeur? And the Rolls Royce?" Maggie asked. "And why plan the wedding in the first place? Why not just move away?"

"That's what I want to know," Graham Lockwood said.

They all jumped, none of them having realized he'd come into the office. In fact, Maggie didn't recognize him for a moment. He looked far different than the passive young man standing in front of the church just two days earlier. This Graham looked more like his brothers, ruddier, muscular, as though anger and frustration had taken root in his body.

"That's why I want to hire you," he said. "I can't believe Bethany would have done this."

He was panting as though he'd just run down Main Street. He too must have just got the news about the bank, Maggie realized.

"She set me up," he cried out. "She made me look like a fool."

His words lobbed into the empty air. No one could say anything in response, because it was the truth.

"Please," he said. "Please. You have to find out why she did this to me."

Agnes shrugged. "We'll need a down payment," she said.

"I'll pay you just as soon as I can. She cleared out all my money."

Agnes looked like she might object, but Maggie stepped in front of her. He'd been her Sunday School student. He was in trouble. And she did genuinely want to know what happened to Bethany, especially if her niece was coming to town. "Of course," she said. "We'll find out what happened."

"Ten hours," Agnes said. "That's it."

"Ten hours," he said. "Thank you, Maggie Dove."

But after he left, Agnes shook her head. "It's a waste of time. You'll never find her, and he'll never pay you."

"But think of the good publicity for the agency if I do find her," Maggie said.

Agnes gazed at her suspiciously. "Why are you really doing this, Maggie Dove? What's on your mind?"

"It just sounds like a challenge," she said, because there was no way in this world she was going to tell Agnes about Livy and that she wanted to make sure Darby was safe for her. Not right now. And perhaps a challenge was what she needed. Anything to stifle that terrible fear that was rising up inside her about her niece's arrival.

Chapter Six

"Adults are allowed to disappear," Walter said later that Tuesday afternoon. "It's not against the law. They do it all the time. It's not a crime. Usually, they're fleeing something unendurable to them."

Maggie had walked up to the police station after her meeting with Graham. She figured the first step in her investigation should be to find out what the police had done. Though it turned out the police hadn't done anything much because they were swamped dealing with the side effects of the storm. Neither did Walter seem especially concerned about Bethany's disappearance.

He seemed significantly more preoccupied with arranging his lunch to his satisfaction. He'd put a blue and yellow placemat on his desk. There was wedge of blue-veined cheese on a plate, a loaf of what smelled like fresh baked bread on a cutting board, and a chunk of salami that he'd cut into neat slices. But it was the apple that was drawing his attention. He was focused on it so intently that his eyes crossed slightly, which reminded Maggie of her cats. There was, in fact, something catlike about Walter, something finicky.

Maggie found herself focusing on the apple as well. She'd been a Sunday School teacher for so long that she could not regard an apple without subtext, but she wondered what Adam would have done if Eve had just held the apple and stared at it.

"Often it's because they're fleeing something unendurable to them," he repeated.

"But surely you're doing something," she said. "I mean, it has been more than 24 hours since Bethany disappeared and she did have a lot of cash with her and it's possible something happened to her. Anyway, it was her wedding day. She loved Graham, I think. What's unendurable about that?"

Walter was a nice-looking man, though he didn't seem so at first glance. He was too stern to be handsome. But he had a thick head of hair and the healthy glow of a man who spent a lot of time outdoors and should probably put on more sunscreen. His white shirt was neatly pressed and he always wore his badge.

"There have been eleven accidents in the county since she walked out of the wedding and she hasn't been in any of them. She's not in the morgue and she's not in the hospital. I understand from Elizabeth Prue that you called the local hotels. So, there's not much more I can do."

"Can't you ping her phone or put out a Missing Persons bulletin?"

"She wasn't kidnapped, Maggie. She's not a victim of a crime. She's a woman who didn't want to get married. We all saw her walk out."

"But don't you think it's odd that she hasn't surfaced, and that she had a huge package of money with her?"

"I think it's plenty odd, but I do not have the resources to go investigate everything odd that happens in this village."

He held the apple up to his nose and breathed in deeply. She wondered if he was intentionally trying to irritate her. Without even thinking she grabbed it out of his hands and took a bite out of it. To her surprise, the fleshy part of the fruit was not the regular apple yellow, but a vivid pink.

"What is this?" she asked.

"According to my fruit merchant it's a Cosmic Crunch. But I don't think that's right."

He spoke so calmly that she wondered if women made a practice of grabbing fruit out of his hands. She was so glad Agnes wasn't there.

"You have a fruit merchant?"

Walter withdrew another apple from a brown bag. "I think it's a Kissane."

He'd worked at a hedge fund in Manhattan before quitting it all to become a police chief in their little village.

"Walter, has it occurred to you that you have too much money?"

He looked up at her, and for the first time that afternoon she felt like she had his full attention. Then he laughed, and shrugged. "All the time."

"I mean seriously, what's wrong with a Red Delicious?" she said, though in fact this was the best apple she'd ever had.

Walter got up and went to a cabinet, over which there were photos of the most wanted men in New York, and he withdrew a plate, and then he cut her some cheese and salami and tore off a chunk of bread, his palms pressing right into a soft spot in the bottom so that it seemed to groan as he tugged it open.

Maggie felt her cheeks warm.

Then he handed Maggie the plate, leaned back into his chair and paused. She sensed she shouldn't speak, and so she didn't, and eventually he said, "My wife left me."

"I'm sorry."

"She said I'm too controlling. And boring. In fact, she seems to hate everything about me. She's taking my children to England. She's found someone more appealing there."

"Can she do that? You're such a good father." She remembered the time he brought his oldest daughter to Sunday School, a gangly serious girl whom he gazed at as though she were Helen of Troy.

"I could fight her, but what's the point? The girls want to go and she's a good mother. It's a great opportunity for them." He shrugged. "When Bethany walked out of that wedding, I thought how many problems I would have avoided if my wife had done something similar. Or if I had."

A school bus rumbled by. School was back in session after the storm. She had to remember to pick up Edgar tomorrow. But for now she felt almost drowsy with contentment. His office was not as comfortable as hers, but Maggie supposed the police were not in the business of providing comfort to their visitors. His desk was made of aluminum and reminded her of the ones her teachers used to have in elementary school. The chairs had no cushion. Yet for all that, she did feel quite comfortable in this room. And although his news was sad, he didn't look especially mournful.

"What do you think of him?" Walter asked. "Graham?"

"The word unlucky comes to mind. He's not bad. He's not incompetent. He's just always in the wrong place at the wrong time. Let me put it to you like this, he was cast as Joseph in every single Christmas play. He's the sort of man who would find out that God fathered his son."

Walter laughed at that. He always laughed at her jokes, which she considered one of his best features. She found herself trying to make him laugh. She always felt just a bit sparkly around him.

"You think they loved each other?" he asked her.

"In a half-hearted sort of way. I mean, I wouldn't have said it was a grand passion." He looked at her intensely, as though she were a person who knew all there was to know about grand passions. "I would have said that she felt as much for him as he did for her. Which is pretty damning, when you get down to it. But the thing about Bethany is that she's loyal. And I would have thought she'd be loyal to Graham, so that even if she didn't want to marry him, she wouldn't want to embarrass him. He's always been good to her and I would have thought she'd respect that."

He took a long slow breath. She breathed in as well. Sort of a nice feeling to breathe with someone. To talk to someone. To trust someone.

"My niece is coming to visit," Maggie said, which surprised her. She'd talked to about twenty people that morning and had not felt comfortable talking to any of them about Livy and yet here was Walter Campbell, and suddenly she wanted him to know. "My niece is coming to visit," she repeated, "and I'm worried something will go wrong."

"Like what?"

She felt relieved that he didn't dismiss her fears, that he didn't say that nothing would go wrong or whatever foolish statement people liked to make.

"Where to even begin? She could disappear. She could get in a car accident. She could eat poison. There could be a killer. She could get hurt. She could die."

She looked into his eyes, but she didn't see mockery. "Her parents treasure her. She's 23-years-old and she's heartbroken and vulnerable and they're entrusting her to me and all I can think of is the terrible things that can happen and now Bethany's missing and I know she's probably figured out a way to take a private plane to Santa Lucia. I imagine her sitting on an island and putting ten-dollar bills into some waiter's underwear, but it's possible that something did happen to her. Bad things do happen and she could be hurt or in trouble and there could be some malevolent force out there and what if Livy gets in its way?"

Walter nodded. He picked up a paperweight and his hands caressed the weight's smooth surface.

"I'll circulate a missing person bulletin," he said. "And I'll call the Westchester County Task force and ask them to check for unreported car accidents. I can also ping her phone. That may be the simplest thing."

Was there anything more wonderful than a man who listened to your concerns and tried to address them?

"Thank you," she said. "That would help."

His phone began to buzz. He scowled at it, then picked it up and began barking into it. She stood up, ready to go, but then he was there behind her, walking her to the door. How close he was. When she got to the door, she paused and looked up at him.

"I wonder if you'd like to come over to dinner."

He had beautiful green eyes, with little gold flecks. "Yes, I would."

"I'm glad."

Without thinking she stood up on her toes, kissing him softly, his lips crinkling into a smile beneath her own, and then kissing her back surprisingly hard. Leaving her a bit breathless as she went on her way, crunching her way down leaves that sparkled as though draped with sugar.

Chapter Seven

The following morning Maggie went to visit the Colemans, who lived on Coleman Circle, which was off of Coleman Street. They'd been in Darby for a long time, which was why Maggie was stunned to see a For Sale sign on the front lawn.

Even more startling was the sight of Ben Coleman hammering at a tree. It was a dainty little cherry blossom that shuddered under his attack. She'd always suspected Bethany's father harbored anger inside him. He was so aggressively virtuous. So enraged by every infraction. He'd actually filed a complaint against Edgar with the minister. Who files a complaint against a child, even if, yes, he shouldn't have got dirt in the baptismal font? He was trying to wash his hands.

"What are you doing?" she called out, running toward him. The poor little tree had a huge scar down its middle.

"Fixing this tree," he said.

"By killing it?"

He stopped hammering for a moment and looked at her. He was an ascetic man, with the face of a medieval monk. Gaunt. Hollowed out. Weirdly sexy. Or maybe it was just that he radiated heat.

Suddenly her mind flashed to Walter, for whom she'd decided to cook a beef stew for dinner. Something hearty and crusty. No mushrooms, just carrots and potatoes and peas. Though maybe he'd like mushrooms. Maybe he'd prefer a beef Bourgogne. She supposed she could try something new. Her face began to heat up, but fortunately Coleman was not really paying attention to her.

"It got hurt during the last storm and it looks like it's going to fall apart. You see," he said, pointing at two screws. "I'm hammering them in. They'll hold the trunk together. Bark will grow around it, and the tree will survive."

Maggie nodded. It made sense, but it also made sense that Ben Coleman would rescue something by hurting it.

"Are you really going to move?" Maggie asked.

"We have to," he said. "We have to pay off all the debts Bethany ran up. No other way to do it. We're going to go to India. I have a brother there, doing mission work. We'll join him."

He didn't look upset, she thought. The way one might if one's daughter had disappeared and you'd been bankrupted by her actions. It was almost as though he was pleased. Like he wanted to suffer. She'd never found any virtue in suffering, herself. She'd always just wanted to run from it.

He lifted up his hammer to pound the tree and she stepped in front of it. Couldn't bear it.

"Have you heard anything from Bethany?" she asked.

"I would have said so."

"You're not concerned about where she might be?"

He sighed and looked up toward his house. His wife was in there. His wife, but not Bethany's mother. That woman had died years earlier, and then Ben had gone to a religious retreat, met up with Abigail and brought her home. Maggie wondered what she thought of going to India, but suspected that Abigail would be supportive. She thought of how they'd looked when they'd walked down the aisle, entwined with each other, in their own world. They had that sort of love that forsakes all others. That takes up all the air in the room, that seems more appropriate for 20-year-olds than 50-year-olds, though Maggie didn't know if she was thinking that because she was envious. She suspected she had a tendency to want to wall herself away from the world. That's what she'd done when she was grieving. There was something so seductive about shutting everything out, and perhaps because of that she'd always been drawn to friends who forced her into the world.

"She wanted a big wedding and I gave her that."

"Why do you think she ran off?"

Just for a moment something blazed in his eyes. But quickly he regained control of himself, and became almost genial. "Because she wanted to get back at me. She's wanted to get back at me for years."

"Why?"

If he wondered why she was asking him so many questions, he didn't say so. He was a man who liked to talk about himself. That was his secret temptation, she suspected. He knew that that was a sign of pride, but it was a whole other matter if someone needed to ask him questions. If someone wanted him to talk about himself. The realization gave her a feeling of power. She sensed he would talk to her all afternoon.

"Graham Lockwood has hired me to find your daughter."

"He's a good man."

"You like him?"

"Oh yes. Very honorable. He would have made a good husband for her. He would have trained her."

"Trained? You mean like a dog?"

He looked toward the house again. What was he hoping to see there? She noticed then that Abigail Coleman was in the window, watching. She had her hand flat to the pane. Sending a signal, a benediction? She was a stunningly beautiful woman with the face of an angel, though she always played down her looks. Never wore make-up. Always had her hair tied back.

"She needed control. I couldn't do it. She fought me too much, but she loved him. She would have bent toward his will."

Maggie didn't know what she found more remarkable. The idea that he saw Graham Lockwood as someone with the power to bend someone to his will, or that he seriously wanted his daughter broken. No wonder Bethany wanted to get out of there. But she was not here to argue.

"You do think she loved him."

"She loved him as much as she could. She loved herself first."

He sighed.

"She wanted to have surgery," he said.

"Bethany? Why?"

"On her chin." He stroked his own chin. The famous Coleman receding chin. "She didn't like it and she wanted to have plastic surgery."

"For the wedding?"

"No. When she was sixteen. Foolishness. I told her she was made in God's image and she should be happy about it. But she couldn't accept it. She didn't want to go to college. She wanted to spend the tuition money on surgery, but I refused. Took her to Nicaragua instead. Spent the summer working with children with scars. Showed her what it was like to really suffer."

"Did that work?"

He looked at her appraisingly. She wondered if he planned to break her as well.

"She could not think of anyone but herself. She had an opportunity to stay in Nicaragua, but she refused. She came back here."

Maggie nodded. She noticed Abigail was still in the window. She pictured Bethany with her beautiful stepmother, self-conscious about her looks. The thing of it was that she agreed with Ben Coleman in principle.

She did think that beauty came from within, and that the most beautiful people she knew did not have the best features. But then she pictured that needy girl, trapped in a house with two adults swept up in their own romance. She'd never before felt sympathy for Bethany, but now she did.

"Is that where you think she is?" Maggie asked. "Do you think she left the wedding and went to have surgery?"

"Yes. She's going to come back here in a week or so with her brand new chin, wanting to show it all off. But we'll be gone."

He smiled then, a skeletal grin, and she shivered. He had an air of satisfaction that she found unappealing. It was as though he knew Bethany was going to let him down, and she did let him down, and now he was pleased about it.

"How much was the surgery?"

"Twenty thousand dollars," he said.

His wife opened the front door just then, to wave down at him and invite them both up for cookies.

At the sight of his wife, Ben's entire face changed. Softened.

So he was capable of love, Maggie thought. She thought of the two of them walking down the aisle. She was developing more and more sympathy for Bethany, nothing she'd never expected to feel. But she also thought it interesting that he quite genuinely didn't seem worried about his daughter.

Although she didn't agree with Ben Coleman on much, she did think he might be right in this situation. She could believe that Bethany wanted to get the heck out of there.

Chapter Eight

Maggie felt weirdly reassured after her visit with Ben Coleman. She thought he might be right that Bethany would reemerge in a week or so's time, looking stunning. She would resume her place at the loan office at the bank and Graham would probably withdraw into himself and become one of the walking wounded, those people in the village who'd been hammered down by life, in some way, and cobbled together an existence. It was sad for him, but it might actually be easier than marrying Bethany. That would have brought him no joy.

Meanwhile, her more immediate task was to get Edgar to the library and do research on the year 1934.

He was enthralled. He loved the library, loved the books, which smelled of dust and history. He held each one up to his nose and breathed in deeply. The librarian, a kind woman, offered them the use of her office, and so he was able to spread out all the old volumes of newspaper articles from 1934.

The first thing Maggie saw was something about Sergeant Enoch Coleman, who must have been Bethany's great-grandfather. He warned youngsters about skating on thin ice on the Hudson. She couldn't help but look at his chin.

"Look, Maggie Dove, look."

Edgar pointed at an article about a young man who'd accidentally killed his mother in a car accident.

"Let's find something more historical," she said, and she flipped the page to the social calendar. There was a concert at night at the Bingley home, offered by the Westchester Chamber Society. That must be some relation of old Mrs. Bingley, who lived in one of the most rarified parts of Darby. There was a Fireman's Ball. Someone was fined for weighing coal without a license.

Edgar was writing things down feverishly, although she pointed out to him that he was only supposed to write down five things of interest.

"How can I stop?" he asked.

Life was not easy for people who had a problem with rules, she thought.

The firemen were in a bridge tournament with the Pastimers, which were, she supposed, a prehistoric version of the Insomnia Club. Then there were all the ads, which were so much fun to look at. The Darby jewelry store, the Darby candy store. A Gristedes ad offered milk-fed fancy fowl and Cuban lima beans and the finest California broccoli. There was also Jell-O for 17 cents. And Lockwood & Sons reminded you to buy your Christmas trees early. Four Lockwood brothers stood, holding axes, in front of a fir tree.

Suddenly Edgar turned the page and yelped.

"What is it?" Maggie cried out. The librarian looked up at her solemnly. *Sorry.*

There, emblazoned across the top of the newspaper article was a headline: "Find Remains Of New York Girl Buried in Woods."

"Oh no," Maggie said.

"Degenerate Confesses to Fiendish Crime," Edgar read out. He was a very good reader.

She read on with horror. Some man had lured a young girl from New York City and killed her at Hollyhock House. Maggie knew where that was. She often drove by it, a pretty white farm houe, but she'd had no idea of its history. There was an old spruce tree in front of it that she loved. One of her favorite trees in the village.

"She was my age," Edgar said.

Maggie grabbed the volume out of his hands. "My love, I'm sorry but this is really not appropriate to read."

"But it's no worse than Jael. And she was in the Bible."

"I know, and there are things in the Bible that are complicated, and difficult to understand. But one thing I do know is that Ms. Sanchez does not want you coming in with information about a murder."

He sank against her. He didn't object, which surprised her. Instead, he seemed thoughtful.

"Am I bad?" he asked.

"Not in the least," she said. "You're a treasure."

He gazed up at her. His little face looked so serious. His blonde hair had a streak of brown going through it. He was changing, growing up, darkening.

"Why would you think you're bad?"

"My mother said so. She said I have bad genes and that I'm going to have to try very hard not to let them overpower me."

The room shook from a train going by.

"Sometimes when mothers get upset, they say things they don't mean. You've done that, haven't you? Remember when you told poor Ambrosia Fletcher that she was stupid."

"But she is stupid."

"No, she's not. And you know that, but you were provoked and you wanted to say something hurtful. Mothers are the same way."

"Were you like that? With Juliet."

She loved the way he said her daughter's name, enunciating each syllable.

"I certainly got mad at her. She wasn't perfect. One time she got into trouble at school and the teacher wrote a note and she didn't give it to me. She ate it."

"What did she do?"

In point of fact Maggie couldn't remember Juliet doing anything horrible, but she thought that this might be an occasion when a lie would be forgivable. "She bit someone," she said. "A little girl. Gave her a scar."

"She was bad?"

"I don't think of children as bad, my lamb. Children are so close to God. Maybe some children grow up to be bad people, but I don't think they start out that way, and in any case, you are not one of them."

"That man, that degenerate, he was bad."

Degenerate. What a word to teach a seven-year-old.

"Yes, he was bad. But he lived long ago."

"Do you think he was electrocuted?"

"It's certainly possible."

"He had to be punished."

She noticed a tear trailing down his face. She clutched him to her. "There is always more good in the world than bad, Edgar. And you are one of the good. Now, I've been meaning to tell you, my niece is coming to visit. Her name is Livy and she speaks Latin and I'll bet she'll teach you ancient words, and I want to get her some new sheets and we can go to Bed Bath & Beyond and you can ride on the escalator, and then we can go to Burger King and get a Happy Meal."

He laughed at that. "They don't have Happy Meals at Burger King. You're stupid, aren't you? Just like me."

He cackled merrily, but she didn't like the sound of it.

But fortunately, there was nothing in the world to Edgar more wonderful than the escalator at Bed Bath & Beyond, the one that you could insert the shopping cart into. They spent a solid half an hour riding it, racing against the shopping cart, and sampling free honey-flavored pretzels, and Maggie was so dizzy at the end of it all that instead of buying plain white farmhouse linens for Livy, which would have been the sensible choice, she bought from the Spice Palm collection. Aqua green with a coastal background and some pineapples stenciled in. So tropical. So colorful.

So inappropriate, she thought later that night, when she'd set everything up in Livy's room. She looked at the sheets and the comforter and the pillow shams and the dust ruffle, and the blue rattan bench she'd bought, and the mirror that had shells on it, and realized she'd created a room for a five-year-old.

She would have to go back to Bed Bath & Beyond, but she didn't have time with all the work she had to do before her niece arrived, and anyway, there was a small part of her that hoped, perhaps, her niece would love it, and then the doorbell rang. Seven o'clock.

It was Walter. He'd come over to tell her that he'd checked the national data base of missing people, and he'd looked through New York records and had even checked with someone he knew at TSA to see if anyone named Bethany Coleman had boarded a plane from New York. Oh, and he'd brought over a beef stew. "If you'd like to have dinner."

She noticed pearl onions, her favorite thing in the world.

"Do you have a stew merchant?" she asked.

He laughed. "A chef," he answered, "but he doesn't live in."

He'd brought wine too, and chocolate from Iceland, which had licorice in it, and she was thought what a treat it was that he'd surprised her. If she'd planned out the dinner she would have obsessed, but this way she didn't have to worry about anything. She could just enjoy his company, which she did, and the happiness she had from that evening floated her for the next two days, up until she was driving to LaGuardia to pick up her niece. Somehow even LaGuardia didn't seem that bad when you were happy. So what if the parking lots were closed and the call waiting lot was full and the traffic was so bad that people were jumping out of their cars and trudging through the slush. A scene similar to that of people fleeing Stalingrad.

She would see her niece.

For the first time since talking to Linus, Maggie embraced the joy of this visit. Why had she let her anxieties ruin her anticipation? This was her niece. This was a good thing. She didn't want to be one of those people who found misery in every opportunity. Where was Livy? Bring her on!

Chapter Nine

The last time Maggie saw her niece she was wearing a plaid shirt, denim jeans and her hair in pigtails. So, Maggie expected her to look something like that, just taller. She could see other people from the plane milling around and that's what they looked like. So it took her a moment to realize that the elegant swan with pulled-back blonde hair and huge sun glasses was her niece. She looked like she got off a plane from Paris and not Indiana.

"Hello," she said, waving at her.

Livy nodded. She had the Dove nose, Maggie saw. A thin, aristocratic nose. Linus traveled the world for his research, she realized. Livy was in a Ph. D program. She'd studied in Paris.

Maggie should definitely have bought different sheets.

"Thank you for picking me up," she said. She had a cultured, accentless voice. She sounded polite. Reserved.

Maggie noticed an engagement ring twinkling on her finger, quite a large one. So, she had not let go of this man just yet. There were vulnerabilities there. Wasn't that always the case?

"I'm so glad you're here," Maggie said, but there was no time to hug because a cab driver swept in behind her, honking her forward.

"How was your flight?" she asked, as she merged into traffic.

"We almost crashed over Michigan."

"Oh my God," Maggie said. "What happened?"

"A plane flew right in front of us. Missed us by less than one hundred feet. The pilot said it was a miracle we're all alive."

"Oh my God." Maggie almost swerved off the road, but then she heard a sound like geese flying south for the winter.

"Just kidding," Livy laughed. "The flight was fine."

"Oh my God," Maggie said. "When do you go home?"

"What?" Livy asked.

"Nothing."

Livy was chuckling to herself, Maggie was driving, trying to think of where to take the conversation.

She'd brought a bag of M&Ms with her, and she gestured at it.

"I remembered how much you liked them."

Livy looked at her as though from a great distance. Maggie wondered if any part of what Linus had told her was true. Had she enjoyed the M&Ms? Had she liked Maggie? Had she any desire at all to be here or had Linus just set up the whole thing? She'd been so preoccupied with keeping Livy safe, that she'd not paid much thought to the circumstances of this visit.

But no. Livy seemed determined to see this through. She tore a tiny little hole in the paper bag and plucked out a brown one and then slowly put it on her mouth. She looked like she was taking communion. Then she gagged slightly, and swallowed. And sighed.

She was like a hedgehog, Maggie thought. All bristles and nose. She remembered how enthusiastic she'd been at the M&M center in Times Square, though that had been more than a decade ago. She was the only daughter of a man who was head of the classics department at a major university. She supposed it made sense that she'd be proud. She supposed Linus was, come to that. All the Doves. They weren't snobs. They just believed they were smarter than anyone. They actually were smarter than anyone else. They always made Maggie feel like an idiot. It was all coming back.

"How are your parents?"

"Papa is obsessed with the new research on Tiberius Gracchus, of course. It's all he'll talk about. That and the Pullman fellowship. And mama is busy with her organizing. Well, you know how she is. Twenty Latin students from Turkey arriving at our house. She's very busy. I should be there," she cried out, and then caught herself. And resumed looking out the window.

Maggie's phone rang just then. Sounding like a fire engine. She realized then that Edgar had reprogrammed her ring tones and he'd made this the sound for Agnes. She didn't answer.

Livy put her head back and closed her eyes.

Maggie felt a longing for her husband that surprised her with its intensity. He would know what to say. He would know what to do. He would ask her something about Petrarch and they could chatter about that for a while. Well, he was gone and she was here and Livy was here for two weeks, so they'd both have to deal with it.

Agnes kept blaring.

Maggie felt sure she was calling to welcome Livy. But now was not the moment. Really no one should talk to Agnes without a good night's sleep. Agnes was definitely a person you had to build up to, and meanwhile she needed to merge on to the Grand Central, which was always a bit of excitement. She tried to think what to say. Did she mention the wedding or not? Who made a joke about plane crashes? All right, she was oversensitive, but it felt hostile. Had her niece been forced to come here?

"My dad told me that you'd also been jilted at the altar," she said. "Before you met Uncle Stuart."

That Linus Dove was a liar, Maggie thought. You assumed because a man sent you notes on blue paper that he told the truth. You assumed that because he put care into his correspondence that he valued his words.

"Certainly, I had some difficult romantic entanglements," she said, which seemed true enough. She'd loved one man and he'd loved her back and then he died. But it took her a while to persuade him to marry her. He thought he was too old.

"He said you suffered from depression."

Linus was a real chatterbox, she thought. Why was he so busy writing letters when he could have simply called on the phone?

"I know what it's like to feel despair. Is that how you feel?"

"No." She looked out the window. Manhattan loomed up in front of them, full of promise and danger.

The phone blared again and Maggie brushed it off with her hand. Not now, Agnes.

"There are times in a person's life when despair is the only thing you can feel."

"I'm not despairing," she said. "Anyway, he's going to call. He's going to realize his mistake. This will all be over soon and then I can get back to my life."

Maggie turned on to the Cross Westchester Parkway. She was tempted to point out that this might be Livy's new life, but Livy didn't seem in the mood for philosophy and she was annoyed at Linus and when the phone rang again, she pressed the on button and Agnes's voice blared into the car.

"Bethany's dead!" Agnes shouted. "Somebody's murdered her."

"What!"

"You heard me Maggie Dove. Someone's whacked Bethany Coleman. With an axe. A dogwalker found her in the woods. He must have chased her. Terrible," Agnes said, in a tone of voice that made it clear she did not find it terrible at all.

"Agnes," Maggie cried out. "I've just picked up my niece from LaGuardia."

"Oh," Agnes said. "Welcome, Livy! Oh, sorry Maggie."

But Livy was unfazed.

"Don't stop because of me," Livy said, finally coming to life. "I'm on the ambulance corps back home. I've seen everything."

"I like a bold spirit," Agnes growled. "So, this is what happened."

Chapter Ten

Darby looked especially lovely that night. Snow sparkled on the buildings, smoothing out all the flaws and hard edges. It looked like an enchanted village. Like something you'd find in Disney World, except without the tunnels for sweeping away the dirt. Here, in her beautiful town, a murderer roamed, and she was bringing her niece home into this. She'd sworn to keep her safe, and she was exposing her to a killer.

"So sweet," Livy said.

Maggie pulled into her driveway and propelled her niece out of the car and up the steps of her porch. She hadn't even locked her front door. She never did. But now she bolted it shut behind them.

Only then did she notice that Helen must have been inside. There was a bouquet of freesias on the table, and a welcome card from the Farraday sisters. People had been walking in and out of her house all day. She felt touched, but frightened too. She was so exposed. How on earth was she supposed to keep her niece safe?

"Aren't you going to call that Agnes person back?" Livy asked.

The cats jumped down to sniff at Livy. She ignored them, which seemed to meet with their approval. They glared at Maggie. *Don't screw this up.*

"Not right yet," Maggie said. "Help me lock up the house."

They went from window to window, pulling down the latches. Livy had strong wrists. The windows rattled as she slammed the latches into place.

"You think the murderer will come here?" Livy asked, as though asking whether mail delivery were disrupted by the storm.

"I don't know. But I don't propose to sit here with my teeth in my mouth, waiting for him to show up."

"You think it's the groom, no? The one she dumped."

Maggie had explained the whole situation on the ride back, after getting Agnes off the phone. She'd not really wanted to talk about it, but Livy was laser focused. She wanted to know about Bethany, and how she'd walked out of her own wedding, and how she'd disappeared with the $20,000 and how Graham had hired Maggie Dove's Detective Agency to find her. She wanted to know every last detail.

Maggie had never in her life spent so much time thinking about Graham Lockwood. In fact, the essential nature of Graham was that he was not a person you spent a lot of time thinking about. He was there. He was like the grass in the field, or the clouds in the sky. He didn't do much. He was a part of the scenery. So trying to transpose that vision of

Graham into someone who had a murderous temper was difficult for Maggie to do.

"I don't know," she said to Livy. "He certainly has a motive. He has the physical build for it, and there are generations of Lockwoods who know how to wield axes." She remembered the picture in the newspaper Edgar had looked through. All those husky men standing one against the other, axe at the ready. For trees.

"I've always thought of him as gentle, but maybe he's just passive."

True, he'd hired her to find Bethany, but that might have been because he didn't expect Maggie to find her.

"You know him well?"

"Not really. I taught him about Noah's ark. It's hard to make a leap from that to murder."

The fact was, Maggie had no idea what thoughts Graham harbored. He'd never been one of those Sunday School students with a lot of questions. Not like Bethany, who was so sure of God. She'd been someone who kept going to church even after Sunday School was over. But Graham stopped going as soon as he was doing with confirmation class. He fulfilled his obligation and he was done. Long way from that though to striking down a bride in her wedding dress in the middle of a snow storm. Maggie couldn't get the images out of her head. Agnes had been quite explicit. Bethany found with her stockings torn. No shoes on. She must have kicked them off to be able to run faster. Through the snow, but not fast enough. She must have fallen.

She was such a strong and powerful girl, and the hatred involved in killing her frightened Maggie. She hoped it was Graham. That would at least make sense. He had a sort of rational reason for his anger. She didn't want to think there was someone else in the village who might have wanted to destroy Bethany, or, even worse, didn't even care if she was Bethany or not. Just wanted to destroy.

"Come on," Maggie said. "Let's latch the upstairs windows."

They climbed up the narrow flight of steps, and paused at the landing, Livy's room to the right. "This is your room," Maggie said, opening the door.

For just a moment they both paused to take in all the tropical décor. The sea shells. Had she really bought a lei?

"Sweet," Livy said.

Then they went into Maggie's room, pulled down the door to the attic and climbed up a narrow ladder.

In truth it was hard to imagine someone with an axe climbing up to her attic in the snow, but Maggie didn't care. She wanted to be thorough. She didn't want to leave anything to chance. Having latched the attic window, they both paused a moment to survey all the boxes. Old photos, old report cards, old phone books. There was something about looking through an old phone book that she loved. So many names.

Livy leaned over and picked up an old photo of Maggie's husband. "The mysterious Stuart Dove," she said.

"Mysterious?" "

He was wearing a kilt in the photo. Maggie stood alongside him, also in a kilt. She remembered that night, in Scotland.

"My father says he was desperate for you."

Maggie laughed. The Doves had always seen her as a wild woman. She suspected in their mind that she was still the 19- year-old who had hurled herself at Stuart Dove. She had been a bit wild, come to that. She knew that they believed she'd tricked him into marriage, though he'd been happy enough to go along with her.

"He was fond of me, certainly."

"Father always said he would have done anything for you."

What an odd thing to say, Maggie thought, but just then she heard someone pounding on her front door. Must be Agnes, come to harass her. She'd probably been ringing the bell.

Maggie raced back down the steps, Livy behind her.

She threw open the door and there was Graham Lockwood.

"Help me," he said. "Help me, Maggie Dove."

Chapter Eleven

aggie Dove had never before slammed a door in someone's face, but this was definitely the moment. She acted without thinking, hurling the door closed and clicking on the lock.

She expected Graham to pound on the door, but he didn't move. He simply stood there on her doorstep.

It was freezing outside. A foot of snow on the ground, her porch not yet shoveled. Joe Mangione always came by and did it for her, but he must be at the crime scene.

Graham wore a light coat. No gloves. Snow dusted his hair making him look like an old man. He didn't look angry, didn't look dangerous. But that didn't mean anything. She'd been in this business long enough to know that people wore masks.

Still. Graham Lockwood.

"Go to the police station, Graham," she called out. "Turn yourself in. They'll be fair with you. You know Walter Campbell. And hire a lawyer!"

"I loved her, Maggie Dove. I would never hurt her like that." He sounded different, she thought. Huskier, like a man who'd been at a football game. He didn't sound like the gentle man who'd stood at the front of the church less than a week ago.

"That's very good to know, but I'm not the person to persuade."

"You think I did it! You really think I did it!"

"Graham, I'm not a jury. There's a process here. You can't hide." Livy hovered behind her, peering through the window. "Go to the police station. Get this all cleared up."

"I knew she was going to walk out of the wedding," he shouted.

"What?"

"She told me. She had it all planned out. She never intended to leave me behind."

Livy gasped. Maggie tried to figure out what that meant, or even if it could be true. It was a sufficiently ridiculous notion that she was inclined to believe it. Graham was the sort of person who always got involved in strange schemes and usually wound up the one taking the blame. She could imagine Bethany coming up with a plan and Graham going along with it.

"Are you going to help him?" Livy asked.

Oh, good Lord.

"Wait a minute, Graham," Maggie called out. "Clear off some space on that bench."

Then she turned to her niece. "Livy, listen to me. Do not get involved in this. I'm going to go outside and I want you to lock the door after me. Do not let Graham into the house."

"I'll watch you," she said. "I'll make sure you're safe."

Maggie turned and looked at her niece. "If anything happens to me, call the police. I don't want you to help me. In fact, it would be best if you went into your room."

"No."

"Fine, but do not come outside."

Livy looked at her with those curved Roman lips. She reminded Maggie of statues at the Met. Heads that had been severed from the bottom of the statue.

"Yes, Aunt Dove."

Then Maggie went to her closet and pulled out two of her warmest coats and a blanket. She wrapped herself up and went outside.

It was arctic. Her bones hurt. Her little oak tree flinched in the wind. She thought of Ben Coleman's tree, pictured it splitting apart at the seams. Graham didn't look especially cold, however. He looked overheated. He sat on her little wood bench. She sat on it as well, though at the opposite end.

"Now start from the beginning," she said. "How did you know she was going to walk out on that wedding?"

"She told me. So don't you see? I had no reason to kill her. I knew she was going to leave. I wasn't mad at her. I expected it."

"Graham, take me back a step. Where did this all begin?"

He took a deep breath. Off in the distance Maggie could hear police sirens. More officers showing up for the crime scene, probably coming from all over the county. She was glad Livy was watching, phone at the ready.

"We made a promise when we were in high school that if we didn't meet anyone by the time we were 30, we'd marry. So on her thirtieth birthday, she came to me and said it was time."

"And you just said yes?"

"I didn't have anyone else in mind to marry, and I did love her and she wanted children. I really want children. Plus, we really liked doing the same things. She was always up for anything, you know. Any sort of mountain sport. She was fun that way. And I knew I could make her happy. She was so unhappy because of her parents and all. She cried so much. But I didn't make her cry. People never understood how sensitive she was, but I did."

He pressed his hands together as though in prayer. "I could make her happy."

Maggie supposed that was a form of love. She was way too much of a romantic to think that was enough, but she supposed you could make an argument for it. She supposed you could do worse than a shared interest in mountain sports.

"So then it got to be the wedding?" she prodded.

"Yes, and her parents were terrible. Fighting her about every single expenditure. Mean about everything. She'd begged them to pay for her to have surgery on her chin. That's what she really wanted. She didn't really care about a big wedding. She just wanted to be happy about her looks, and she told them we'd have a small wedding, if they would just pay for the surgery."

"But why didn't she just pay for it herself?"

"That wasn't the point," he exploded. "She wanted them to recognize it was important to her. She wanted their support, and they wouldn't give it." He clenched his hands together and banged them against the bench. Maggie felt his fury. Bethany and her father were locked in unmoveable positions. They were each so sure of where they were, both so aggrieved by the other.

"So she decided to take revenge on him?"

"Yes, she thought that if he wouldn't spend $20,000 for the surgery, that she'd force him to spend as much as she could for the wedding. And then she'd just walk away from it all. She couldn't wait to see the look on his face when she went storming out of the church."

Maggie thought of the look on Ben Coleman's face, which had been more in the nature of calm acceptance. Perhaps that's why he hadn't seemed that upset at the time. Perhaps he'd known all along what she planned to do.

"Then what happened?"

He shook his head. "I don't know. She was supposed to go and get the surgery and then we'd meet up in the city and get married and go away. But I think the snow messed everything up."

"Where was she having the surgery?"

"I don't know. She just told me that I should make sure to go after her in my car, because that would distract everyone and then she'd be able to get away. She was supposed to call me at 6:00 and tell me where to meet up. But she never called." He paused. "I had my bags packed. I could show you," he said.

"I'm not sure that a packed bag is much of a defense against murder," Maggie said.

"But you do believe me, don't you?"

Maggie believed that Bethany wanted revenge on her father. She believed she planned this all out. She'd always had a manipulative side. She liked playing games with people. What she wasn't sure of were Bethany's intentions with Graham. She'd wound up making him look like an idiot. Was that her plan?

Poor Graham. So often the butt of the other kids' jokes. So eager to belong. A boy stuffed into a trash bin by his brothers. She thought of Joseph, who'd loved Mary, even though he risked humiliation. She wondered if love meant making yourself look like a fool. For some people it did.

"Do you have any idea the name of the surgeon?"

He shook his head.

"No, she wanted to surprise me. That was the thing. She didn't even want me to go with her." He paused then. He was the sort of person who, when he thought, his whole body came to come to rest. Like he had to focus all his energies on that one thing. "I have an idea that his last name was Irish. Or German."

"Oh."

"You have to help me, Maggie Dove."

"I don't see how I can, Graham. I want to, but this is way more than I'm capable of handling."

"But no one else will believe me," he said. "You know me. You know what I'm like."

He knelt at her feet, in the snow. "I'm desperate, Maggie Dove."

"Oh good grief," she said, and at that moment her front door swung open. There stood Livy, looking like a goddess. Her hair had come loose and flowed in the wind. Her cheeks were pink, her eyes flashed.

"I believe you," she said. "I'll help you."

Graham looked stunned. He rose to his feet as though pulled by an invisible string. His mouth opened slightly. Livy reached out her hand. Maggie could almost feel Cupid's dart go shooting by.

And then, for the second time that day, Maggie pushed someone through a door and slammed it closed. But she had a terrible feeling it was too late.

Chapter Twelve

Maggie lay rigid against her bed that night. Like a sarcophagus. She couldn't seem to move her shoulders. Livy had gone into her room. Locked the door, though not before glaring at Maggie to make it clear, in no uncertain terms, that she'd let her down. She was not the sweet little Maggie Dove she'd been expecting. No laughing at her now.

The cats lay outside Livy's door, though Maggie wasn't sure if they were there to stop Livy from leaving or to stop Maggie from going in. Whatever the reason, they were decidedly hostile. They glared at Maggie. In less than an hour she'd gone from sweet ditzy aunt to monster. All because she'd not wanted her niece to get involved with an axe murderer. A potential axe murderer. A hypothetical axe murderer.

Just to occupy her mind, Maggie got out of bed, opened her phone and googled a list of plastic surgeons in Westchester County. There were 1,137 of them. In Manhattan, there were 2,005. She scanned the names. There were a bunch with obviously Irish last names— O'Connors and O'Keefes. But what about Guthrie? Did that count? It was like looking for a needle in a haystack. And what if Graham was completely wrong?

She felt her heart pulsing. It was going to be one of those nights. A night filled with darkness and anxiety. She hadn't had one of those in a while. She tried to pray, but her mind was filled with images of Bethany. Agnes's descriptions swirled around her, and her imagination did the rest of the work. Bethany in a wedding dress. Something that symbolized hope and a future. Bethany cut down. Bethany kicking off her shoes so she could run better. Bethany afraid.

That bothered her most of all, because Bethany was fearless. Reckless. The first person to take on a dare. She hated to think of her dying afraid.

At midnight her phone pinged with a text. It was Walter, wanting to know if it was too late to call.

Please call! she responded

Immediately her phone chimed. "How are you?" he asked.

She pulled the comforter over her, pressed the phone against her ear. She was convinced she could smell him over the phone. A warm soapy scent.

The words burst out of her and she told him about everything that had happened, up to and including the fact that the cats had refused to budge from Livy's door and were staring at her with contempt. *Clearly you are not up to handling this issue.*

He chuckled at that, which encouraged her to go on and tell him her great fear, which was that Livy had somehow fallen in love with Graham. That she'd taken one look at him and swooned. Romeo and Juliet on the Hudson.

To her great relief Walter didn't laugh. Didn't tell her she was crazy. Just listened and absorbed. You could love a man for that reason alone, she thought.

"I have this stranger living with me, and I guess I figured she'd be the way she was when she was ten. Or I thought she'd be like Juliet. Or I thought she'd be normal. I mean I guess she is normal. I just thought she'd do what I'd ask her to do. I can't figure her out. Of course, I've only known her about two hours. But she just seems so volatile."

Nothing seemed so bad when you could talk it over with somebody else.

"But what about you?" she remembered to ask. "What about Bethany? What about the crime scene? Did Graham go to the police station?"

He had, which was a relief. He'd told Walter everything he'd told Maggie, about how he knew that Bethany was going to walk out of the wedding.

"Bethany must have been killed not long after she fled the wedding," he said. "No sign of the money. No sign of her phone."

"And the car. Did you find a Rolls Royce?"

"No," he said. "I don't know how she got there. We can't follow the tracks; they've been covered over with snow. There is one odd thing, though. The axe that was used on her was old."

"How old?"

"I can't tell yet, but the handle's hickory, the head is iron. It looks like it was designed to split wood. But someone restored it. I smelled vinegar on it."

"Vinegar?"

"People use vinegar to restore axes. It takes off paint or grim."

"Someone restored the axe because they intended to use it on Bethany?" Maggie asked, trying to fold her tired brain around the issue.

"Or she was in the wrong place at the wrong time. She did have a bag with $20,000 in it," he said.

"And just happened to run into someone with an old axe?"

Walter sighed. "Was she the unluckiest woman in the world?"

A bride runs away from her wedding and just happens to run into a person with an old axe, who wants to kill her. Maggie believed in bad luck. Her daughter had been killed while stopped at a traffic light. She knew that sometimes the forces of the universe could swallow you up whole and she didn't understand it. It frightened her. You couldn't protect yourself. You couldn't protect the people you loved.

"I wonder if she lied to Graham when she told him she was going to meet up with him. Maybe she had someone else lined up," Maggie said.

"Do you have someone in mind?"

"No, but it's weird that she didn't give him a meeting-up point. That she didn't want him at the doctor with her. Maybe she really did plan to walk out on Graham, but needed his help with the getaway. Maybe she met up with a different person and he killed her."

"For the money?"

"She was sort of gullible," Maggie said, "now that I think about it. I mean, she didn't seem gullible, but she was always so sure she knew exactly what she was doing. She was confident in herself to the point of foolhardiness. I spent a fair amount of time working alongside her at the bank, and she was always strutting around, saying that she knew better than anyone, and I believe she genuinely meant it. So I could imagine her going into a situation and feeling like she knew exactly what she was doing, and then finding out she'd messed up."

"You don't suspect Graham?"

She'd seen him on Sundays for years. His father had a terrible temper, she knew that much. He got mad at the minister once and grabbed him by the throat. Graham had always seemed the complete opposite. But just because someone repressed feelings didn't mean they didn't have them. She thought of the Colemans, who, from the outside looked so cold, but actually burned with savage lust. It was actually easier for her to picture Ben Coleman going after his daughter with an axe. But he was her father.

"I just don't know. It's very hard to look at someone you know and try to see them as a murderer."

"We have a lot of information to process," Walter said. His voice sounded heavy.

She imagined him inside the bedroom of his own house. She'd never been there, had only seen it from the outside. An intimidating modernist structure with a huge wood door that probably cost more than many people's houses.

Walter started talking about something he'd learned in policy academy. He'd gone comparatively late in life, after a successful career on Wall Street. She shut her eyes and listened to him talk. He had a very soothing voice. She suspected he'd have a nice singing voice. A tenor. She wondered if he played the piano. Her eyes started to droop. She settled back into her pillow. She woke up the next morning with the phone pressed against her heart, the sound of Walter's snoring coming across it.

She could have just lay like that all day, but suddenly realized what she needed to do. What she should have done hours ago. Before it was too late.

Chapter Thirteen

She called Linus, but he didn't answer, which was all right, because it was his wife, Nora, on the phone. Maggie was quite fond of Nora. She was the only member of the Dove family you could talk to without mentioning Herodotus.

"Oh Maggie," she said, as though she anticipated what was coming.

Maggie launched into her explanation. Saying that Livy was a lovely person and under normal circumstances she'd love to have the opportunity to know her better, but there was an axe murderer in the village and no one knew who he was and she just couldn't take the risk of something happening to Livy and she thought it would be best if Livy were to go home. Possibly tonight.

Maggie pictured her sister-in-law's soft, serious face. She was the sort of woman described as sensible. No-nonsense. She wore long skirts and comfortable shoes and she cut her hair herself.

"But doesn't this happen quite a lot in New York?"

"No," Maggie said. "I mean maybe in New York City, but not in my part of New York."

Maggie heard a noise downstairs. It sounded as though Livy were in the kitchen.

"I'm sorry to hear this, but she can't come home," Nora said.

"I beg your pardon? I'm talking about an axe murderer, Nora."

Nora sighed. Maggie remembered then that quality about her. She often sounded like wind blowing through trees.

"We should have told you this and I wanted to, but Linus was afraid you wouldn't take her."

"What's going on?" Maggie whispered. She could hear Livy clattering around downstairs.

"She's developed a bit of an obsession with Shiv. She's having trouble letting go. Following him around. That sort of thing. He promised he wouldn't press charges if we could get her out of town."

"She's a stalker?"

"Not a stalker. She feels things very strongly, and she was shocked when they broke up. It was abrupt. She couldn't process it, Maggie. She's a girl who's never failed at anything."

"But love isn't a failure."

"It is to Livy. And it was very public. She's always just thought that if you worked harder at something than anyone else, you would win. She just couldn't understand how she wasn't good enough for Shiv, and it didn't help that he's her father's top assistant, and that he's in line for many of the same awards she is."

"Have you considered getting her help? There's no shame in going to a therapist."

"She can't."

"Why?"

"She's applying for a very important job with the government. Top-secret. Code-breaking. They do a psychiatric background check. If she has any mental illness in her background, she'll be disqualified."

"That makes no sense," Maggie said. "Wouldn't the government want to make sure its people are stable? That they have help?"

Nora sighed. "We did have a friend of ours talk to her. He has a Nobel Prize. He says she's fine."

Maggie wondered how two such brilliant people could be such idiots.

"Oh, Maggie. I know this is a big ask, but we were desperate, we needed to get her out of here and we remembered that special bond."

"Nora, please. Don't insult my intelligence. That girl barely remembers me, neither do we have a special bond."

Another sigh. "You have what she needs, Maggie. You're loving and accepting. It's such a pressure cooker here. Please."

Maggie sat and thought about it. That girl with the honking laugh. That girl with a big, if misdirected heart.

"All right, but listen to me, Nora. If she's going to stay here, she has to talk to my minister."

"Your minister?"

"She's a lovely woman and she's trained in counseling and she won't try to convert her to Chrisianity, and she won't report her to the U.S. Government, but she can help her. And she will know if something serious is going on. This is non-negotiable."

"Do you know where she got her degree?"

"Somewhere in Ghana."

"Oh."

"She does not have a Nobel Prize. But she has wisdom."

Another sigh.

"Linus won't like it," Nora said. "But I accept. Thank you, Maggie Dove."

Then she hung up. Fast.

Maggie called Reverend Sunday and spoke to her, and as she expected, she was amenable. Then she went downstairs to try and figure out why she smelled French toast.

Chapter Fourteen

"Will you be working for Graham today?" Livy asked, the moment Maggie walked into the kitchen. She was standing in front of the stove, cooking French toast, which was the only thing that stopped Maggie from snapping something savage in reply.

"I don't want to talk about Graham," Maggie said. "I want to talk about you."

"What about me?"

She flipped the toast on to a plate and brought it over to Maggie. She sprinkled confectioner's sugar on top, and handed her a pitcher of warmed maple syrup.

All right, Maggie thought, so her niece might be crazy, but she could learn to live with her.

"I talked to your mother."

"Oh," Livy said.

She had circles under her eyes, and her blonde hair was pulled back tight and then twisted into a figure eight that stood atop her head. She had on slim jeans and a white shirt. She looked fragile, and young, and vulnerable.

"You've had a hard time."

"It's over."

"Things don't always end when you think they should."

"No," Livy said. "It's over."

"Nonetheless," Maggie said, and explained about Reverend Sunday and her deal with her mother. "That's my condition for staying."

Livy's face f ushed red, but she didn't argue. "She'll see you this afternoon," Maggie said, and then she turned her attention to the French toast, which was amazing.

"Butter?

"Apple butter," Livy said. "I always have some with me. Want more?"

"No. Are you going to have any?"

"Right now," she said, and stacked three on too a plate.

She ate heartily, which Maggie approved of. She did not like people who were tepid about food.

Maggie leaned back into her chair and scanned her kitchen, a tidy little room built for a time when servants did the cooking and weren't expected to use much space. No island. Barely enough room for a refrigerator. She had chickens everywhere. Mugs in the shape of chickens and chicken-shaped oven mitts, and salt and pepper chicken shakers. She didn't actually like chickens all that much but she'd bought a chicken tea pot at the Attic Sale one year and somehow word had gotten around that she collected chickens and next thing you knew… Your whole life could be determined by inadvertent decisions.

The Bible was in the corner. She read it every morning, and always turned to the front of it, where the family tree was. There were her grandparents' names, written in their patchy old ink, her parents, and then her own name, Margaret Rose Leigh and next to that, her husband's name and under that, Juliet's name. Birth and death.

"Are you going to be doing work for Graham today?" Livy asked softly, as though she hadn't already asked.

"No," Maggie said. "He went to see the police, and they're investigating the murder now and they referred him to a lawyer."

"What about your detective agency?"

"He can certainly go talk to them," Maggie said. "But I'm on break while you're here. I thought we could go into the city. The Frick has an exhibit I've been wanting to see. We could have lunch."

Livy nodded slowly. Up and down, up and down.

"I also have a 10,000-piece jigsaw puzzle, all in white. I've been saving it for just such a day."

Maggie knew how Doves loved puzzles. She'd probably want to wear a blindfold to add to the challenge. But all Livy said was, "Uh hum."

"The thing is," Livy said, "don't you feel like you are uniquely positioned to help Graham. Having taught him Sunday School and all."

"I taught him to recite the Lord's Prayer," Maggie responded. "I did not do a thorough analysis of his psyche."

"But surely he showed some important interiority to you during that time."

Maggie had never thought of Graham as having an inner life. He liked marshmallows and going outside. He loved when they had a vegetable garden.

"But you don't really think he did it, do you? It seemed from the way you were talking to him last night that you cared for him."

"I do care for him. My judgment is clouded." She thought of what it had been like to try to defend Peter Nelson, and he was someone she loved. It was hard work defending someone when you had a personal relationship with them.

"This is not a game, Livy. These are high stakes. Someone is dead, a girl not much older than you. Who loved him."

She gave that honking laugh. "She didn't really love him."

"What makes you say that?"

Lily faltered for a moment. "Because she walked out on him."

Maggie considered herself a good-natured person, but she did not consider herself an idiot.

"Livy, listen to me. I am not getting involved with this while you're here. End of story. I'm not risking it."

Livy got that Dove look that Maggie associated with her daughter. The face stayed calm, but something steel seemed to go through it. But Maggie did not lack for steel herself.

"We are going to let this be. We are going to work on a puzzle and talk and get to know each other and bond and it's going to be fabulous."

"What will you do if the axe murderer strikes again?"

"What?"

Kosi stalked by and looked at her. *You fool.*

"What if everyone is busy paying attention to Graham, and meanwhile the axe murderer strikes again? Wouldn't you feel like you had that death on your conscience then?"

"For Pete's sake, Livy. I'm not Batman. I'm a 62-year-old Sunday School teacher with grief issues. If there's a killer prowling around Darby, all I can really do is keep you away from him."

"You don't believe that," Livy said, leaning forward, putting her slightly sticky hand on Maggie's own. "You're a person who helps. I know that about you. You must want to do something. However small."

Maggie thought about Bethany, and her parents, and that tree, and Graham. She thought about what it would be like spending the next two weeks arguing with Livy. She thought she was probably right.

Livy looked at her hopefully. Maggie noticed a little chip on the chicken cookie jar's beak. So that's why Edgar had looked so crest-fallen last time he was there.

She had an inspiration.

"Okay, I have a job that's probably impossible, but I'll give it to you."

"Really?"

"I have a list of about 3,000 names of plastic surgeons. We know that Bethany was going to see one of them. Or at least we think we know that, if Graham's not lying. Or mistaken. I'm going to put you in charge of calling them. See if you can find out which one Bethany was planning to go to."

"That's a great idea," she said. "You're so creative."

"Well, I don't know about that."

"You really listened to me. Thank you, Aunt Dove."

It was a hopeless task. A doctor's office would never give out that sort of information. Maggie was struck with the depths of her genius. She felt like Sisyphus' aunt. She would give Livy this task. It would occupy her for two weeks. She could not get into trouble calling plastic surgeons. Then she would go home. Win. Win.

Soon after Livy went up to her room, Agnes came by to talk to her about the drama. "Where's your niece?" she asked, and Maggie explained she was investigating. Agnes nodded, and went on to talk about Walter and how he was having a fight with the state task force because they wanted to come in and take it over and he wanted to handle it himself. "He's not making himself any friends," she said, and then told her that the Colemans were still planning to move away, though they'd scheduled a memorial service for that week. She also said there was a communion chalice missing from church and that Bethany might have stolen it.

"When? She was barely at the front of the altar."

Agnes shrugged. She took some of the French toast left on Livy's plate and poured some more syrup on it. Then she started to eat. "Bethany had folds in her dress. She could have picked it up in all the commotion. No one was looking at her dress, at that point."

"But why?"

Then Walter called to see how she was doing, and she talked to him briefly, because she could not have a prolonged conversation with Agnes eyeballing her, and then Helen called, sounding harassed, because Edgar's gymnastics class had been canceled because of the snow. Maggie heard Edgar clanging in the background and so she chatted with him for a bit on Facetime, and then Livy came in. Burst in.

"Aunt Dove," she said. "I found it."

"Found what?"

"The plastic surgeon. I found where Bethany was going to go."

"How on earth did you do that? It's only been an hour."

"I figured she'd go for the one with the best yelp review. Dr. Huang."

Huang, she thought. That Graham was a moron. Irish or German.

"But how did you get them to give you the information?"

"I paid her. Venmo, Aunt Dove."

"You paid her to give you information?" Maggie was awestruck by the boldness of it.

"How much?"

"One hundred dollars."

Maggie felt like she was going to swoon. Meanwhile Livy looked at her serenely.

"Don't worry," she said. "It's a business expense, right? Anyway, I figured it was a small price to pay to get the answer. "There was no other way she was going to give me the information and I had to get it. Are you worried about the ethics? I mean, she's not going to tell. She'd get in trouble herself. But this proves what Graham was saying, right? Bethany really did have an appointment with a plastic surgeon. She was planning to go there. The appointment was for Monday morning at 7:00 a.m. She must have planned to go into the city that night, stay over, have the surgery and then come home and surprise everyone with how she looked. He's innocent." She beamed at Maggie. "He was telling the truth."

"How do you know she gave you the right information?" Agnes asked.

"You're eating my French toast."

"This is one of the detectives I work with," Maggie said. "Agnes Jorgenson."

"Do you have any proof that what she told you was true?"

"She was reading it off the computer," Livy said, sinking down into one of the chairs. "I could hear the sound of the keys.

Agnes cackled, and headed for the door. "Nice to meet you," she said. "Livy the Younger."

"You think she lied to me? To get my $100?"

"It might have been an awful temptation," Maggie said. "We can certainly check it out. But I wouldn't offer anyone else money."

Livy put her head in her hands. "What's wrong with me?"

"It was a bold plan," Maggie said.

"It's like when I did the research on Persephone and I didn't take account of the wanton women. I just forgot all about them. I don't know what happened. I had to withdraw the article."

"We all make mistakes."

"Shiv said he wanted to marry a real woman. Not someone so immature."

Maggie thought of Edgar, how vulnerable people were to cruel words. "Then you're lucky you didn't marry him."

Livy looked down at her empty plate. Maggie had a horrible feeling Agnes had licked off all the syrup.

"When I talk to Graham, he just talks to me like I'm so special."

"Talk to Graham. When do you talk to Graham?"

"Just on Facebook. Don't worry, Aunt Dove. I'm not going to see him until this is all over."

Facebook.

Just then the phone rang and it was Abigail Coleman.

"Thank you for answering," she said.

"Of course."

"I have a favor to ask. Would you give the eulogy at Bethany's service?"

"Me?" Maggie said.

"She was always so fond of you."

Maggie paused. She had made a bona fide effort to stay away from this case. A sincere effort. She had done everything she possibly could and yet fate, or God, or bad luck, kept throwing it back at her. Maybe it was time to surrender.

"Would you mind if I came by, Abigail? I'd love to talk to you a bit about Bethany, to get material for the eulogy."

"Oh, I don't know. Ben's not here right now."

"And I have my niece staying with me. Would you mind if I bring her? She's assisting me."

"I guess that's all right."

Maggie looked over at her niece, who eyed her speculatively, and who then emitted a soft honk of laughter.

Sometimes it was better to try to walk alongside someone than to push against them.

Chapter Fifteen

aggie told Abigail she'd be there in five minutes, but walking up Main Street was never a straight-line proposition.

The first thing they saw when they turned on to Main Street was a Missing Persons poster for Bethany. There she was, taped on to a lamp post, underneath an ad for dogwalkers and a notice of an apartment for rent for $3,000 a month.

It was odd to see Bethany's picture outside of the actual Bethany. In person she was vivid and loud, Maggie thought, but in her photo, she looked like anyone else. Her eyes seemed narrow and suspicious, her hair was tidy. So much of Bethany was movement and vibration. Maggie couldn't help looking at her chin, the body part that had caused so much trouble. She'd never really thought about it before, but now that she focused, she could see it was pronounced. She understood why it bothered her.

"Sad," Livy said.

"Yes."

Perhaps Livy was finally realizing that a young woman had died. That a tragedy had taken place. She looked like she might cry. She held on to Maggie's arm for a moment, and they continued up the hill, where they ran into Mr. Cavanaugh, who was out with his little dog Fidelio. "Livy Dove," he said. "Why is that name familiar? Do you play the piano?"

She blushed.

"Of course. You were in the Meyerstein competition, weren't you?"

"I only placed fifth."

"Brilliant playing," he said. "I look forward to hearing you perform."

They continued up Main Street until they reached the detective agency, which was empty, being a Saturday, but Maggie had a key. She could see Livy was impressed by the whole operation, as was Maggie. She still couldn't believe she was a detective. Then they went past the barbecue place that had great food but was never open, and then past the bagel place that was always out of bagels. Then past the candy store, the fire department and the police office, and then past Joe Mangione, who was shoveling the walk in front of D'Amici's deli. He was a passionate shoveler, very precise, but he stopped what he was doing when he met Livy. "Ah, you look like a Red Sox fan to me," he cawed.

"I don't watch football," Livy said.

That pushed him right over the edge, he'd be talking about that to the end of time, but Maggie dragged her forward and thought perhaps she could take a few moments to stop in the church and introduce Livy to Reverend Sunday. Livy, it turned out, had spent some time in Ghana and she spoke a little of the language, and she could see the two of them would get along.

She knew she was procrastinating.

She had to go see Abigail, but as they left the church, Maggie was surprised to hear someone yelling. Even odder was that it was Sibyl, a real estate agent who was renowned for her good humor.

"You'd better get to the bottom of this," she shouted. "There are people's lives at stake here."

"What is it?" Maggie said, after she'd hung up.

"Ugh," she cried out. "It's that house on Hollyhock Lane. I'm trying to sell it and the poor owners have done so much work on it. It's gorgeous. But every time I run an ad, someone puts up a comment about how it was involved in a terrible murder ninety years ago. It scares people away. No one wants to buy a house where a murder took place."

"Why would they be doing that?

"To force down the price of the house. It's already dropped by $200,000 and if it goes any lower, the owners are going to be out serious money. They're good people, Lady Dove. I hate to see this happen."

"But why would anyone benefit from lowering the price of the house?"

Sibyl smiled over at Livy, who stood stunned alongside Maggie. "Sorry," she said. "You must be the brilliant niece. I'm not normally a raving lunatic."

Then she looked back at Maggie. "I thought it was Bethany, truth to tell. We had an argument about something and I thought she was doing it to get back at me. She liked games like that, but she couldn't be doing it now. It must be someone else."

She died in a part of the woods not far from Hollyhock House, Maggie thought. Could she have been involved in some real estate scam and the victim felt betrayed?

"Who owns the house?" Maggie asked.

"The Collins," Sybil said. "I don't think you know them. They never did live there. No sooner did they fix it up that he lost his job and they moved in with their son in Connecticut while they put it on the market. It's really cruel what this person's doing, but I suspect it seems llike a game to him. Meanwhile, the Collins are going bankrupt. I hate cruelty," she said, and then her phone started to buzz and she headed off.

"That's a motive for murder," Livy said.

"The Collins? I don't know. I can't see someone downtrodden going after someone with an axe."

"No, not them. Sybil. She has a terrible temper and she's strong."

"Sybil! No. She's one of my favorite people in Darby."

"She could be dangerous."

"No," Maggie said. Not Sibyl. Though she couldn't help but remember the time Sibyl tried to run someone over. But she'd been drinking, and it was a long time ago. Still, someone in this village had attacked Bethany Coleman with an axe. Someone who she knew and might well like. Or someone she didn't know. So many new people had moved in over the last few years. Maggie had a sudden feeling that things she took for granted might not be so.

Chapter Sixteen

bigail Coleman had, in the span of a week, watched a wedding implode and suffered her step-daughter being murdered, so Maggie expected her to look upset. Or preoccupied. And yet she looked exactly as she always did. Hair pulled back, dressed sensibly, no make-up.

She was a stunningly beautiful woman, but she did everything she could to downplay her looks. Her blue eyes were huge, her nose like something from a sculpture, and her chin was absolutely perfect. The sort of chins movie stars have. Maggie fought to keep her hand from stroking her own chin. That was the sort of woman Abigail was. You always found yourself checking yourself in her presence.

"Thank you for having us," Maggie said. "This is my niece, Livy."

Abigail smiled warmly at Livy. "Welcome," she said. She had a slight Texas accent. She gestured for them to come into the living room, which was a barren place. No signs here that a wedding had been planned, or now a funeral. No cards. Flowers. Gifts. Maggie suspected they'd thrown everything out, or more likely donated everything.

She guided them over to a dark brown couch. Maggie felt certain they'd bought it at an Attic Sale and she recalled that Abigail had some sort of strange requirement for her furniture. She didn't approve of bare legs, so all the furniture had to be skirted. No TV. One family photo of them in a tropical location. Bethany looked about sixteen. One painting on the wall that had a vivid sunset splashed across it. All oranges and reds and violets.

"This is a passionate painting," Livy said.

"Is it?" Abigail said. "I painted it in an art class and Ben loved it. He insisted on putting it up."

"You're an artist?" Livy asked.

"No, I only painted that one painting."

She blushed, deeply. "I guess I only had that much to say."

Or that was as much as Ben wanted her to say, Maggie thought. He was a controlling sort of man. She could imagine him wanting to control Abigail's artistic expression, and yet he had hung the painting up. What did that mean?

"What would you like me to talk about in the eulogy," Maggie said. "Any points you want me to make?"

Abigail shrugged. She assumed her more familiar diffident expression. "I'm sure you'd know best, Maggie Dove."

"Still, any insights you might have."

"She…" Abigail paused. "Oh, I wish Ben were here. He's better at these things. He knew her better. But he had to go see the real estate agent."

"I'm sure you have some insights too," Maggie pressed. "What was her favorite TV show? I think she told me once she liked *Project Runway*."

"I don't know. We don't watch TV."

"What about that picture?" Livy asked. "Was that taken in Nicaragua?"

She pointed at the photo of the three Colemans standing on a beach. They were surrounded by children with hare lips. Bethany was the only one in the picture who didn't look happy.

"Yes, the summer she turned sixteen, we took her on a mission trip to Nicaragua," Abigail explained. "We wanted her to see there was a different path. That there were children who were really suffering. That it was foolish to be so upset with her looks. Her chin."

"She doesn't look happy," Livy said.

"It wasn't about being happy," Abigail said.

Maggie pictured Bethany, growing up in that house, her father desperately in love with her beautiful stepmother. She so conscious of her looks. She agreed with Abigail that it was good to remember others' suffering, but she also thought that you could do a good thing with tremendous cruelty. She began to feel oppressed. There was something airless in that room

"Could we go in her room?" Livy said. "Maybe we'll get some ideas there."

"Why yes. Of course," Abigail said. For the first time since they arrived, Abigail seemed to lighten up. She was a sensitive enough woman, Maggie suspected, to be ashamed of how she'd treated her stepdaughter. Or maybe she just wanted to be rid of them.

She gestured toward a hallway. "Take your time."

Then she turned in the direction of the kitchen.

As soon as Maggie went in to the bedroom, she was hit by Bethany's strong scent. She favored a heavy spicy aroma. Overpowering.

The room itself must have been the original master bedroom. There was a bathroom attached. So somehow Bethany'd wrangled the best bedroom in the house, and the Colemans slept in the guest room. She pictured this family life as a continual tug of war, with bitterness on both sides.

Bethany's room was more colorful than the rest of the house. One of the walls was painted red. A huge black TV hung on it. A TV big enough to anchor a bar. Maggie could imagine the sound from it seeping into the house. The parents singing hymns on the piano and Bethany watching *Real Housewives of New York*.

The bed was stripped. The closets empty. They must have bagged up all her clothes and donated them. A calendar from the bank remained on the wall. No dates marked off. No photos of Graham. No computer. No phone. The bathroom was more cluttered. Here were stacks of Bethany's make-up. Had she taken some with her? It was impossible to know. There was one of those professional mirrors with lights bulbs all around it, the better to see your pores. Or your chin.

Maggie went back into the bedroom and looked around. There was a bureau. She pulled out the drawers, which were empty except for the bottom one which was stuffed with things from the bank. Notepads. Calendars. Pens. Small petty stuff that she probably enjoyed stealing. Maggie'd recently handled a petty theft incident at a restaurant and she thought Bethany was exactly the sort of person who would become a thief. Someone aggrieved, someone unappreciated. She'd worked at the bank for years. She'd know a lot of secrets. It would not be impossible to imagine her blackmailing someone. Could that have led to her murder?

"Why didn't she just move out," Livy asked, as they left. "She had an income. She didn't have to stay there."

"Sometimes people get trapped in bad situations, but Bethany never struck me as someone who couldn't break her way out. She must have planned this whole wedding thing for years."

They were both silent as they contemplated that. Bethany in her bedroom, festering, plotting, planning. Hating.

Chapter Seventeen

That night Maggie dreamt of her husband in a way she hadn't done for years. He was young and strong. He made love to her, and she could feel herself, even inside her dream, crying out for him, and she woke with a start and found her cats staring at her, stunned. Their camera eyes clicked. She'd twisted the sheets all around her, and they were wet with sweat. Her heart felt like it might pulse right out of her chest.

"Stuart," she whispered.

How she missed him. How she'd loved him. All this talk of weddings and love and Walter had resuscitated feelings she'd thought were dead. Feelings she'd forgotten. Now they flooded over her. Lying in her bed she remembered another night, long ago, when they'd traveled to Ireland. The inn had no central heating, so the owner gave them a steak-and-kidney pie to put at their feet. How they'd laughed. How they'd loved.

She remembered their wedding, which had been at the church she still attended. The ladies of the church cooked the wedding supper. Pork roast and potatoes and carrots drenched with maple syrup and butter. Her father gave a toast. Mrs. Pillsbury made the wedding cake, and the church choir came and sang to them before they left on their honeymoon. She wondered if it was possible that all that had happened in the same lifetime as this one. It was as though life came in waves. You rode one as long as you could, and then it crashed, and then there was another wave. She thought of Walter, which it was hard to visualize in the context of water. Not a fluid man. More of an arboreal presence. A tree that would not crash.

Now Maggie's heart felt like it would surge right up her throat. She could hear it pulsing in the room, and she reached for Shadow, thinking he might offer some comfort, though he went hard at her touch. Poor rescue cat who had suffered who knows what hidden pains, and so she let go of him and got out of bed.

She grazed downstairs and logged into the Insomnia club, but she was so wired that she couldn't focus and everyone was getting mad at Leona Faraday because she refused to pause. So while everyone else was trying to come up with the right answer, Leona just listened to the contestants and entered the right one, and when her sisters started to complain, Leona said that she was just having fun and she didn't understand why everyone got so serious about these things, and then they all started to argue about something related to the church. And they started to ask her about Livy and what she was like and how it was going and Joe said she heard she was talking to Graham on Facebook.

"You can't allow that," Leona shouted.

"How am I supposed to stop it?"

"Take her computer away from her."

"She's 23. Not a child."

"Have you talked to her?"

Maggie began to feel claustrophobic. It wasn't that she disagreed, she felt overwhelmed and all the shouting was making her dizzy.

That was when she happened to look out her front window, and noticed that there was a light on in the van Dorn house.

That was odd. She knew they'd moved out. The whole street was empty and dark, except for Mr. Cavanaugh's house and that was at the bottom of the road. Was it a light or a flash light?

"I've got to go," she said to the Insomnia Club. Clicked off the computer, and then, without even thinking about it, she grabbed her coat and went out the door.

Chapter Eighteen

The cold staggered Maggie when she got outside, so much so that she almost slipped down her front steps. She grabbed onto the railing and looked over to her little oak tree, shivering in the cold. She thought of Ben Coleman hammering a screw into his tree. For a moment she considered going back into her house, but no. She wanted to know what was going on. She was curious. She walked over to the van Dorn house and rang the bell. No one answered, of course.

They'd divorced and moved away.

The moon was out. Maggie looked back at her house, so welcoming, with two cat silhouettes in the window. She thought sure the van Dorn's door would be locked, but it wasn't. She opened it.

She'd never been in the house when the van Dorns lived there. They were not friendly people. Of course, she'd never had them over either. But it was strange to walk through a deserted house. People on the news were always surprised when they found out their neighbors were running meth labs or burying bodies in the backyard, but the fact was that there was no way to know what your neighbors were doing unless you walked around looking through windows. One thing she'd learned from being a private detective was that people were not always what they seemed. A surprising number made up facts about themselves, even in this time of google.

She walked into the living room and saw that all the furniture had been pushed toward the center, as though someone planned to start a bonfire. A stained towel lay on the floor. There was an empty Gatorade bottle and the room smelled of cigarette smoke. The curtains were yanked off the railings. The van Dorns had lived in this house for ten or more years, but it felt like a hotel room after a bachelor party. Anonymous chaos. And deserted.

Had Bethany done this?

Had she planned to hide out here. Leave the wedding and hole up out at the van Dorns house. She would know it was empty. As a loan officer at the bank, Bethany would know the location of all the empty houses in Darby. It would appeal to her sense of humor, she felt sure, to hide out in one of those houses. To watch the consternation in the village as people searched for her. Maybe the chauffeur was her lover. Maybe the Rolls Royce was parked in the van Dorn garage.

She might also have enjoyed being not far from Maggie Dove. She was a person who enjoyed knowing something others didn't. Could she have been blackmailing someone?

Maggie smelled something. Was it Bethany's scent? Or was it lilies? From her bouquet?

Maggie wandered around, into the kitchen. The refrigerator had old milk and eggs in it. It smelled rank. This room must have been where so many of the van Dorns' arguments took place. She thought of the sound. Never clear what they were arguing about, just angry voices raised. They were brassy people, over-tanned with dyed hair. If happy couples seem to look like each other, they should have been happy. She could only recall one conversation she'd ever had from them. It was during a black-out and they'd all gathered outside and talked about Con Edison. Suddenly Maggie faltered, exhausted. All her nervous energy gone.

She wanted to go home, to her bed and her cats. She felt so tired her legs hurt. She should leave this monument to unhappiness. But first she wanted to check one more thing. The garage. She went over to the garage door and opened it, but there was no Rolls Royce there. She didn't see any tire tracks and she thought there would be because it was so wet outside. There was another jumble of things, this time old dolls. Here was the source of the light she'd seen. Someone had been in the garage. She was surprised the electricity was still on. Was that Bethany's doing as well?

She couldn't puzzle it out. She couldn't believe that this empty, frightening house was right next to her own.

She started back toward the front door, but something silver caught her eye. It was buried underneath some towels, but she was drawn toward it. It was the chalice from church. A silver goblet that they used for communion. She'd spent enough time as a Deacon that she recognized it quite clearly. It was a gift to the previous minister. She looked on the bottom and saw his initials engraved into it. This cup had been used in every communion service she'd been part of. It wasn't the silver that made it valuable but the meaning. She knew it had been at the church at Bethany's wedding because she'd noticed it. It was always in the center of the altar. Bethany must have been here. But why did she take the chalice? How did she take it? She'd certainly not had it in her hand when she walked down the aisle.

Had she perhaps circled back to the church? Waited until everyone was gone and then snuck back in? The church would have been locked, but almost everyone in Darby had a key. But why would she have done that? Maggie supposed for the same reason she'd gone walking out in the first place. Because she was angry? Because she was vengeful?

It was unnerving.

Suddenly something flew up behind her.

Pushed her out of the way. She stumbled, startled, tried to get her hands out in front of her but wasn't fast enough. Fell onto a pile of debris, heard someone running out of there. Tried to get up to chase them, but she couldn't. Her ankle hurt. She had to sit for a moment and get hold of the pain.

"Stupid," she whispered at herself. She felt embarrassed. She could only imagine what Walter would have to say. She would have to be more careful.

Someone angry and violent was out there. She thought of Livy, which gave her the strength to get home. Fortunately, her room was dark. She listened. No sound. She was asleep. She was safe. She wondered then if Livy was talking in the dark to Graham. It would be interesting to know if he had an alibi, or if he had been at the van Dorn house.

Chapter Nineteen

Bethany's funeral was at 4:00 Sunday afternoon, almost exactly a week after she'd gone storming out of her wedding.

Livy'd dressed for the occasion in a prim blue dress and she had a scarf wrapped around her head.

"You actually don't need to wear head coverings to church," Maggie pointed out. "I think that's what the Catholics used to do before the 1960s."

"And you're not Catholic?"

"Presbyterian," she said. "It's a different approach to the whole thing. I have a book if you'd like to read it."

"Interesting," she said. Maggie eyed her. She didn't seem to be sarcastic.

Maggie limped up Main Street, her ankle killing her. She figured she deserved the pain for being stupid.

They kept walking up the hill until the church came into view. It was a beautiful old building made of rock quarried in the Hudson Valley. Maggie always felt happy at the sight of it, except that in this case, to her surprise, she saw Joe Mangione out by the front door, yelling at people to go away. They did not often shun people. They did not generally yell at people to leave the church, except for one truly unfortunate incident with the Lambert family, but as they neared, she could see it was the press. They were trying to get in to interview people and Joe was trying to keep them out, which seemed a Sisyphean task if ever there was one.

Livy looked appalled, as though this confirmed her worst fears about religion, and Maggie was on the verge of trying to explain, except that it was so cold she felt like her nose would fall off and her ankle hurt and all she really wanted to do was get inside and give a eulogy for someone she didn't really know.

Then Walter stepped out in front of the church, inserting himself in front of Joe.

He wore a suit. No coat. He must have decided he could tough out the elements. He looked imposing, she thought. Not that the press seemed intimidated. They began waving their mikes. Lights went on. Cameramen jumped into action.

"Have you arrested Graham Lockwood?"

"We will arrest no one without proof," Walter said. "We are still in the preliminary stages of our investigation and are gathering information."

"Is it true that you are deploying a state-of-the-art drone force."

"Yes," he said.

"Do you wish you'd done that sooner?" another reporter shouted. "Do you wish you'd discovered Bethany sooner?"

"Bethany died soon after she disappeared, so I don't think it would have made any difference."

"Can you be sure?"

"Will you be calling in the state police for help?" an older woman shouted.

"Why would I do that?" he snapped.

Oh dear, Maggie thought. She hoped he didn't lose his temper.

"Do you have much experience handling murders of this type? You seem like you might be in over your head."

"Is that your boyfriend?" Livy whispered. "The one who calls at night."

Walter looked like his head might fly right off.

Maggie felt like this might be the moment for her to intervene. She headed toward the church, pushing through the reporters, and pushed Walter through the door. She was clutching the chalice and felt like she was running a football through a field. Pressing up against Walter was a bit like pressing against a rock, except fortunately he was so startled that he stepped backward and they all sort of staggered into the church, where rows of people awaited and then someone, she wasn't sure who, started to clap and then everyone was clapping and Maggie thought this had to be the most surreal religious experience ever, but it also reminded her of how someone had started to laugh at Bethany's wedding. Something she hadn't really thought about at all, because she'd been so distracted by everything else, but that was an important avenue to pursue.

The Colemans stood hand in hand in front of the casket. Graham waved at Livy and she waved back, which all of Darby observed. Reverend Sunday waved Maggie forward to give the eulogy.

It went all right, but she was dissatisfied. She wished someone who'd flat-out loved Bethany had spoken for her, but the only real candidate was Graham, who might have killed her and now seemed involved in a flirtation with Maggie's niece. She caught herself frowning and stopped herself, looked up and saw a young woman's eyes on her. She wasn't someone Maggie knew and yet she felt she'd seen her around town. Her eyes were made up like a cat, as Bethany's had been, and yet she was pretty sure she hadn't been at the wedding. She looked at Maggie with dislike, which made her feel all the more off balance.

When the funeral was over, everyone went into the parlor, where the Deacons had prepared a huge spread of food. Maggie wondered if some of it was leftover from the wedding feast. Bethany would have been pleased by the turnout, she thought, as she watched the crowd grab for deviled eggs. You could not make enough deviled eggs for a church event.

She noticed Agnes wrapping one in a napkin to take away, which was cheating. You should really only eat one at a time. Graham was surrounded by his brothers. Maggie guided Livy over to Helen and indicated, she hoped, with her eyes that Helen should keep her away from Graham. Helen nodded.

The room was crowded with Coleman relatives, but she saw that Ben and Abigail were standing to the side. Even at their daughter's funeral they made a point of isolating themselves. Alone among the people there, they weren't eating anything.

She was about to go up to them, but Graham got there first. He hugged them. Interesting that there didn't seem to be any bad feeling between them. If you didn't know what had happened, you might have just thought they were friends having a chat. They seemed more glad to see Graham than anyone else there. Maggie wasn't sure why. She'd like to believe they loved him because he'd loved their daughter, but she had the discouraging feeling it wasn't that simple. She wondered if in running out on the wedding, Bethany had proven something the Colemans had long wanted to prove. That they were in the right. Their daughter was willful and proud and now look what she had brought down upon herself.

Maggie started to go in the direction of Bethany's grandfather, when Walter tugged on her arm and yanked her back into the Sanctuary.

His face was red. He looked more agitated than she'd ever seen him.

"Are you okay?"

"I should have sent the drones earlier," he said.

"Well, I think you've handled the whole thing admirably," she said. "No one thought Bethany was in danger. You know what she was like." She felt touched that he would confide in her. She'd never known him to express the least self-doubt.

"The press have been hounding me. I didn't expect all the politics."

"Then you, my friend, have never been active in a church. I remember the time we wanted to move the coffee table from one window to another. It's the closest I've ever come to being assaulted. Trust me, being harassed by the press is nothing compared to being harassed by an angry 90-year-old."

He smiled. "Makes me want to get more involved."

He looked around. No one was there. Everyone had gone for the deviled eggs. There was a beautiful stillness to the place. Sunlight floated in from the Tiffany windows, making everything glow. He smiled down at her.

"Am I too old to feel this way?"

"I hope not," Maggie said, "since I feel the same way."

He pulled her toward him and kissed her slowly. His lips were warm, like coffee.

An acolyte poked his head in, then darted out.

She looked into his serious eyes. She thought she could look into them forever. She reached up to touch his hair, which was surprisingly smooth. She breathed in his warmth, and she touched the small line at the edge of his mouth. The place where he smiled.

Walter's phone buzzed, and he pulled away, hunched into it.

She knew she had to get back to the real world. She'd left Livy alone. With Helen, and she was reliable, but how long had she been away. What if she ran off with Graham? Oh good grief. She dashed back into the parlor. Helen was talking to old Mr. Ridgefield. She didn't see Graham, or Livy. She ran to the center of the room.

Agnes appeared out of nowhere, handing her the napkin with the deviled egg. "Didn't think you'd have a chance to get one," she said.

"That's so thoughtful."

"You thought I was taking an extra one."

"Nonsense. Have you seen Livy?"

Agnes squinted. "She's over there, isn't she?" She pointed toward the far corner of the room and there was Livy in an animated discussion with the young woman with the cat's eyes she'd noticed earlier. As she glanced at her, the young woman leaned toward Livy and said something. Livy honked with laughter.

"It was a nice speech you gave."

Maggie looked over and saw Bethany's grandfather addressing her. Captain Coleman. She supposed he had a first name, but she'd never heard him called anything but captain. He'd settled into one of the couches in the corner of the room. Whenever people moved they donated furniture and it was quite nice. An expensive couch. Lovely end tables. Fine lamps. A piano. She moved over to where he sat and perched on a chair across from him.

"You captured her vitality."

He was a bluff man with red cheeks and rough hands. He looked like he'd spent many winters outside without gloves.

"You were close to her?" she said.

"My favorite granddaughter. And I had a number of them, but none of them like Bethany."

He was the first person who'd spoken of Bethany with true affection and she was touched.

"She was brave. Got my genes. Impatient. She'd do anything for a dare. She loved to hear my stories. I could tell her them over and over again."

Maggie liked talking to older people, partly because it was a relief to know that there were still so many people older than she was, but also because she found the elderly unsentimental. They could tell facts without embroidering them. Having to spend every day thinking about death, they seemed willing to confront hard facts.

"I was always surprised she didn't become a police officer," Maggie said. She settled herself into a chair across from him. Nice firm chair. "Seemed like it would be a natural job choice for her."

He nodded. "I thought so too, but Bethany got into some trouble when she was in high school. Foolishness. Never understood it, but once she had it on her record, she couldn't be a cop. She didn't seem to mind though. She liked being a loan officer. Liked going behind the scenes. She was good at her job too. Tripled the amount of loans they were giving. Damn fools were always telling her to slow down. Telling her they didn't want to grow the bank so fast. What's the point of that? Bethany had no patience for them. She would have taken over the bank one day."

Maggie wondered how many risks Bethany was taking. She remembered talking to someone on Main Street who'd refinanced her house because Bethany had talked her into it, but then, by the time she paid the refinancing fees, she was out a lot of money. She was going to talk to the president of the bank about that. Could Bethany have swindled someone out of money? She thought of the closet full of notepads and pens. But would that provoke someone to go after her with an axe? And how would that person know she was going to go running out of her wedding? The only person who did know was Graham. Unless…

"Did you know Bethany was going to walk out of the wedding?"

"No," he said, "but I wouldn't have stopped her. Always told her she could do better than that. She could have anybody. Why would she want him?"

He glared at Graham, who must have felt the heat from his gaze because he looked up at that moment and met Coleman's eye. He didn't look away, Maggie noticed.

"What don't you like about Graham?"

"He has a temper. They all do, all those Lockwoods. You don't see it because he bottles it up, but that makes it worse."

"You've seen him lose his temper?"

"No, but I've seen all the rest of his damn fool brothers lose their tempers. Why should he be different?"

Suddenly he looked up and smiled, and Maggie, following his gaze, saw that Livy had come over to join them. She perched on the chair that Maggie was sitting in, a bit like a cat. "This is my niece," she said. "She's come to stay with me for a few weeks."

"You're lucky."

"This is Bethany's grandfather."

"Oh, I'm sorry," Livy said, and she did look sorry. She looked sincerely sorry. She put out her hand to him and he held it. Maggie felt touched. Her niece was always surprising her. She looked around and noticed Graham had gone. Most of the attendees had. The funeral was winding down.

"You're helping your aunt with her detection," he said.

"I'm trying."

"You must be a great comfort to her. You stop by and see me," he said. "I'll tell you about my granddaughter."

"I will," Livy said.

"Don't just focus on the surface of the village," he said. "There's a lot going on in here. Bethany got involved with something bigger than her. I don't know what it was, but be careful. Promise me."

"Yes, sir," Livy said, though Maggie noticed her glance quickly down at her phone.

Chapter Twenty

"**I** need your help, Aunt Dove."

It was an hour after the funeral and Livy had dragged her off to a new waffle restaurant that Maggie didn't even know existed. She said there'd been a lot of chatter about it on-line. It was a cute old-fashioned place tucked on the other side of the train station, in an area of Darby Maggie rarely walked. One of the waiters wore roller skates. He swirled around, holding a plate, then put the waffle in front of you and sprayed it with whipped cream so it looked like an elephant.

"Livy, there is really nothing more I can do for Graham."

"No," she said. "This isn't about Graham, it's about Gunvor."

"Who?"

"That girl I was talking to at the funeral. After it."

"The girl with the cat's eyes?" Maggie asked. The one who looked at her so sneeringly.

"She's having a terrible time," Livy went on. She leaned toward Maggie, so focused on what she was saying that she didn't even touch her waffle. Maggie put down her fork.

It was already dark outside. She longed for spring. Her ankle hurt and her feet were cold from slush. She wished she were stronger, younger, as passionate as Livy.

"She's an au pair and she works for a family that's terrible. They have five children or six and the mother never lets her have any time off. And they never pay her. She's supposed to get $195 a week, but a lot of times they just don't have the money. She has no money. And she's supposed to have time to take an English class, but they don't let her do that. They treat her like she's a slave."

"Isn't there an agency she can talk to?"

Livy looked down at her waffle. "She was with an agency when she first came here, and she had a really good experience with her host family, but then the mother got sick and she got really jealous. So she just left."

"Is she here legally?"

Livy shook her head. "I don't know the status of her visa, but she found this family through a message board. But does that matter? She's trapped. She can't leave because she'd never find a job anywhere else."

"Where is she from?"

Some girls walked by and waved at Livy and said hello. She waved back. Maggie took a bite of her waffle.

"Norway, but she's had a really hard time. She doesn't want to go back. She was supposed to be at that camp where people were shot a few years ago. So many people she knew died. She would have died except that she was sick and couldn't go, but it's changed how she feels about her home. She's traumatized. She can't go back there. It would be torture for her."

"Who are the people she works for?"

"The Windsors. They live on Woodland Drive."

Maggie did not think she could help at all. She didn't know those people and she wasn't sure what she could say, but something about Livy made her want to be better than she was. She always looked at her so hopefully. She couldn't get over how many people her niece knew given that she'd only been here two days, and the remarkable thing was that she knew all these people Maggie didn't know, which was odd because she would have said she knew everyone in the village. It was almost as though there was a whole parallel Darby running alongside the one she knew. Then there was an underground Darby. There was so much she didn't know. That felt like a sin to her because it meant she'd kept herself walled off.

Bethany too had crossed between these worlds, because of her job at the bank. She met all the various people coming to Darby. Maggie had a feeling that something in that intersection caused her death, but she didn't know enough about Darby to know what that was.

It occurred to her suddenly how restricted her circle of acquaintances was. She knew everyone at the church, of course. She knew people who'd been in the village a long time. But she didn't know many of the people Livy's age. She didn't know the au pairs. She didn't know the outsiders. That seemed wrong to her. She realized she should make more of an effort. It was her responsibility to widen her circle.

"What do you think I can do?"

"Aunt Dove! You'll do it? Maybe you could just talk to them. The mother. The father's always at work."

"If I do this, will you give me a reprieve. Do I have to save anyone else in the village?"

Livy laughed her great honking laugh. Everyone in the waffle store turned to smile at her. "Then you'll do it?"

"I'll go to see her. I should be able to think up some reason. But I think that Gunvor is going to have to figure out this legal situation."

She nodded, and put a big piece of waffle in her mouth. "She was good friends with Bethany."

"She was? I'm surprised their paths crossed."

"They were in a basketball league together. They liked to do meet-up things. Rock climbing. Extreme scavenger hunting. She's fun."

"How did you meet her?"

"There's a whole discussion board about Darby on line. People give tips, and so on. You should look at it, Aunt Dove. You'd be amazed."

She took a big spoonful of cream and put it in her mouth. For just a moment she looked like that girl in the M&M store in Manhattan. Nice to have someone around who thought you were wonderful and powerful and better than you were. Maybe she would become better.

"I'm glad you're here," Maggie said.

"Me too."

"Oh," Livy added. "We should also go talk to Amber at the eye salon."

"Amber?"

"Yes, she was another one of Bethany's friends. We can go by tomorrow morning. Gunvor thought she might know if Bethany was seeing someone else. Matter of fact," she said, "I made an appointment for tomorrow morning. I thought she'd be more comfortable if she thought we were regular clients." *We?*

"You're not looking for a job as a detective, are you?"

Honk.

That night Walter called to check in, and she could hear the frustration in his voice. The weather was making finding clues difficult. They were exactly where they had been three days earlier, when Bethany's body was found. The state was making noises that it might come in and take over. He was irritated. She told him about her plan to talk to Amber and he said that's fine, though he was obviously distracted. She was going to hang up and then he said, "Why were you limping?"

She was going to make up some story, but she pictured Livy and thought perhaps she should tell the truth. "You went into that house by yourself?"

"Walter, I repent."

He cleared his throat. "Okay," he said. "But I can't have anything happen to you."

"I will not do anything so foolish again. It was really scary."

"You didn't see who pushed you."

"No, but it was with force. More than just a 'get out of my way' push."

"You and Livy could come stay with me until this is solved. You'd be safer."

She could hear Livy's laughter in her head. *A man has asked you to move in with him, Aunt Dove.*

"I will consider it," she said.

Chapter Twenty-One

Maggie was entranced by the Amber Eyes salon the moment she walked in. She hadn't been in the building since it was an organic pharmacy and it had changed considerably. Soft carpets were strewn about the floor. There were several velour pillow chairs to sink into and a display case full of colorful boxes. There was also a director's chair in the corner, which was where Amber guided Livy.

Bethany would have loved it here, Maggie thought. She would have loved all the colors and mirrors and all the focus on her. That's all she really wanted. When you got right down to it, the whole reason she was killed was because she wanted attention. She could have simply run away, but she didn't want to do that.

She wanted shock and awe. She wanted everyone thrilled by her disappearance.

Something about the way she left the wedding led her to die, but that was the conundrum. Did she leave the wedding and just happen to draw someone's attention because she was wearing a wedding gown and holding $20,000? Was she the unluckiest woman alive? Or, did someone, knowing who she was, set up her up, and then, take pleasure it. That was what she felt as she looked around Amber's room. She had the sense of the murderer knowing what sort of person Bethany was and taking pleasure in bringing about her death.

That brought her right back to Graham, because who knew her better than he did?

But how well did he know her? The more she heard, the more it made sense to her that Bethany would have spewed all her love and passion onto someone else.

"Now which one of you is Maggie Dove?" Amber asked.

"That's my aunt," Livy said. "She's getting her eyes done for a big date."

"Me?" Maggie hissed.

"It has to be you," Livy whispered back. She smelled of lemons. "The person in the chair can't talk and I thought it would be better if I asked the questions."

"Oh dear."

Maggie leapt up onto the director's chair and Amber began peering at her face. "You have to relax," she said. "No lines. No tension in the jaw. Do you wear make-up?"

A plush sort of person, Maggie thought. Not so much overweight as well-developed. Her lips were stained wine colors, her blouse was tight and low fitting, her eyes sleepy. She looked like Dionysus, Maggie thought.

"Not much," Maggie said.

"With her bones she doesn't have to," Livy said.

Amber nodded.

"But I thought you could play up her eyes."

It felt strange to have someone looking at her so closely. Iphigenia looked at her when she cut her hair, but she didn't pay that much attention. She was usually busy talking. Maggie'd always fantasized about a transformation. She loved movies where the protagonist got done over. She'd watched *Pretty Woman* twenty times.

She started to ask a question, but Amber put her finger on her lips.

"Sssh, you can't talk. It will ruin the lines."

"You've been doing this a long time," Livy said.

Amber nodded. "I got my start in *Little Shop of Horrors*. Off Broadway," she said.

"That must have been exciting."

Amber began rooting around her colors, now picking out a little swab and began stroking it against Maggie's cheeks. Her skin glowed. She looked like she'd just come back from Bermuda.

"I loved it. Every night was something different. Then I got a job on *Lion King*."

"Wow," Livy said. "That's got to be the Mount Everest of Cosmetology." Maggie looked around the room. There was a framed *Playbill* on the wall. A pair of purple pants tossed in a pile in the corner. Was she living in the studio? Or probably renting space upstairs.

"So why did you move to Darby? It must be a huge change."

She paused for a moment. Stopped to put on a bit more mascara. "I wanted a change. Working on Broadway is tough, and I happened to read an article about best places to live in the Hudson Valley and they mentioned Darby and I thought, why not?"

Seemed sort of random to Maggie, but all right.

"I'm new here myself," Livy said. "Just got here four days ago. Gunvor was telling me about you."

"Oh Gunvor, she's great."

Amber began flicking a soft brush over Maggie's eye lids. It felt so soft, like the way the cats did when they licked her face.

"She was telling me about Bethany. You did her eyes for her wedding?"

Was it Maggie's imagination or did Amber's hands shake a little bit? She stopped putting on the eye shadow and began mixing some colors in a pot.

"That was sad."

Livy paused, waiting for her to say more, but Amber seemed to have clamped up. She looked at the clock. Maggie could feel Livy thinking, the energy pouring off her.

"I guess I can relate to Bethany in a way because my wedding fell apart too, though it was my boyfriend who walked out on me."

Amber looked over, curious. "He walked out on you?"

"He realized he didn't love me. Just like that. He was sitting at a traffic light and he saw a couple go by and he realized he'd never love me like that. He wanted more passion in his life."

"Oooh," Amber sighed. "Jerk. I had a boyfriend like that. Not exactly like that, but he didn't like my toes. My pinkie toe is really small and he couldn't get over it. What could I do? I had to wear socks all the time, but that didn't work. He broke my heart. We were together for seven years."

Maggie could feel that Amber's hands were on auto-pilot. She thought how right her niece was that she was the one to ask the questions. She could never have got Amber to open up llike that.

"Do you think Bethany had a change of heart like that? Was that why she walked out?"

"No, she loved Graham and he loved her. He was wild for her."

Maggie could feel Livy flinch from across the room. "You're sure?"

"Oh yeah." She smiled. "She used to tell me about the things they did. No, she loved him. She wanted to marry him and he wanted to marry her."

"Then why did she walk out of the wedding," Maggie asked. She couldn't help herself though Amber screeched and told her to "mind your lines!"

She looked over to Livy and saw her rubbing her eyes. Had it never occurred to her that Graham really had loved Bethany? What had he been telling her?

"I think it had to do with her parents," Amber said, which brought them right back to the beginning.

Bethany wanted revenge on her parents, walked out of the wedding and ran into someone with an axe. Someone who wasn't Graham, if what Amber said was true. Maggie felt like the more she learned about Bethany, the closer and yet the more far away she became. She was a woman with friends, but none of them were in her wedding party. She was a dishonest woman, and yet seemed devoted to Graham. She seemed so proactive and self-directed that it was hard to picture her death as a random act of violence, and yet randomness was always hard to understand.

"Are you okay?" she asked Livy when they walked out of the store.

Livy looked subdued. Even her hair looked flatter. It was only 10:00 in the morning and Maggie was made up to go to a ball. She was glad Livy was going to see Reverend Sunday later that day.

"You'll think me insane, but I never envisage Graham with her."

"You've only known him four days."

She whirled on Maggie. "But you only knew Uncle Stuart one day and you fell in love with him. Isn't that so?"

"Yes, but he'd not just been engaged and no one had accused him of murder. He was just a professor."

"Are you so sure?"

"What are you suggesting? I was married to the man for twenty years. I'm reasonably sure of who he was. Is there something I don't know?"

She flushed. "Nothing. Nothing. I'm just all turned around. I've got to get over to Reverend Sunday."

"Okay," Maggie said. "I'm going to be picking Edgar up at school later, if you'd like to come with me. I think you'd like him."

"Sure," she said. "Sure."

She had been married to Stuart Dove for twenty years, Maggie thought. She felt reasonably sure she knew him. Not all of him. All those trips to Russia, the phone calls at night, the Russian immigrants showing up. She assumed he had some secret work with the government. And he was a man who kept to himself. Not a chatterbox. He loved nothing more than to sit in his library, reading, with Maggie in the next chair, reading, and his daughter at his feet, reading.

This was not a man with a dark secret, she thought. She hoped.

Chapter Twenty-Two

"You look stunning, Maggie Dove," Edgar sang out as he lunged toward her. "You look like a cat." She'd decided not to wash off the make-up. She knew how much joy it would bring Edgar, even if it would lead to a frenzy of licking.

"This is my niece, Livy," she said. As she suspected, Edgar was intrigued. A beautiful and sympathetic woman. The boy was no fool.

She figured they could all go down to the park, but just then she noticed Ms. Sanchez heading her way.

Head down, on a mission.

"May I speak to you for a moment," she asked.

Poor Edgar clung to her like a tic, but she had to let him go. "I didn't mean to talk about the axe."

Ms. Sanchez stroked the back of his head. She was a kind woman, though a stern one.

"I'll watch Edgar," Livy said. She knelt down in front of Edgar and held out her hands. He paused for only a moment. Then Maggie set off behind Ms. Sanchez.

"It's completely my fault," Maggie said, as she walked into Edgar's first grade classroom. "I should have looked through the newspapers before I showed them to him. It just never occurred to me that there was a murder in Darby. I wasn't even worrying about it, quite honestly, and then I told him not to talk about it, but that was asking a lot."

"He does have a preoccupation with violence," Ms. Sanchez said, "but that's not what I'm concerned about."

She gestured Maggie to sit down across from her desk. It was a bright and energetic school room. The desks were set in circles so all the kids could make eye contact with each other. There were posters all over the wall showing the water cycle. Ms. Sanchez had a degree in chemistry and was renowned for her passion for the Hudson River, or any other body of water. Occasionally she joined the Insomnia Club and always did well on questions about water ways.

"There's something else?" Maggie asked. She began to get that anxious pumping feeling that she got when she was about to get bad news.

Some kids began yelling and laughing and Maggie turned to the window, recognizing Edgar's voice. He was riding on the zip line, Livy racing alongside him, laughing as she tried to keep up. The au pairs were running with her, all of them laughing. She recognized Gunvor, the young woman with the hostile host family.

"This is awkward," Ms. Sanchez said, "and I shouldn't be talking to you. I should be reporting this to social services, but I know how much Edgar and his mother love you and I'd rather not raise this to the next level without trying to intervene."

Report? Maggie heard. Social services?

"What's happened?" Could he have hurt someone seriously? She supposed it was possible, though he was more bark than bite. Except for the time he went after Ambrosia Fletcher with scissors, but that was some time ago. And the scissors were plastic.

"I'm concerned that Edgar is being abused."

Maggie rocked backward, knocking her knees against the desk so hard that tears came to her eyes. "Abused. What do you mean?"

"No, no, no," Ms. Sanchez said, putting her hand on her's. "I'm not talking about physical abuse. I'm talking about emotional abuse."

"I don't understand," Maggie said.

"If a child feels uncared for, unloved, it can be as damaging as a slap," Ms. Sanchez said. "Children like this cannot learn to express emotions safely, so they have to learn to hide them, but being children, they can't tamp them down completely, so they erupt in other ways. Difficulty standing still, anxiety, an inability to regulate themselves, isolation."

"But he's loved," Maggie said.

Ms. Sanchez sighed. "Have you ever watched his mother with him? Really watched her?"

"I've certainly been with them enough."

"Have you ever seen her praise him, or tell him that she loves him?"

"She's not an effusive sort of person, that's true. But that doesn't mean she doesn't love him. The fact is, she's having a very difficult time," Maggie said.

She couldn't give out more details without betraying a confidence, but she knew that Helen had not loved Edgar's father, that she had been afraid of him, that he was a dangerous man and she worried that his genes would work their way through Edgar. She'd always been open about her concerns. She'd always said she was being intentionally strict because she wanted to make sure Edgar didn't turn out like his father.

But even as she spoke, she remembered the last time she'd been with Helen. The way she'd berated Edgar. The way she had of tuning him out. The pained look on his face when she turned him away. Poor little boy with the circles under his eyes.

"She needs to see a counselor," Ms. Sanchez said. She took a business card from her desk and gave it to Maggie. "This therapist specializes in counseling parents with this issue."

Maggie felt the embossed print on the card. She couldn't imagine handing it to Helen.

"This can't wait," Ms. Sanchez said. "He's a very special little boy and she's damaging him. I can give you a week to talk to Dr. Blake, but if she won't go, then I'll have to report her. You understand?"

Maggie went outside and found Edgar still on the zipline, though at the sight of her he jumped right off.

Pummeling right into her. The Edgar hug. It rearranged your organs, but it packed a lot of love.

"Am I in trouble?" he asked.

"No, lamb," she said, hugging him tightly.

"What did Ms. Sanchez want to talk to you about?"

"It's a grown-up thing, but you've done nothing wrong."

Livy walked over then, with the au pair Maggie recognized from church.

"This is Gunvor," she said. "And this is my Aunt Dove."

"Nice to meet you," Maggie said.

Gunvor mumbled a reply.

"Livy tells me you're from Norway."

Gunvor rolled her eyes. Maggie began to feel some sympathy for her host family, whoever they were.

The girl oozed contempt. Maggie did not like being dismissed. Part of the pleasure of being in a small village, or in a church, is that you're seen, even if you're not young and beautiful. Maggie did not like being ignored. The sin of pride, she told herself. Exactly, she responded.

"What part of Norway are you from?" Maggie asked.

"You've been there?"

"Matter of fact I have," Maggie said, which happened to be the truth, though she would have lied. There was only so much contempt a person could endure. "I had a friend in Bern," she said. Her husband's friend really.

A professor at University of Oslo. Suddenly the image flashed in her mind of her husband skiing. He was a fluid skier. Completely fearless. That had surprised her about him. She hadn't expected an academic to have that level of athletic competence. Stuart was also good with cars. He would have been intrigued by the mystery of the Rolls Royce. He would have loved that she had a detective agency.

"Beautiful country," Maggie said.

"Beautiful country," Gunvor repeated. Truly an annoying person.

"We were thinking of getting coffee at the new coffee shop," Livy said. "Would you like to join us, Aunt Dove?"

"No thank you," Maggie said. What new coffee shop? "I'm going to spend some time with Edgar, but I'll see you later. You think you'll be back for dinner?"

"You have to report back," Gunvor said to Livy.

"No, it's not like that," Livy said, looking flustered, but Maggie had no desire to talk any longer to Gunvor. Life was way too short.

"I'll see you later," she said, and kissed her niece on her cheek, and then put out her hand for Edgar. There was a library in the school that he loved. He always did well in quiet places, oddly, where there was less stimulation. He loved to sit in those beanbag chairs and cuddle, and she felt a burning desire to give this child a hug right now.

"Would you like to go to the library?" she asked.

"Don't I have to go home right now?"

"Not yet. We can spend some time here."

They walked down the hallway, in the direction of the library. The walls were filled with posters and Valentine's Day hearts. She remembered how back in her day that was such a controversial holiday. So many tears over who got valentines or not, and the teacher always having a talk about fairness. She'd been a popular girl and proud of it. She had not always been kind. One of the people she'd teased so much had been little Agnes Jorgenson, one of seven children, the girl who always came to school with sweat stains under her arms and smelling of chicken soup and onions. She regretted that, but was grateful that Agnes had forgiven her and become one of her closest friends. She wondered if Agnes would be a good person to help Edgar. Somehow, she'd managed to survive her childhood, and thrive.

Bethany had also not been kind, Maggie thought, but she hadn't had a chance to repent. Maybe that was the grace involved in getting older, that you had a chance to make up for all the stupid things you did when you were young. Life was so much longer than she realized when she was young. Had Bethany lived, what would she have thought of her wedding? Who would she have loved? What was she running off to on that cold afternoon? Or who?

"The blue seat," Edgar said. It was his favorite chair, and pity the poor child who was sitting in it when Edgar got to the library. But now it was empty. They had the space to themselves. The librarian came over and gave Edgar a hug and gave him a new book that had just come in. "I thought you'd like it, Edgar. It has military weapons in it."

"Thank you," he said, grinning widely, his little face dissolving into dimples. He clutched it to his chest as though trying to absorb the words through his heart. Then, after Mr. Hurston had gone away, he turned to Maggie.

"Why did Ms. Sanchez want to talk to you? Is it to do with Ambrosia Fletcher?"

"No," Maggie said. "But whatever you're doing to Ambrosia, stop."

He nodded and snuggled against her. He ground his bottom into her lap, as though trying to permanently insert himself. "Then what did Ms. Sanchez want?"

How could she begin to explain this to a seven-year-old when she didn't understand it herself? Emotional abuse. How on earth to raise the subject with Helen, and yet she had to talk to her before she could even begin a conversation with Edgar. Abuse. It was hard to imagine loving someone who was an abuser. It seemed the ultimate taboo, and yet she loved Helen. She was a ferocious friend, a good person. How to reconcile that?

"Maggie Dove?" he pressed.

She hugged him tight. "Ms. Sanchez wants me to talk to your mom about something, but you're not in any trouble, and I promise you that I'll explain it all to you when I can. Is that fair? Can you trust me on that?"

He looked at her closely. She thought of how the cats looked at her, as though able to intuit something that went far deeper than what she knew she was projecting. She felt, as he gazed at her, that he was going into her very soul, and she hoped she was worthy. The moment clicked by. His pupils widened and then she must have passed his test because he nodded and said, "That lady that was killed. It was with an old axe, wasn't it?"

"Yes," she said. "How did you know that?"

"I saw it on the news," he said. She pictured him, up at midnight, watching the news on his phone.

"That man, that 'degenerate,'" he said. "The one in the newspaper article, Maggie Dove. He killed that girl with an axe and then he threw it in the woods and the police never found it."

"How do you know that?" she asked.

"Because it's on-line. I went and looked it up on my mommy's computer last night. You can access the newspapers on line. I was reading about it and that's what it said. Here, give me your phone."

She looked into his eyes and saw a 35-year-old staring out of a seven-year-old head.

He began pressing buttons and then he called up the library website, and clicked some more and soon a very small newspaper photo was in front of Maggie. It was an issue of *The Darby Gazette*, the same newspaper they'd looked at at the library, but this one had been transferred on-line. The print was impossibly small, but she was able to zoom in and read it. It came from January 1935, which was after the articles she and Edgar had read. It was titled, "Search reveals clues."

"Investigators examining Hollyhock House have discovered several clues relating to the heinous murder of young Daisy Calhoun." It went on to say that they'd found a saw, and a knife, but they believed an axe to have been involved and couldn't find it. Teams of police officers were roaming the Darby woods, but without success.

Hollyhock House, she thought.

That was the very house that Sibyl was talking about that had stood empty.

A house with a murderous past.

A house that Bethany could have driven past on her way to the airport, or wherever she was going. Maggie'd assumed she'd take a direct route because the roads were so bad, but it was possible she'd taken a back route. Could she have broken down at Hollyhock House? Or could she have intended to go there in the first place? Was she meeting somewhere there? It was empty. Maybe it was part of a network of empty houses people went to.

But Walter said someone had cleaned the axe. So it wasn't just a random find. Had someone found the axe in the woods and cleaned it and then brought it back to the house?

"Edgar," she said. "I think you've discovered something important. I think we should go talk to Walter Campbell about this. Would you be all right with that?"

"Yes," he cried out.

Chapter Twenty-Three

The police station was under siege. An army of news vans surrounded it and a line of newspaper reporters stood outside. They didn't seem bothered by the cold. Each reporter had his own territory and a camera man and they were all recording something as Maggie walked past. She felt their eyes on her, but figured they dismissed her as a grandmother who happened to have on a lot of make up, with her grandson. She suspected she did not look to fit in with the salacious bride murder they were covering. Incognito!

They walked through the doors and found Mercy Williams glaring at them. That was her natural demeanor, however. It didn't mean she was actually angry. Though she was actually angry. She was a very polished young woman who'd transferred to Darby from the Bronx and, in one of her first acts, had given Maggie a parking ticket, and in her second and third acts, two more. She was rigorously honest and completely humorless, and because Maggie knew she didn't like her, she managed to annoy her at every step, which she felt bad about.

"How are you?" she said to Mercy. "Lot of disruption."

Mercy just glared. She wore her dark hair cut very short, and no make-up, and yet she managed to be stunning and feminine.

"We'd like to see Walter, if we might."

"He doesn't have time for this. He's busy. He's inundated."

"We have a clue," Edgar cried out.

Just then a door slammed open and a young man came scurrying by, closely followed by Walter, who looked like he was going to strike him. "You stay away from my family," he shouted, as the man went vaulting right out the door. Walter stood there, panting, and then his eyes focused on Maggie and he smiled.

"What are you doing here?" he asked.

"I tried to keep her away," Mercy said.

"That's quite all right. And young Edgar, too. This is a treat."

He beckoned them past the entry way, into the private corridor that led to his office. Past the holding tank where the occasional felon was locked up, past all the administrative offices, and then into Walter's room. It did not look as neat as it had a few days previous. Stacks of paper were carefully piled on his desk. Walter pulled over a second chair so that they might talk.

"Intense?" Maggie asked.

His face was red from anger, but his white shirt was as fresh and neat as it always was. He looked imposing. Maggie was impressed that the young man had tried to challenge him.

"Edgar's uncovered something that might be helpful," Maggie said.

"Please."

She nodded to Edgar who launched into his story about the missing axe. Walter listened intently. Maggie found herself eyeing him surreptitiously, noticing a scar under his chin that she hadn't seen before. She loved the way he listened so carefully to Edgar. He could not have been more different than her own husband, she thought disloyally. But Stuart would really not have approved of Edgar. He was not really a person who liked children, though he did adore his beautiful and well-behaved daughter. But Edgar would definitely have been high-energy for Stuart's taste. She wondered how he would have handled it.

"So a killer throws an axe in the woods almost ninety years ago," Walter said. "It sits there all that time, and then someone finds it and uses it." He paused. "On someone."

"Or maybe," Edgar said, in a surprisingly strong voice, "the degenerate never threw it into the woods. Maybe he hid it somewhere in the house and someone found it."

"Someone who might have been staying there," Maggie said. "Walter, do you have any idea how many empty houses there are in Darby? People get divorced. People can't sell them. People go away. And then other people sneak in. You know how people are about security here. Everyone thinks it's safe, and so these people, these strangers, or not strangers, come and stay in the houses. I don't mean like squatting, necessarily. I mean like airbnbs. They stay there for a night or so, or maybe longer. But maybe someone was staying at Hollyhock House. Bethany knew about these empty houses," she went on. "In fact, I get the sense she might have encouraged people to stay." She thought of what Sibyl said. Maybe she was actually trying to manipulate the price of houses.

Walter buzzed his phone. "Mercy," he said. "I want you to get hold of the bank and get a list of abandoned buildings in Darby. Thank you."

Then he turned to Edgar. "Thank you, young man. I'll make sure that you'll get a commendation for this."

Edgar looked like he'd swallowed the moon.

Walter shook Edgar's hand. "Nice work. Both of you. I'll be in touch."

They were being dismissed, but Maggie did not plan to go quite so easily. "You know," she said, "if you get in your car and drive to Hollyhock House, all the reporters will follow you. But if I swing by the back lot, no one will pay any attention. You can sneak out."

"You plan to drive me to Hollyhock House?"

"You will have to fit yourself into an Audi TT, but yes, that would be my plan."

He grinned. "Why not?"

"Can I come too?" Edgar asked.

"No," they both replied.

"My car's in front of the detective agency," Maggie said. "I'll drop off Edgar with Agnes, retrieve the car, and then come get you. I'll park in the back lot."

"I don't like Agnes," Edgar whined.

"I'll get the Forensics team up there as well," he said.

Walter stood to his full height, which had to be hovering around 6'4". Maggie was not, in truth, sure how to get him on to the TT. It would be easier to tie him on the roof, like a Christmas tree. But she suspected that good humor and resourcefulness, would solve the problem, and in fact, Walter wound up being far more flexible than she had expected, though it did require some prying to get him out of the seat. But then there they were, at Hollyhock House.

Chapter Twenty-Four

Someone had put a lot of money into Hollyhock House. It gleamed with fresh white paint. It glowed with fancy solar-powered walk lights. The curtains in the windows were perfectly hung, neat little waves that dipped evenly in each room. Yet for all that, there was something dispiriting about it, Maggie thought. Empty houses gave off a particular vibe. As do people who were lonely. There was an emptiness in them that longed to be filled. Or maybe she was just imagining things. Maybe it was just hard to look at a house like this and see anything but the crime that had once taken place here. Someone, a child, had suffered terribly here. That had to leave a mark.

That terrible man had kidnapped a young girl from New York City. He'd told her parents he was bringing her up to Westchester to go to a nephew's birthday party. The parents were simple people, excited that their daughter had an opportunity to shine. They let him take her, told her to be good, and only when the day had passed did they recognize something was wrong and they called the police. But it took the police years to track down the missing girl. They searched diligently, but there were no clues. She disappeared into the mists and it was only a weird coincidence that finally led to the discovery of her body. An off-duty police officer, years later, happened to see the man walking by. He had an unusual face and that triggered a memory of the wanted poster. The police officer followed him back to his home, and the murderer, confronted, confessed.

After Franz Stanger was caught, the trial was a three-ring-circus. This was only a year after another man had been tried and executed for killing the Lindbergh baby. Like Bruno Richard Hauptman, Stanger was a German national. There was a lot of feeling against the Germans, and that was part of the rage his murder provoked. Darby convulsed with hate, people drove their cars down this very road for hours. Lines of cars, headlights on, wanting to look at the site of evil. A line of cars. Maggie remembered how when Juliet died, lines of cars went by her house. She wondered what human need it was to want to see firsthand where a tragedy took place.

But there'd never been any question that Franz Stanger was guilty, or that's what the newspapers said. He confessed to the murder, and to several others, and when he went to the electric chair, he was eager.

Could the footprints of such crimes not leave a mark?

Could the house not absorb the fear and anguish that lived here? She'd read once that trees absorbed the feelings around them.

Two giant hemlock trees grew on either side of the house. They would have witnessed the crime, Maggie thought. She noticed both were bare of leaves in their midsection. Was it possible that the evil had spread outwards like the waves of a nuclear blast and destroyed everything in its path?

Walter strode up the steps, to the wrap-around porch, and then to the front door, where he reached under the mat and pulled out a set of keys.

"Sibyl told me they were here," he explained.

He turned the key in the lock and it swung open.

A large foyer loomed in front of them, grander than Maggie would have imagined. There was something almost theatrical about it, as though intended to be a stage. The wood was highly polished cedar and there were darker pieces of wood inlaid. To the right was a large solid stairway, also with inlaid wood and wainscoting, and beyond it was a huge empty room, probably a dining room. A chandelier hung from the ceiling but there was no table. Next to that Maggie could see the gleam of a stainless steel kitchen, also clean, also empty. She stepped forward and saw nothing though she thought she smelled something. Was it Bethany's perfume or was she imagining it? She remembered Bethany saying that she was having a special fragrance made for the wedding. She should have asked Amber about it.

"Do you smell that?" she asked Walter.

He closed his eyes and breathed in deeply. "Gardenias?"

"I think it's the perfume Bethany was having made up for the wedding."

They walked further into the house. Their footsteps echoed against the walls. The house sounded empty. She imagined Bethany running in out of the snow, dressed in her wedding dress. "If she ran in here, she would have to be planning to change out of her wedding gown. She had a bag full of money. Maybe she also had some spare clothes."

"She'd go upstairs," Walter said, "to the master bedroom."

Maggie nodded and started toward the stairs. She felt confident this house would have an opulent bathroom, and in fact it did. When they opened the door to the master bathroom, they were stunned. You could turn the shower on simply by pushing a button right at the doorway, and then the shower burst forth like a rain forest. The floors felt warm. But there were no towels here, no sign that anyone had been there. Maybe she was wrong. It all made sense that Bethany would have come here. It felt psychologically right, but there was no clue.

She walked toward a large window that faced out onto the woods. These were the very woods Maggie walked in almost every day of her life, but they looked different from this angle. Where Bethany had died was clearly visible. The trees were bare. No sheltering leaves and she could see the yellow crime tape. "She must have come up here, intending to change, but then she found something here that frightened her, and so she turned around and ran down the steps and out the door."

"Did she interrupt someone?" Walter asked. "Had someone been squatting here and found the axe?"

"But where's the money? Where are her clothes?"

"Maybe still in the car."

"No, that makes no sense. She chose this place. She must have. She was a loan officer. She knew it was empty. Maybe she'd squirreled her stuff away in advance. Came up here, planned to retrieve it. Got interrupted. But where?"

The room was empty.

Bethany was cautious. She would not risk losing $20,000. Then Maggie caught sight of the tree scraping against the window. She tried to open the window, but it stuck. Bethany was much stronger than Maggie. She beckoned Walter over and he opened the window and reached out and there, in the tree, was tucked a package that contained money and clothes.

"She was here," she said.

Walter began talking into his phone, but she stood in the room a little longer. Trying to understand the burst of emotions inside of her, feeling scared for the first time. Someone evil had been here, someone with hate in his heart. He hadn't wanted money. He hadn't wanted Bethany physically. He had only wanted to inflict harm. She could feel it in the house. Evil gave off a smell. She thought of a place in the woods she used to walk that always made her unhappy, so much so that she stopped walking there. One day Joe happened to mention that that's where the public works department tossed the bodies of animals hit by cars. She'd felt the same dankness there as she felt here.

She suspected Sibyl was going to have a terrible time selling this house, regardless of whether someone kept playing games on google. It wasn't a happy house. There was an undercurrent. The only question in her mind was whether the person who waited for Bethany was looking for her or not.

Chapter Twenty-Five

Maggie picked up a pizza for Livy, but when she got back to her house, she found it deserted. Livy had left her a pizza and a note. "Going out with Gunvor tonight. Don't wait up. Don't worry. Love, love, love."

Gunvor.

That was better than Graham.

She had two pizzas and plenty of people happy to share them, but she was worried about Livy and she needed to worry alone. She didn't think Livy'd lie. She hadn't lied yet, though perhaps she'd exaggerated. But Gunvor struck her as the sort of person who would cover if Livy wanted to go out with Graham.

Maggie took a slice and sat down at her kitchen table, which was covered with the start of an all-white puzzle.

They were already a quarter of the way done. Livy approached a puzzle with military precision. She looked at the pieces, her eyes clicked a few times, and then she began putting pieces into places. Funny how an all-white puzzle made you pay more attention to shapes. Made you work harder.

Maggie sat down to work on it and immediately Shadow jumped on top of the puzzle. Completely incorrigible. She just stared at Maggie, this little cat who did not like to be touched. *I did not push her away,* Maggie said. *She wanted to go out with friends. She's young.*

Shadow got up, disgusted with that line of reasoning, and three white pieces clung to her fur. Maggie scooped her up and poor Shadow went rigid. Kosi came in to watch, curious to see the torture Maggie was inflicting, and then she curled into a ball and began to lick.

When they were all settled, Maggie looked back at the puzzle and tried to think.

Bethany planned to walk out of her own wedding. That was a fact. Graham said so, and Maggie believed him because of the person that laughed. She had to have set that up in advance. Plus, they'd found the money and clothes. She'd planned it out.

Maggie wished she could figure out who laughed, but that was an impossible task. She could hardly wander around Darby telling people bad jokes. Come to think of it, it was odd that with all the money Bethany had spent, she hadn't had the wedding filmed. Because she didn't want people to be able to track her down, though knowing Bethany, Maggie found it hard to believe that she hadn't had someone take a picture of her. She would want to admire it. Gunvor, maybe, or Amber. She wondered what would be involved in getting Gunvor to laugh.

She knew she'd have to go and talk to Mr. Ridgefield and talk to him about the Rolls Royce. He was the most likely person to know who owned one. He was so unpleasant, though, but she'd have to get over that. Detectives couldn't restrict themselves to interviewing pleasant people.

She began making a list, though she found herself writing Livy's name over and over.

She was absolutely sure she was with Graham, but she didn't want to call Livy because she pictured Gunvor's sneering face. She could only imagine what she'd have to say.

Then she had an inspiration.

Graham answered on the first ring. That was reassuring. At least he wasn't at a bar with Livy. Or the bar was incredibly quiet.

"Have you found information?" he asked.

"Did you and Bethany ever fight?" she asked.

"Never."

"Graham, that's ridiculous. She was a tempestuous person. You must have had an argument with her at some point."

"I didn't like to argue with her. She scared me."

"Well then why on earth were you marrying her?"

"I've spent the last week trying to figure that out. I think there's something wrong with me. I think I should talk to Reverend Sunday."

Maggie was beginning to think she was sending everyone in Darby to therapy, which reminded her of something else she needed to do. Helen. She had to talk to her.

"We argued over the extreme scavenge hunting. She got really involved in it. She and some of her new friends. I didn't like it. I thought it could lead to trouble."

"What was it?"

"It was like a scavenger hunt, but you had to find more difficult things. Like the keys to someone's car."

"Or a chalice from a church?"

"Exactly."

That's why it was in the van Dorn house. It was part of a game.

"Who was in this club?"

"Amber, Gunvor, Liesbeth."

Who the heck was Liesbeth?

"All women?"

"No, there was Justin, and Demuth."

"And you?"

"No, I didn't want to do it. I don't like sneaking around and stealing things, even for fun. Even if they're going to give them back. She said I was judging her."

It was the first thing he'd ever said that made Maggie like him. Maybe Livy was right. Maybe he had more of a backbone than she realized.

Would that be enough, Maggie wondered. Would Graham's decision not to join a scavenger hunt club be enough to turn Bethany against him. After years of devotion. It was hard to say. Bethany was very sensitive. The least slight could set her off. She might view that as a betrayal. Or more likely, if she'd found someone else, that might be the justification she needed to break with

Graham. Maggie could imagine her working herself up about it. She was the sort of person who could start with a seed of anger and nourish and water it until it grew into something large.

"Thanks," she said.

"Did that help?" he asked.

"I think so."

"Wait," he said. "Mrs. Dove, I have to say something. This whole thing with Livy. I just want you to know I treasure her. I know it seems sort of fast, but that doesn't mean it's not real."

"Graham, you do know she's going home in less than two weeks."

"What does time matter?" he asked. "What does anything matter?"

Never had she felt so old.

Now, for the first time, she had an opportunity to focus on what Ms. Sanchez said. Maggie felt embarrassed that the idea hadn't occurred to her sooner, but you didn't think of people you loved as abusers. It was such an ugly word, such an ugly act.

She'd known Helen was depressed about motherhood since the first time she met her, napping in the church library, struggling to keep her eyes open. She liked to sleep in the library while Edgar was in Sunday School. Some people criticized her for that, but Maggie thought there were many paths to God and sleeping might be one of them. She supposed she'd thought of Helen as somewhat cold and overwhelmed. But not abusive.

How to even begin that conversation?

Maggie took out her phone and googled "emotional abuse" and "children." The signs were exactly as Ms. Sanchez had said. Abused children lack basic social skills and have trouble making friends. They struggle to regulate emotions. Parents belittle them. The adult always assumes the child is at fault. All of this was true with Helen and Edgar, but it was also true of Graham Lockwood, come to that. His parents had been terrible with him. Always mocking. And he'd grown up to be unhappy. She wanted more than that for Edgar.

She downloaded a book onto her phone that gave advice about how to talk to abusers. She took notes on questions to ask, ways to manage the conversation, resources she could steer Helen too. When she finally had a full page of notes, she was surprised to see it was almost midnight. Livy wasn't home yet. She checked her phone though she knew she hadn't received any texts.

So she went into the kitchen and had some more pizza. She had some tea with that. No alcohol. Just in case she had to drive out somewhere. She knew she could call Walter, and yet she didn't feel she could share her thoughts about Helen. She felt a vein pulse over her eye. It was too early for the Insomnia Club but she logged on and found the Faraday sisters were there already. They were chatting about the new kitchen going in to the church parlor and whether it had enough drawer space. This was the sort of controversy that people had quit the church over and could occupy you for a while, and Maggie, who had lobbied for 3 drawers, jumped in, relieved to be distracted, and then before she knew it it was time for Jeopardy, and no sooner did it come on that the door slammed open and Livy was there.

"Aunt Dove. What a night! Graham said he had a good talk with you. I'm so glad. I learned so much from Gunvor. Oh, Aunt Dove, she's having such a hard time. I took a lot of notes. What is this?"

"Who is that?"

Maggie followed her gaze and saw that she was staring at Alex Trebek.

"He looks like Uncle Stuart."

"I don't think so," Maggie said, though that might be why she was always so fond of Alex Trebek. "It's a game show. *Jeopardy*. Have you ever seen it?"

Livy leaned forward, eyes sparkling, lips slightly parted, more excited than anyone Maggie had ever seen at the prospect of playing *Jeopardy*. She smelled a bit of whiskey.

"How much can we win?" she asked.

"Nothing," Maggie said. "We're playing along with an on-line group. The show is on TV, and we watch it on TV and then pause when he asks the questions and type in our answers."

"But you could just watch it on TV."

"We could."

"And you could just google the answers."

"We could, but what would be the fun of it?"

They were already on the Double Jeopardy round and Alex Trebek was introducing the characters. *Men of Science. Bad Heir Day. Their Roman Equivalents.* And three Maggie didn't hear, and then it got going.

A pale looking contestant chose *Their Roman Equivalents* for $400.

"Zeus," Alex Trebek said.

Quickly they paused the TV.

"Jupiter," Livy typed in.

"No," Agnes crowed. She'd signed on as well.

"What do you mean?" Livy asked indignantly.

"It has to be a question." Agnes typed in her response. "Who is Jupiter? Ha. I got it. I got it."

Livy got a look similar to the ones that the cats got when Maggie scolded them for knocking over their water bowls. She hunched her shoulders, looked like she was about to pull a gun out of her pocket. And got every other question right.

She knew which Italian scientist discovered that electricity could make dead frogs' legs contract. She knew the scientist for which the Institute of Physical Scientists at the University of Copenhagan was named. She knew that June 28, 1914 was the last day for this heir to the European throne. The only one on which she faltered had to do with the TV show *Parks & Recreation*, but no one knew the answer to that.

"Hey Maggie. Did you suddenly become a genius?" Leona Faraday asked.

"My niece is here," she typed in, but now they were on Final Jeopardy and the question related to the Hanseatic League and Livy just grinned. "This isn't even difficult," she said, and sure enough, she pounded in the question before anyone else could.

When the game was over everyone was agog. Agnes said they'd have to talk, but Maggie told her she could not swipe her niece. "She's mine," she said, and they both laughed together. "She's mine."

"Oh Aunt Dove," she said, "I found out so much information tonight. Mr. Ridgefield was at the bar. Nasty old man, but he told me that Eleanor Hunt's father has a Phantom 3 Rolls Royce. She's in Tibet right now, but she'll be back soon. Then I got the name of Bethany's bridal consultant in Manhattan. I thought we could see her. Oh, and Gunvor asked when you could see her host family."

"Gunvor wants me to do something for her?"

"She likes you," Livy said.

Then Livy tipped her head against Maggie's and went to sleep.

Chapter Twenty-Six

Gunvor's host parents lived in a ramshackle Victorian. It was one of those homes that seemed to sprout rooms the way trees sprouted burls. A bedroom bulging out of the left side of the house, another one coming out the front. A huge wrap-around porch filled with toys. A summer pool out front filled with snow. A sled in the middle of the lawn sticking up like a gravestone. Hockey sticks flung all over the lawn, along with a beach towel that had some characters on it from Frozen. Not a deserted house, Maggie thought.

On either side of the house grew an aspen tree.

Maggie had complicated emotions about aspens. She couldn't understand why their leaves didn't fall off when other leaves did. Or why they didn't hang on the way evergreens did. Instead they did their own thing, clinging to the branches throughout the winter, withering away like cancer patients, and then finally dropping to the ground when all the other trees were erupting into bloom. Seemed overly needy to her. A bid for pity. Give her an oak tree any day with its stern weathered bark and its uplifted arms.

Kacie Windsor opened the door. She looked familiar to Maggie, but she didn't know why. Mainly she looked like a woman overwhelmed. She held a baby in her arms. A toddler clung to her leg. Several children shouted in the background. A three-legged dog that Maggie felt confident was named Lucky barked at her side. It was pandemonium. Maggie wished Livy had come, but she was still sleeping off her night with the au pairs.

"Yes?" she said.

"I'm sorry to bother you," Maggie said. "I can see you're busy. My name is Maggie Dove, I'm here because…"

"Oh, I've heard of you. You have a detective agency. Is this to do with Bethany?"

"Bethany?" Maggie said. Didn't see that coming. She had a whole script planned about how she was there to raise money for hurricane relief and then somehow, she was planning her way around to how she was overworking Gunvor. This was an unexpected twist.

"You knew her?"

"Yes, yes," Kacie said. "Come on in. Welcome to the nightmare."

The first thing Maggie noticed was a murky fish tank, saw a flash of yellow. Maggie was surprised at how run-down everything looked. She assumed that people with an au pair were wealthy, but now she reconsidered. Wealthy people probably had full-time live-in help. Au pairs were more of a stop gap affordable measure.

"Sorry it's such a disaster," she said. "I have an au pair but she's completely useless. Seems to think she signed up for a travel program. Every time I ask her to do anything she cries. She's sleeping off a hangover right now. Vomited half the night."

The toddler was hopping up and down. Clearly had to go to the bathroom. Kacie looked at him, puzzled. She wore a loose smock. She had straight blond hair which she pulled back with a headband. She wore loafers, no socks. Her feet looked swollen. She had a pretty smile, but her face was mottled. Maggie wondered how many children Kacie had. What a boon for the Sunday School if she could scoop them up!

"Look at that," Kacie said, pointing up at the ceiling. "See that?"

There was a water stain. "Gunvor was giving the kids a bath and they were splashing around too much and it all leaked through. I docked her a week's salary for that. It's not fair that we have to pay for it."

"I thought there were limits to how many kids au pairs could watch," Maggie tried.

"We have an informal arrangement," Kacie said. "We pay her extra. Not that she wants to do anything at all."

"My grandmother was one of eight children," Kacie said, as though reading her mind. "She was always telling me stories about what it was like to grow up with so many brothers and sisters. It sounded like so much fun, but I don't know. I think I'm going to stop here. What is it George?"

"I suspect he wants to go to the bathroom," Maggie noted. "Would you like me to hold this little one?"

"That would be great," she said, and handed her over, dashing off with George, who seemed to just make it in time.

Meanwhile, Maggie gazed down at the little one in her arms. She was a pretty baby with big blue eyes and blond hair. She was wearing a stained onesie that Maggie suspected had gone through an assortment of children. She felt damp. Maggie thought she would take a shower when she got home. How Stuart argued about having one child at all. He didn't want any restrictions on his life. Maggie wondered what he would make of this.

Kacie came back into the room, closely followed by young George, who then ran off into another room to join his siblings. She smiled at her little daughter and kissed her, but made no move to take her out of Maggie's arms.

Then she paused for just a moment, trying to gather her wits. Maggie sympathized. This was an insane asylum.

"So you knew Bethany," Maggie tried. She was conscious of having a limited amount of time. Kacie began getting out pans, opening the refrigerator, lifting up a Brownie mix box and looking at the expiration date.

The baby began to fuss. It was like a coffee maker beginning to perk. "I think she may want you," Maggie said.

"Oh no," she said. "She's fine. Aren't you, Elizabeth?"

Elizabeth began to sputter. Maggie tried an airplane move she remembered and it seemed to work. For a moment.

"What did you think of her?"

"Really a sweet girl," Kacie said.

Bethany Coleman? Of all the adjectives you could use to describe Bethany, sweet was not the one that came first to mind.

"Matter of fact she was helping us."

"How?"

Maggie was swinging the baby back and forth, trying to calm her. It had worked for Juliet, but did not seem to be as effective with little Elizabeth. For the first time she felt truly sorry for Gunvor. No wonder she was so irritable.

"How?" she shouted.

"She was working to get us a great deal on a house. Ah," she said, stopping to take an egg shell out of the batter. "That's it. Yes," she said, pushing her hair off her face. "She had a plan to get us Hollyhock House."

"Hollyhock House," Maggie repeated. "That big white farmhouse."

"There was a murder there, you know. A long time ago and Bethany thought that would work to our advantage. She thought we could get the house for cheap if we could scare other people away. She kept posting stuff on line about the house, so that it would rise to the top of the search engines. Any time anyone did a search on the house, the articles about the murder would come up. They started off asking $1.5 million, but they're down to $700,000 and Bethany thought she could get it down to $500,000. That's the offer we were going to put in."

"Wouldn't it have bothered you to live there?" Maggie asked.

The brownies were done and in the oven and Kacie came over and retrieved her baby and at that moment a terrible thump came from the room where the kids were playing. Someone started to cry and Kacie yelled out, "Put on the TV. Stop that rough-housing."

"No," she said to Maggie. "It happened a long time ago, and who even knows if it really happened and the kitchen has granite countertops and the bathroom has steamed heat flooring. We could really live well there. Though I don't know what's going to happen now that Bethany's gone. She was so committed to working for us. I've never had someone work like that on my behalf before."

"Why do you think she was working so hard for you?" Maggie asked. "I mean it does sound like it was a lot of work."

Kacie's entire face changed in that moment. She turned from someone who looked vaguely cheerful and distracted to someone disappointed. It aged her. Maggie suspected that was the face she would grow into. "There was this real estate woman she was having an argument with. Sibyl something. She was causing trouble for Bethany at the bank and she wanted to get back at her." Then Kacie sighed. "We have no luck," she said. "Our one chance at a nice house and it gets ripped away from us. We'll probably be in this starter house for the rest of my life."

"Don't you have someone who could help you? Family?"

"No," she said. "It was always just me and my grandma, and when she died, I lost everyone."

"What about your husband?"

"He travels a lot," she said. "Though he's very good when he's here."

The phone began to ring, but she didn't move to answer it. When the voice mail clicked on, she heard a man's voice. "We're calling about your Visa bill. Will you be paying the minimum? Please give us a call at your earliest convenience."

A little girl came through and put her lips on Maggie's arm and began making buzzing noises. It was exactly the sort of thing Edgar would do. She had to get out of there. She was feeling claustrophobic. She'd grown too used to living in her neat and tidy house, but she made a final effort. She did think Gunvor needed help. She thought Kacie needed help. She thought this whole thing was a disaster.

"You know," Maggie said. "I belong to a church and we have a play group there for mothers with young children. You might like it. It's not a religious thing. Just a way for young parents to get together."

"Church," she laughed. "Oh no. I don't do things like that."

"It can be really helpful to have another set of hands."

Suddenly Kacie's expression changed yet again, and she looked at Maggie with sharp suspicion. "You're one of those religious fanatics, aren't you?"

"I really would just like to help," Maggie said.

"No," Kacie said. "No thank you. I think it's time that you left."

She slammed the door on her as Maggie stepped out on to the walkway. She noticed, up in a far window, that a curtain was twitching. She suspected Gunvor was hiding out in her room, hiding from the madness, and who could blame her? Maybe Gunvor should come to church. Maybe if Kacie thought she was a religious fanatic, she'd fire her. Didn't seem right.

Maggie went home and showered and then, when Livy drifted downstairs, she said to her, "I have to get out of Darby for a bit. Do you want to go into Manhattan? To Kleinfeld's?"

"Heck, yes," Livy said.

And they were off.

Chapter Twenty-Seven

That afternoon, Maggie and Livy set out for Kleinfeld's and Maggie thought she'd never been so relieved to be out of Darby. There might be axe murderers in New York City, but they were one in nine million as opposed to one in six thousand. The odds were much more in her favor.

The whole city seemed to unfold in welcome. She always liked going there, had always been glad to be only a half an hour's drive from the city, but now it felt like sanctuary. She felt as though she'd been crammed in a hot house these last few days. Now she could breathe.

And the city felt so expansive. It felt warmer even. It had been terrible looking at people and wondering who could be filled with such hate, wondering who might strike again. Because surely the nature of an axe murder was that it was not something to be contained. That type of anger could not be tamed. It must burst out again. Whoever commit just one?

Maggie had no idea what they could learn at Kleinfeld's, but it had to be better than sitting around waiting for something terrible to happen. And she could keep Livy safe here. Every day that ticked by, every new friend Livy made, every time she went out, Maggie feared she was stepping closer to danger.

She parked over on the west side, which was her guiding philosophy to driving in New York City. She didn't care if she had to walk three miles. She would not deal with mid-town traffic. So she parked near the Hudson River and they walked. The air was brisk, bordering on frozen, and it blew right into their faces. But Maggie was happy to have Livy at her side. Away from Graham. Phone turned off. Focused on this experience, and Livy was surprisingly enthusiastic about visiting Kleinfeld's.

"You sure this won't upset you?" Maggie said, though the words came out mumbled because they had to make it through her scarf. She was thinking about how it had only been a few weeks ago that Livy was planning her own wedding.

"Why?"

"Never mind." They pushed on, past a restaurant that served 25 different kinds of meatball sandwiches, and Maggie made a mental note to stop off there on the way back. She'd only had cereal for breakfast and she knew she'd be starving by the time they were done. She wondered if Kleinfeld's had chocolates, but probably not in a place with so much white. Unless they had white chocolate. That would be a treat.

Kleinfeld's was easy to spot because there was a cluster of women standing in front of it. Even in this weather, they were outside and laughing. The sound of laughter was such a relief. Maggie hadn't heard much of it the last few days, with the whole village weighed down by the press of murder. It was a good sound. In front of Kleinfeld's there was a very oppressed looking plane tree. Maggie suspected that many brides had taken photos in front of that tree, and maintaining a cheerful aspect must have worn it down. She stopped to look at it, but Livy kept going, in through the doors, and then they both stopped.

"The happiest place on earth," Maggie whispered, though Livy was not one to catch a Disney World allusion.

It was a huge open space, divided into lots of smaller spaces, and each little tableau was filled with a bride. There were all shades of bride, all sizes, all ages, all sexes. One bride looked to be Maggie's age, and she looked at her speculatively. She wore a lovely French style dress that Maggie thought would have suited her. So different from the heavy silk of her own wedding.

"They all look so hopeful," Maggie said, to no one because Livy had gone up to the front desk, which was manned by two elegant women with blunt cut hair styles and black outfits.

There was something so hopeful about brides, Maggie thought. These were not hopeful times, and pragmatically you had to know that you stood a fairly good chance of getting divorced, and yet for that moment, there was a person who was willing to commit his whole life to you. It was a tremendous honor.

Only then, after almost a week, did she realize the enormity of what had happened to Livy. She'd been so preoccupied with keeping her safe, and worrying about Graham, that she hadn't stopped to think about what Livy'd been through. A man she loved, who she planned to spend the rest of her life with, had told her he didn't think she was good enough. No wonder she was so smitten with Graham, who seemed awed by her. She was vulnerable. In her own way she was just as lost as Bethany had been, one because of anger and one because of pain. Two lost brides.

Maggie had to calm down about Graham, she resolved. She didn't think he'd killed Bethany. No one really did. She needed to provide comfort.

"We're here to speak to Tasmania," Livy said to the receptionists.

"Do you have an appointment?"

"She's expecting us."

Maggie noticed overhead was a sign that cautioned that cameras were filming and that you should be prepared to be on the TV show. She pictured herself appearing on TV. Life took strange hops.

The receptionist handed them both bottles of Kleinfeld water and pointed them toward a set of stairs to the far side. "She's downstairs in her office."

Downstairs turned out to be the hive where all the alterations took place. It was a little more business-like than upstairs. Decisions had been made. A woman swished by carrying a huge white bag. There were arrays of accessories. Shoes and tiaras and bags. Livy paused for a moment to look at the tiara. Maggie wondered if she wanted one or if she was planning a paper on the role of the princess mystique in the feminist archaeology. She realized then that she had no idea what sort of wedding Livy had planned. She'd been so preoccupied with keeping her away from Graham that she hadn't thought about Shiv.

Suddenly an older woman in black and impossibly high heels came dashing by holding a bottle of water.

Everyone peered in the direction of a fitting room.

"She fainted," someone said.

Another one added. "Happens all the time. They don't eat before the fitting and then they have to stand there for hours and they fall right over."

There was a flutter of people running back and forth and then a very slender bride, held up by her mother and a very patient looking woman in black, came by and settled herself into a comfortable looking pouf. Someone else ran up with some cookies and handed her one.

Livy said nothing, just stared wide-eyed at it all. *The role of body image in the American wedding culture.*

Tasmania had a small office in a little warren of offices toward the back. She was a tall woman with light tan skin and a black outfit and high heels. She greeted them and gestured for them to sit in the chairs crammed into her office. Maggie noticed her wall was covered with postcards from exotic locations. "Honeymoons," she said, catching Maggie's glance. "My clients like to send me cards when it's all over. Bethany told me she'd send me a card. Is it true that she was…" She stopped, clearly unable to say the word. This was a place for dreams, not axes.

"Yes. I'm sorry."

"It was such a beautiful dress," Tasmania said. "She put such care into choosing it. Special ordered it."

"Really?" Maggie said. She couldn't remember what the dress looked like though she'd seen it when Bethany walked down the aisle.

"I have a picture of it," she said. "Just a minute."

She began clicking around the computer, and then pulled up a picture. "See," she said. "It's unusual because it's a convertible dress. It has a zipper sewn into it, so after the ceremony's over, you can unzip the bottom and then you have a regular cocktail dress. That way you can dance without having to hold up your train the whole time. You can really enjoy your reception."

Neither Graham nor Bethany struck Maggie as people who were going to really enjoy their reception.

Tas began to sniff. She got out a tissue. She had a huge satin-covered box of tissues, and she blew her nose. "She never got to unzip it."

"Did she say where she was going on her honeymoon?"

"Yes, Santa Lucia. She'd booked a hotel that was in the middle of the jungle. It didn't have a fourth wall so you could let the jungle right in."

Had Graham mentioned that?

"She talked about it a lot, she and her friend."

"Her friend?" Maggie asked. "Who was that?"

"She came with her to all the fittings."

"Was it Eleanor Hunt?" Maggie tried. "That was her maid-of-honor."

"No, it wasn't a name like that. It was a foreign name. Something violent sounding."

"Gunvor?" Livy asked.

"Yes, that was it. Gunvor. The two of them seemed very close. She must be broken-hearted."

Maggie looked over to Livy. "Did you know that?" she asked.

"No, she never said anything about it. I mean, I knew they were friends but I didn't know they were that close."

"I wonder why she wasn't in the wedding party."

A mother and daughter began arguing in the booth next to them. The mother had tried on the daughter's wedding dress and now the daughter didn't want it anymore. She thought her mother looked better in the dress. Maggie began to feel dizzy. There was so much input. She looked over at Livy, who also looked puzzled.

Just then Maggie's phone rang, which startled her, and she was even more startled her because she thought she'd turned it off. Then she saw saw Helen's name on the screen. What had Edgar done? Was he in trouble?

"They've arrested the murderer," she said, when Maggie answered.

"What! Who is it?"

"A young man named Jeremy Kessler. He escaped from a group home. They found him at the house at Hollyhock. He's been living there. It's over."

"You're sure."

"He's confessed. It's done. You don't need to worry anymore, Maggie Dove."

She couldn't believe it. She looked at Livy, who stared back at her, puzzled.

"We have to get home."

Chapter Twenty-Eight

It was a sad story.

Jeremy Kessler was a young man, raised in wealth. His parents doted on him. He excelled in sports, academics, social life. He went to good schools, succeeded. Got a job in an investment bank, began taking pills to up his stamina. His personality began to change. His parents got him counseling, but he got more and more erratic. He got in a fight with his boss and lost his job. Came home and got another job, not as good. Seemed listless. Turned thirty. Fired again. Decided he didn't want to be in finance. Went into carpentry. Seemed to create a life for himself as a carpenter, found a girlfriend, but things started to go wrong again. He began to hear voices. Was convinced aliens were reading his mind. Got depressed.

One day he attacked his mother. Tried to stab her with a pen. He said he saw an alien being in her eyes and wanted to protect her. They had to get him out of the house. Tried to get him into a group home, but there was no room. They took out a second mortgage on their house to be able to place him in somewhere good, and for a time he did better, but once he was released he began to struggle again. They sold the house. Put him in another place, but then the money ran out. He was on his own. Began living on the streets.

At one time he was arrested for vagrancy and that was a relief. He was in a safe place. He couldn't harm anyone. But that didn't last. They lost track of him. For the last three months his parents had been searching for him. They had no idea he'd wound up in Darby, that he was living in the woods and seeking shelter in the outbuilding behind the Hollyhock House. That day, the day Bethany was murdered, he'd gone into the house to take shelter. It was so cold that day. He was burrowed into the house when she came racing in. All he saw was a creature all in white. He thought she was an alien and he chased her. Killed her with an axe he'd found.

The police found him hiding in one of the caves in the woods. Actually, the drone found him. He was terrified, whimpering. He confessed immediately.

Maggie could tell from the moment she drove back into Darby that the mood had lifted. The sun had come out. The streets sparkled with melting ice. More people were out. They were smiling, laughing. It was good to see her village back to life, but she felt uneasy.

"Would you mind," Livy asked, when they got back to the house, "if I go out with Graham tonight? Now that everything's settled."

Maggie wanted to say no. Wanted to say it all seemed too easy, that there were still questions about the Rolls Royce and how was Gunvor involved and who'd laughed at the wedding, and what was Bethany really planning to do? But there was no question Jeremy was in custody and had confessed. They were quite clear about that on the news.

Jeremy would be absorbed into the criminal justice system, his parents would be heartbroken, Bethany was dead and perhaps no one would ever fully understand what she intended to do. Livy would be going home in a few days. Life would go on and Maggie would go back to her normal life.

The important thing was that Graham had been cleared. There was no longer any reason to avoid him, except for common sense.

"Of course," she said to her glowing niece. "Have fun."

Chapter Twenty-Nine

Not ten minutes later, after Livy dashed upstairs to primp for her date, Graham showed up at Maggie's house. He arrived there so quickly Maggie suspected he'd been circling round and round until Livy gave the all clear. He carried a bouquet of freesias.

"I remembered these were your favorite flowers," he said, as he handed them to her. His hair was growing, as was his beard. He reminded her of plants after you put on Miracle Gro. She supposed that was one definition of love.

"They are? Aren't they?"

"Yes," Maggie said, breathing in their scent. She'd always had a fondness for them. "But I can't believe you remembered such a thing."

"I remember everything you said. I used to love being in your class. It was the one place I felt safe."

The hair dryer sounded and he looked up, and blushed. "I remember the time you pulled me out of the trash."

"Well, yes, though I think any Sunday School teacher would have done that."

She gestured for him to sit down. Funny how you can know someone his entire life, and yet not know him at all. Something about this young man was extremely compelling to Livy and Maggie wished she could figure out what it was. He had a gentleness to him that she liked. She supposed she had a hard time seeing his charms because he was so tied up in her mind with being a victim and it was sort of hard to love a victim. But that wasn't his fault. She thought of Edgar. Would someone someday think that of him? Yet she loved Edgar passionately.

She was surprised to see the cats go over and jump on him. They lounged on his lap. Kosi, who had the coloring of an angry waiter in a tuxedo, purred so loudly that the room vibrated. Never had he purred for her. That had to mean something, didn't it? Cats didn't like evil people, did they? Or perhaps cats did like evil people. Perhaps they preferred them.

"Oh, and I wanted to give you this," he said, handing her an envelope. "It's the balance of the payment I owe you for your detective work."

Based on the size of the envelope, he'd paid her with singles. But she respected him for honoring his commitments.

"I was sad to hear about that guy they found. I was sad to think of Bethany surprising him."

"It seems incredibly unlucky," Maggie said.

"She used to say you make your own luck."

He looked down at the rug on her floor. It was a beautiful carpet that her husband had brought back from a trip to India. She remembered how he'd taken it out of his suitcase. It had been all folded up to the size of a newspaper, and yet when he started unfolding it, it got bigger and bigger. It took up most of the floor.

Suddenly Maggie heard movement behind her. She watched Graham's face change. Here, truly, was the look of a groom seeing his bride for the first time. He rose to his feet and Maggie turned to see her niece floating in her direction. Her hair looked like it glowed with an inner light. Her dress was sleek and elegant, and her face beamed.

She stepped out of the way. Even the cats stepped out of the way, and they were hardly oversensitive. Livy moved into his arms as though she belonged there, and then they floated toward the door.

"See you later, Aunt Dove," Livy remembered to call back, though Maggie doubted it.

She watched him hold open the door for her. He drove a beat-up Subaru, but in this context, it was a golden chariot. She got in, buckled her seat belt, and they drove off. Only then did Maggie realize how hungry she was. She'd meant to take Livy out to lunch after Kleinfeld's, but got side-tracked by the call from Helen. Helen, whom she had been meaning to talk to and kept putting off.

She called Helen. "Hi there. I wondered if you and Edgar would like to come over to dinner tonight?"

"Oh, I'm sorry, Maggie. I'd like to but I have to help him with a homework assignment. He's put it off to the last minute and he'll get into trouble if he doesn't get it in on time, and then the teacher will blame me. Can we make it in a few days?"

Maggie wanted to say, "Of course," but she knew she couldn't. She'd put this off long enough. "Tell you what," she said, "how about if I come over to your house? I'll bring dinner with me and I can help Edgar. Would you be up for that?" She was pretty sure she had a macaroni and cheese casserole in the refrigerator.

"Okay," Helen said, though she sounded wary. She was smart and intuitive. Maggie wondered if she knew what was coming.

Then Eleanor Hunt called.

"Hi Ms. Dove. Sorry to be so long getting back to you. I've been traveling. You wanted to talk to me about a Rolls Royce?"

Maggie wasn't sure it was necessary anymore The murderer had been found, and yet she was still curious. Someone had driven Bethany in a Rolls Royce to Hollyhock House and then had left her there. That person had to know what Bethany was intending.

"Could I come by tomorrow and talk to you about it?"

"That would be lovely," Helen said.

Then she had one more call before she left.

She wasn't sure Walter would answer because he must be having a busy day, but he answered on the first ring.

"Just thinking about you," she said. Honestly, this was so ridiculous. How she couldn't stop smiling. "Everything okay?"

"I've spent the day with psychiatrists. We're hoping to get Kessler into a hospital bed while we try to figure out what happened."

"But you're sure he's the killer?"

"He confessed."

"That doesn't always mean anything."

"He has a history of violence with knives. He's a big man. He keeps talking about an alien in white. Everything fits."

He paused. "What's worrying you, Maggie?"

"Livy and Graham. They've gone out together. I don't know. He seems nice enough. The cats like him. She's 23. I can't stop her from seeing him."

"Where are they going?"

"If I were to hazard a guess, I'd say to his house."

Walter laughed softly. She thought about how precious his smile was to her. It wasn't easily earned. In fact, she didn't think she'd seen it for the first few months she'd known him. So it still felt a sort of triumph when she knew she'd provoked it.

"Why don't I send Officer Williams out to drive by his house. She can look for signs of trouble."

Oh dear. Officer Williams had such a dislike for her. Now she was going to spend a cold night sitting in a car. On the other hand, it would make Maggie feel better.

"Is that legal?"

"Legal enough," he said. "I'd be happy to stake out your house too," he said. His grin came through the phone.

She blushed. "I really think I'm too old for a stake out."

He laughed. Then his voice softened. She pictured him pressing the phone against his ear, his strong hands cradling the phone, the scar under his chin. "I don't think so," he whispered.

But she couldn't continue. She had to go off and see Helen and she dreaded it.

"Soon," she told him.

Chapter Thirty

Helen and Edgar lived in a tiny coach house on the grounds of an old estate in Darby. It was a jewel of a place, fashioned with stones that had been mined locally. Mullioned windows, iron detailing, a park-like location. Helen had told her once that it cost way more than she'd intended to spend, but she knew right away that it was what she wanted, and she didn't second guess herself.

Lights shone in every window. The sidewalk was carefully shoveled. For all that Helen herself, and Edgar, often looked tired and disheveled, the house looked perfect. Vastly different than the Windsor house, which was not that far away. Somehow Maggie doubted the two women knew each other.

Helen greeted her at the door, holding a glass of wine. She held it out to Maggie, who took it gladly. She would need some form of courage and, if it came in liquid form, that would do, though she knew Reverend Sunday would tell her to pray. She whispered a quick prayer, and just then Edgar came running in her direction, but stopped at the sight of his mother. His blonde hair went in every direction. His pale face cracked into dimples, but then immediately went back to looking somber.

"Did you finish packing up those Legos?" she asked him.

"No," he said. "Not yet."

"Do it now."

"Cleaning up?" Maggie asked.

"No, he has to give up his Legos. He didn't clean them up when I asked, so now we're giving them away."

"All of them?"

"We're starting with the Stars Wars ones. We'll see how he does."

Maggie wanted to point out that he loved those Legos, that they engaged his mind and kept him out of trouble, but the look on Helen's face was so intimidating that she held back. She loved her, but she was a little scared of her. However, she could help Edgar pack up, which she did.

"I can keep these at my house. Then, when he's gotten out of trouble, he can have them back."

Helen pursed her lips. She'd grown up on a farm in Kansas. Her parents valued hard work and independence, Maggie knew, and she suspected Helen was not asking anything of Edgar that had not been asked of her. Did that make it wrong? "I just want him to take responsibility for his things."

"I know," Maggie said. "Oh, and here's the macaroni and cheese."

Helen thanked her and went into the kitchen to warm it up, and meanwhile Maggie and Edgar picked up the Legos.

The living room was immaculate, except for a few Legos. The furniture was white, and clean. Helen, she realized, was one of those sneak cleaners. She told you to relax and be comfortable, but if you spilled anything she tiptoed over and cleaned it up.

"How long do you think it should cook?"

"Half an hour?" she said. "Until it bubbles."

"Thank you, it looks great. What sort of cheeses?"

"I didn't make it, I have to confess. But that's a good thing. Magnolia dropped it off for me. She thought I'd had surgery, which I hadn't, but I figured I might as well keep it."

Helen laughed. She was as difficult to make smile as Walter, Maggie thought. She wondered why she liked solemn people so much. More of a challenge?

Maggie sipped the wine, which was just as wonderful as she expected. It was so light.

"It's from a small vineyard in Spain. I happened to be visiting there last year."

That was the other thing about Helen. She didn't have a lot of things, but what she had was first rate. If she offered you a glass of wine, it would come from a vineyard she visited, and Maggie suspected it would be quite expensive. Maggie suspected the furniture was expensive as well. Everything was so lovingly tended except for Edgar, who now came toward her holding his box of Legos.

"Put it in the closet," she said, and he nodded solemnly and walked down the hallway, toward a closet that Maggie suspected was filled with many loved toys. Then he came back and sat down alongside of Maggie. One brief sob emerged from his throat, and then he burrowed in. Helen looked at him as though she wanted to say something, but thought better of it. Instead she went into the kitchen and Maggie took a quick moment to squeeze him tightly. This was an impossible position. How do you tell a mother she's not doing a good job? Mothering was such an impossible job to begin with. She thought of Kacie Windsor and all those children under foot. But if she didn't do something, Ms. Sanchez would file a report.

Helen came out then with a plate of cheese and French bread. Maggie put some on a small plate that came from Morocco, and she started to pass it to Edgar, but Helen stopped her.

"Nothing for Edgar," she said. "We had an incident with Juicy Juice that doesn't bear going into."

Maggie nodded. She set the plate down. "Actually, I need to talk to you about something and it might be better if Edgar wasn't here. It's an adult thing," she said to him. "Would you mind playing in your room for a little bit?"

"Maggie Dove," he cried out, as though betrayed, but she hugged him and said, "This is important." So he trotted off and closed his door, and Maggie turned toward Helen.

This was a young woman she admired and loved, she reminded herself, but when Helen turned her attention on you she could be scary. Some deep anger bubbled inside her. Like Bethany. Both with some justification, she suspected, and yet their anger had caused both of them to act in ways injurious to themselves. Bethany's determination to get back at her parents got her into trouble and Helen's anger seemed to be seeping out toward her son.

"I need to talk to you about something Ms. Sanchez said."

"What's he done now?" Helen asked. She sank into the chair across from Maggie.

"Actually, Edgar hasn't done anything."

Helen twisted her mouth, making a disturbingly middle-aged face. The sort of face that people wore when they'd been ground down. She'd never met Helen's mother. Never came to visit. Helen never spoke about her, or to her. All she knew was that she came from Kansas and that somehow she knew one of the Clutter family members.

"She's concerned about him."

"I'll bet she is. It's a miracle they haven't thrown him out of that school. I owe that to you, Maggie. I appreciate it." She took a sip of her wine. Maggie noticed she'd written the word "Legos" on her hand.

"He's a bright boy," Maggie said. "You should be proud of that. Ms. Sanchez said he's one of the brightest kids in the class."

"What good is it going to do him if no one can see past his behavioral issues?"

"I think people can see past it. I think you are the one having difficulty with it."

Helen went still. Maggie's cats did something similar, right before they swatted at her hand. "What does that mean?"

Maggie noticed a painting on the wall. It showed a flat open landscape. Looked like something Edward Hopper would have painted had he turned his attention to the Midwest instead of New York. It was bleak and yet beautiful. Maggie wondered if Helen had painted it.

"She feels like you're abusing him."

"Abusing him!"

"Emotionally."

"What is she talking about? I have standards for him. You should have seen the way I grew up if you think I'm tough. You should have seen the things my parents did to me. It makes you tough."

Maggie breathed in deeply. "Edgar's teacher thinks that his behavioral issues may be a result of emotional abuse."

The air seemed to burn right out of the room.

"What does that mean?" Helen asked. She clenched her fists. Maggie knew she was struggling not to lash out.

"When a child grows up without affection, it can affect the way they inhabit the world."

"I've never hit him. Not ever."

"It's not physical. It's emotional. You're critical of him, always. You never hug him. You never show him affection."

"That's not fair."

"I'm not a therapist, Helen. I'm simply a friend, and all I can tell you is that if you don't do something, Ms. Sanchez is going to report you, and then there's going to be a host of problems."

"But you think she's right? You don't disagree."

Maggie wanted to say she did disagree, but she thought of that closet full of Legos. She thought that her primary concern had to be for Edgar. She thought of how many children Ms. Sanchez taught.

"I don't disagree."

"He has to be tough. It's a cold world."

"We're not in a war, not now. We're in a small village in Westchester New York and all the other kids are being coddled and Edgar's being raised like a Marine."

"Edgar's being raised like I was raised. To be tough and self-reliant."

"He's struggling," Maggie said. "You can see that. He doesn't have friends. Don't you want to do whatever you can to help him?"

"What am I supposed to do? What do the thought police want from me?"

"You could go to counseling."

"Oh yes," she said, jumping to her feet. "That's the answer to everything."

Maggie reached for Helen, but she twisted out of her grasp. Turned on Maggie and spit out the words.

"You just don't want to face what his real problem is. That he has in his genes an evil strand, and if he doesn't learn self-control, it will destroy him."

"Helen, if you can't get him help, Ms. Sanchez is going to do it. She can report you to the authorities. Isn't it better to get in front of this? You love him. I know you do. You want what's best for him, and I'll help you however I can."

Helen stood up. "I want you to leave now."

"Helen."

"I'm so tired of your moralizing and always knowing what's best for everyone. Please just go."

Maggie flinched under her gaze. There was nothing to be done. At least she'd made her point and she suspected, after a while, Helen would listen to her. She got to the door and turned. "Helen, you're angry at me and I understand why. But I just want you to know that I love you. I hope you can hear that too."

She wanted to go back in time. She couldn't stand the thought of losing her. She wished Ms. Sanchez had told someone else. She thought how tired she was of having responsibility, and she knew Livy wouldn't be around tonight. She would most certainly be off with Graham.

Maggie got back to her house, which felt so quiet. She'd gotten so used to having Livy around and it had only been five days. She could feel the reverberation of her laughter in the living room. There was the all-white puzzle that they worked on. She was such a vivid living person and soon she'd be returning to Indiana and Maggie would miss her awfully.

The doorbell rang. She wasn't expecting anyone.

She wiped off her eyes and went to answer it, and there was Walter, standing there with a bag of groceries.

"I thought you might like someone to cook dinner," he said.

"How did you know?" she whispered, as she folded herself into his arms. "How did you know?"

Chapter Thirty-One

"What happened to Walter?" Agnes asked the next morning.

It was a quiet Wednesday, and Maggie had just walked into the detective office. She noticed immediately that Helen wasn't there, but Walter's face occupied a large part of the TV screen. He was giving an update on Jeremy Kessler, explaining that he'd been moved from the jail to a mental health facility. "Right now, Jeremy Kessler is being assessed by social services. They will make the determination as to whether he is fit to be tried. It's out of my hands, at this point."

However, in spite of the seriousness of the topic he was addressing, there was no denying that Walter looked cheerful. For Walter.

He looked quite handsome, Maggie thought. His jaw was a bit looser. He looked relaxed. She thought of the way he'd smelled last night, of spruce and laundry detergent. She thought of how warm he'd felt when she'd sat alongside of him, the press of his lips.

"I don't know," she said. "He must be relieved to have the crime solved."

"Is that it?" Agnes asked. She was dressed in pink today. Maggie wondered if that had anything to do with Valentine's Day, which was only a week away. Or it might equally have to do with heart disease. With Agnes there was no way to tell.

"You're blushing, Maggie Dove."

"I am not," she said, because when all else failed you could always fall back on behaving like a teenager.

"But you are certain the killer has been caught?" the reporter asked.

"Yes, and I want to give credit to my able police staff for catching him so quickly and before anyone else was hurt."

He looked straight ahead then, and Maggie felt quite certain he was talking to her. Looking for her.

With the Bethany Coleman case wrapped up, Maggie could turn her attention back to the more mundane work that had been occupying her time. She still had a lot of resumes to check on for the bank. A new matter had come in from a local restaurant owner who was looking to sell a share of his restaurant, but wanted to be sure that the potential buyer was a good citizen, as he put it.

She started pulling out papers, but Helen's empty desk worried her. She hoped she hadn't quit. She hoped she hadn't run off in the middle of the night with Edgar. She called the school and asked to speak to Ms. Sanchez and after a bit she came on the phone, and Maggie told her how the conversation had gone.

"Is Edgar at school today?" she asked.

"Yes, he's here."

Thank God, Maggie thought. "Will you keep me posted, if you see anything that concerns you?"

"I will not let this rest," Ms. Sanchez said.

After she hung up, Maggie tried to focus on work, but her mind kept going back to Helen. She wondered if it would help to call Helen's mother. She knew Helen and her mother weren't close, but she did often use her as a model for her parenting. Maybe her mother could offer her some comfort. She didn't have her number, but she knew the town she lived in and she could track her down. When it got to be about noon Kansas time, Maggie called her.

Helen's mother answered on the third ring.

"Hello," she said. "I'm a friend of your daughter's."

"What has she done now?" Helen's mother said, in a tone that echoed her daughter's so precisely it broke Maggie's heart.

"Nothing," she said, and ended the call.

Livy called then to say that she and Graham were going to go into the city and visit the Museum of Modern Art, and that she'd probably be gone all day. "Is that all right?"

"Of course."

Livy laughed. "I know you're not really happy about it, Aunt Dove. But thank you for trusting in me."

"I love you," Maggie said, surprised as the words came out of her mouth because she hadn't intended to say them. "Just take care of yourself."

"I love you too," Livy whispered. "Don't get sad. We'll do something fun tomorrow."

Maggie laughed. She really was an open book. Good thing she didn't play poker.

"Oh, and I was talking to Gunvor and we thought it would be fun to have an early Valentine's Day party, before I leave. We thought we could have it at your house. What would you think?"

"I'd love that."

"Maybe we could get rid of some of your chickens and replace them with hearts."

"Why not? I'm ready to explode my horizons."

Livy laughed and went off to be with Graham. Agnes ran off to do something with the Board of Elections. Maggie was alone in the office. It was peaceful there. The village was peaceful. She could see the news vans were clearing out. The weather was starting to warm up a bit. More people were out. Life was going back to normal, except for Jeremy Kessler, and his family. She thought of what a long struggle they had in front of them, and how hard their life had been. She thought of him moving throughout the village, finding homes to live in. She imagined him in the van Dorn house. She wondered how many empty houses there were, how many families torn apart by mental illness. How many hidden dangers there were. She wondered if he was the person who pushed her.

There didn't seem to be any doubt that Jeremy Kessler was the murderer. He'd confessed. He was known to be violent. It all made perfect sense. As Walter had explained it to her, he'd been hiding out in Hollyhock House. He couldn't remember how he'd come to know about it, but he'd been hiding there for some weeks. He was resourceful, had found parts of the house that had not been touched since the 1930s. The house was built into a hill, and it had a secret exit. Stanger must have figured that out and so did Kessler, and it was on one of his forays that he found the axe.

It was just all so neat. Also, he'd thought to wipe off the fingerprints. That seemed fairly lucid, and yet he'd also had the wits to hide there for weeks.

Walter said she was like one of those people who liked conspiracies, though she didn't think so. Though she also didn't think Lee Harvey Oswald killed Kennedy, but that was a different situation. She supposed it was possible that Bethany was just the victim of incredibly bad luck. That on the day she decided to walk out of her wedding there should be a snow storm that prevented her from going into the city and so she stopped off in a house she knew to be empty and there ran into a man who, of all people, was frightened of aliens and thought she was a threat.

The randomness of it disturbed her. She was a person who built her life around order. Who believed the very universe was ordered by a supreme being, and this all felt so disorganized.

She suspected she should just surrender and let justice take its course.

But she wasn't quite ready to write it all off yet. She was not a great person for letting go, evidently.

She'd heard the sound of someone laughing in the church. Bethany's face going red. Screaming as she stalked out of the church. Got into a limousine that someone drove. That person dropped her off at Hollyhock House. Bethany took her bag with her $20,000 and went inside, intending to get changed she supposed. Or at the least unzip her dress. But first she went upstairs, and put the money out on a tree. That's when Jeremy Kessler must have surprised her. He wasn't a big man, but she must have been startled. Had to get out of there fast. So she ran down the stairs, but of course there was no one to help. No cars were on the road. The cell service was bad. She wouldn't have time in any event because Kessler was running after her.

She wished she knew who had laughed in the church. She wished she knew who drove that Rolls Royce. She wished she knew where the Rolls Royce was. That was one question she might answer when she talked to Eleanor Hunt.

Chapter Thirty-Two

*E*leanor Hunt's home was one of the grand old houses of Darby, the perennial last stop on the annual fundraising tour for the historical society. Maggie'd never actually been inside because tickets to the tour were $250 and she just could not bring herself to spend that much money, and she kept waiting for a fundraiser for the middle class, so she felt a little bit thrilled as she stepped up to the front door. It was a vast pink octangular house, built during a time when octangular houses were the rage. It had a lot of windows and angles and Eleanor Hunt opened the door, and welcomed her in.

She was a tall young woman with perfect posture. She worked for her father, who was a well-known politician, and one of the few people in that world who had a good reputation. They were known for their noblesse oblige view of life, sort of Franklin Roosevelt combined with Spiderman. *To those to whom much has been given.*

She wore a soft wool shirt that clung to her slender frame. Maggie had a feeling that it came from happy sheep in Ireland. She couldn't imagine anything violent to do with Eleanor.

The house had the casualness of old money. They had nothing to prove. No decorator had worked here. Everything was comfortable and slightly bent. But it was all first rate. Eleanor had been in the same Sunday School class with Bethany and Graham, but whereas they had gone to Playland for the holidays, Eleanor went to Switzerland. She never bragged about it, but there was a sort of unconscious entitlement to her. All over the walls were portraits of various Hunts. They all seemed to be dour men with pink cheeked wives and hunting dogs. Eleanor herself was pink cheeked and had the sort of posture that, in Maggie's mother's time, young woman got by holding a broom against their back. She had one of those thin, well-behaved dogs that stood at attention at her side, but, when she clicked her fingers, lay down with a sigh at her feet.

"Max," she said. "Poor thing's getting old."

"He looks like a faithful companion."

"He would give his life for me," she said. "And I would give my life for him."

"Dogs do make you want to sacrifice," Maggie said, leaning over to pet his soft fur. "I suppose we respond to perfect love by wanting to give perfect love in return." She felt like she'd just said something profoundly important, but wasn't sure what. Her mouth was working ahead of her mind. Was she thinking of Graham? Certainly, he'd not been the recipient of perfect love. Or was she thinking of Walter, who'd somehow known that she needed him.

"Meanwhile," Maggie said, "I have two cats and I can assure you that no one in our relationship is looking to sacrifice for anyone else."

"I'm sure that's not so," Eleanor murmured.

She picked the dog's paw up in her hands and held it, as one might hold a child's.

She had incredibly long fingers. She was bred to be long and fine, just as this dog had been, Maggie thought. Generations of Hunts marrying generations of long boned, fine looking, intelligent women. That made her think of the Colemans, producing generations of pugnacious police officers. One of the things about being part of a small village was that you got to see the way generations played out. Her own family had been school teachers for generations, and librarians. There were still a lot of books in the library that had donation plates from her father. One of the hardest things about losing Juliet was losing the last of the Leighs. She thought of how the line came to the end at the bottom of the family Bible. She'd loved looking at that line when she was a girl, imagining all the people who would come after her, never expecting to be the last one.

"How did you come to be Bethany's maid of honor?" Maggie burst out.

Eleanor flinched. Maggie was surprised to see her look so unsettled. The Hunts were not unsettled people.

"I was so sorry to hear about her death, but I had to leave right after the wedding. I had business in Tibet. Going back there tomorrow."

"You were able to fly out?" Maggie asked, thinking of the torrential snow storm.

"Private plane," she said. "You have a lot more latitude."

Maggie waited. She knew Eleanor had heard the first question. She would answer it. She was bred to be polite and answer questions. The dog slumped against her knees. Sunlight poured through sparkling clean windows. Eleanor shifted uncomfortably.

"To tell you the truth, I was surprised that she asked me to be her maid of honor."

She stroked the top of the dog's head. The room was silent.

"You're the only person I can tell this to, Mrs. Dove. I know that it will go no further."

"I can't promise that," Maggie said, "if it's something that the police need to know, I'll have to tell them."

Eleanor plucked at her sleeve. She wore no jewelry, Maggie noticed. No engagement ring. No decorations. She was like the house in that she needed no adornment. What she was, was sufficient.

She sighed, or the dog sighed. "That will have to do," she said.

"Some years ago, Bethany did me a kindness. We were on a band trip in high school. I got into some trouble. It involved drugs. My father was in the midst of an important campaign, and had this information been revealed about me, it would have been very damaging. I couldn't see a way out. I was guilty. I knew I'd have to take my medicine, and I got so far as to go to the principal's office to confess, when Bethany came out. She'd confessed for me. She told me it didn't seem fair that I should lose so much over such foolishness, whereas she didn't have much to lose. It was the most generous act of sacrifice I'd ever seen."

"And then?" Maggie asked.

"Yes," Eleanor said. "And then. You understand. I didn't. I felt so badly at first, you see. It went onto her record. It prevented her from being a police officer. She couldn't pursue her dreams."

That's what old man Coleman had been talking about, Maggie recalled. That's why she couldn't become a police officer.

"A few years after that, I was in the bank. I hadn't seen her for years. I'd been studying at Oxford, and she was working in the bank, and she called me into her office. She was very proud of it. She said that if we were going to be refinancing the house, she could get us a good deal. She said it was funny how things worked out, that because of what happened she was now in a position to help me. We didn't need to refinance our mortgage. It cost a lot to do, all the points. But I didn't see how I could refuse her. You know I had the strangest feeling in that moment that she planned the whole thing out. Is that possible? Could she have known as a seventeen-year-old what she intended to do with her whole life?"

"What did you do?"

"We refinanced the house. I couldn't risk it. Then, I wouldn't hear from a while and when I least expected it, she'd come up with a small request. Could I introduce her to someone? Could I write a recommendation?" That was how she'd risen so quickly at the bank, Maggie thought.

"So then when she came to you and asked you to be maid of honor."

"I said yes."

Eleanor sighed. "My father is in a very difficult campaign. Things in politics have gotten so ugly. The least hint of scandal."

It was a motive for murder, Maggie thought, though it was hard to imagine Eleanor Hunt with an axe. But maybe she was the sort of person who would only murder if she snapped, and maybe Bethany had pushed her hard enough.

"Mr. Ridgefield told my niece you have a Rolls Royce."

"Yes, a Phantom 3. My father's joy."

"Did she ask to borrow it?" she asked.

"Yes. How did you know? I didn't tell my father. I didn't want to upset him."

"Did she return it?"

"I don't know. I haven't looked. It should be back in the garage. We could go see."

Eleanor went to a closet and retrieved a camel's hair coat and a mohair hat. She tucked her hair underneath and wrapped a scarf around her neck. Then she wrapped a coat around Max and they went through the house and out a back door. There was a woman in the kitchen and she waved at her. "I'll be back soon, Irina."

Then they were out in the backyard, walking under trellises that would bloom with roses in the spring. They continued further, on a plowed path, until they reached an outbuilding that was only a little smaller than Maggie's house. Eleanor tugged open the door and they went inside and there was the Rolls Royce.

Maggie'd been thinking about it for so long that it was startling to see the actual thing in front of her.

It was a magnificent car. It was much larger than Maggie expected. The lines were so sensuous, the half circles around the wheels and the parallel silver lines on the trim. There was something childlike about the big lights in the front and the glistening grille, and then there was that Rolls Royce hood ornament that looked a little like a bride—a woman in white leaning forward, arms outstretched. Maggie peered inside, but knew she shouldn't touch anything. She wished she could reach inside and smell it and see if it smelled like Bethany.

She needed Walter to send someone with the fingerprint kit, but she hesitated to ask him. She knew what he'd say. The case was solved. The murderer in jail. She hesitated for a moment, but then punched in his number. This was important. She could fight for this. She called him and said, "Walter. I've found the Rolls Royce. I think you should send someone to look at it."

"I'll be right there," he said.

"Oh."

Maggie sent Eleanor back inside, but she waited in the garage. She started to feel seriously cold, but minutes later he showed up. He got out of the police car and strode toward the garage, closely followed by Mercy Williams, who was holding an equipment box. He was grinning foolishly, and Maggie felt herself warm.

"Mercy," he said. "Check it out."

Then he came and stood alongside Maggie. He radiated heat. He wore the sort of winter coat sea captains wore out on the ocean. She pictured him at the helm of a ship. He looked like he could command a platoon of men. They would follow him to their deaths. He would command loyalty. Because he was brave and would go down with the ship if attacked.

"Do you sail?" she asked.

"Matter of fact I do."

"I'd like to go with you sometime."

He leaned toward her. He smelled of apples. She pictured him having his lunch. Cutting up his apple, and eating his carefully chosen cheese. There was something so intimate about knowing how a man spent his lunch hour.

"Sir," Mercy said. They both jumped.

"There are no fingerprints on the car."

Walter frowned. "How is that possible?"

He went over to the car and looked at it.

"Whoever drove this car back, cleaned off his fingerprints. That's why we haven't been able to find the chauffeur. Because he doesn't want to be found," Maggie said.

Walter nodded. "He must have dropped her off. Did he watch her get murdered and not do anything?"

"Or maybe Jeremy Kessler isn't the person who murdered her. Maybe something more intentional happened."

Walter crossed his arms, but she knew he heard her. He would listen. He would act. But if Jeremy Kessler wasn't the guilty party, that meant there was still an axe murderer at large. There was more to this story than it seemed, but she'd known that all along, hadn't she? You always hoped it would be the first and easiest choice, but it so rarely was. Which meant that Graham could still be the suspect. Graham who was out with Livy.

"He confessed, Maggie. All the forensic evidence points to him."

"Then how do you explain this? Who put this Rolls Royce back here?"

"I can't explain it. Some friend of hers who got caught up in her scheme and didn't expect it to end in murder. Someone's who's embarrassed or frightened by what he's done. It doesn't mean the person who drove the car killed her."

"No, but it means that there's more to the story than we know, and that scares me. Who laughed? What really happened to Bethany? Who else is out there?"

"Oh Maggie," he said, and he hugged her, but she wasn't in the mood for comfort. She wanted action.

She wanted to know. She wanted answers. She'd always been able to accept a certain amount of her life on faith, but no more. Not with this, not with her niece.

But she just didn't know what to do.

Nine days until Livy went home. Nine days until she went back to safety, and the only thing Maggie could think to do was follow her around like a shadow, which was not so easy since she was involved in a passionate romance with Graham and didn't seem to leave his apartment much, except when she came home, smiling and happy, and worked on their white puzzle. Fortunately she was too preoccupied with love to wonder why her aunt stuck to her like a starfish. Maggie, for the first time in her life, realized just how treacherous love was. It made you vulnerable, it made you blind, it made you joyful. It made you unsafe.

She also, realized, that unfortunately, she loved her niece desperately.

Chapter Thirty-Three

"Tell me your deepest feelings about these chickens," Livy said later that week. Maggie's house had been convulsed with people preparing for the Valentine's party, which was to be the party to end all parties in Darby.

"Do you really love them?"

Maggie surveyed her kitchen, the chicken plates and the chicken cups and the chicken clock and the chicken egg timer. And so on. "I suppose it is a bit much."

"What if we were to get rid of all of this and paint it a beautiful silver gray."

"We could paint the cabinets Jericho blue," Graham added. "It would be lavish."

"Lavish," Maggie said. "Well, all right then."

She could tell Livy had something on her mind, something more than chickens. "I found out something, Aunt Dove. I don't know if it's going to upset you."

"What is it?"

"It's about Sibyl."

That was the last thing she was expecting. Sybil, the real estate agent who she liked so much. "She reported Bethany to the bank. She told them she was cheating people. She told them she was going to file an official complaint and that she should be fired."

"I didn't realize she felt that strongly about it."

"It all related to the Collins and the Hollyhock House."

"Was the bank actually going to fire her?"

"I don't know. Maybe. But the important thing is that Bethany declared war on Sibyl."

"What does that mean?" Maggie asked, though knowing Bethany and what she did when she was angry, it could mean anything. She wondered if Sybil represented the van Dorns. She wondered if it was only Sibyl's houses that were being occupied by strangers.

"Remember, I told you that she looked angry enough to kill."

Maggie shook her head. Though the fact was, of all the people she knew, Sibyl was the most likely to go tearing after someone with an axe. She was hot-blooded. She remembered then a time she'd been at a bar and got in a fight with another woman. But she was also a kindly woman who'd helped Maggie a lot.

"I don't believe it," Maggie said, but she could read the expression on Livy's face. Why then was she so doubtful of Graham.

"I'll think about it," she said. "I'll tell Walter."

Satisfied, Livy got to work reconstructing her house. Maggie was so glad to have her there, in her house, in her view, that she figured it was worth the loss of a few chickens and the fact was she'd never liked them that much. She'd wanted one chicken, not a flock.

When they were done, she was stunned. The kitchen did look lavish. Elegant.

"It looks like you," Livy said. Graham nodded.

But the work for the party went on.

Gunvor worked to give the party a Norwegian vibe. Putting signs all over the place that read *Elsker*. Love. *Jeg elsker deg*. I love you. *Du er min Valentine*. You are my Valentine.

Edgar came by and helped to cut out hearts. Agnes came by, mainly to sit around and gossip. Sibyl came by to talk real estate and to rest her feet. Joe brought everyone donuts from D'Amici's deli. Mr. Cavanaugh sat alongside Livy on the piano bench and they played together. Then there were all the people who came by who Maggie didn't know, didn't even look familiar. People of all colors and sizes who hugged her and said how nice it was to meet her and what could they do? Would she like a mural? The only people who didn't come were Helen, and Walter, who was busy. Maggie loved the commotion more than she would have expected. She loved the voices and the laughter and activity. Maggie felt that sort of wistful happiness you feel when things are absolutely lovely and you know they are going to end. A week from now, Livy would be back in Indiana. Her life would go back to normal. It was a sweet and savory feeling. There must be a German word for it, she thought, or a Norwegian one.

She would have asked Gunvor, but Gunvor did not want to talk. In fact, although she'd spent the better part of the week at Maggie's house, she made an effort to not be in the same room as Maggie at any given time. Maggie found herself apologizing any time she found herself in the same room as Gunvor, which was ridiculous. But there was something about Gunvor that made you feel like apologizing. Something judgmental about her. When she looked at you, you felt like she saw all your weaknesses.

She did make an effort to talk to Gunvor about her host family. She told her she thought she was in an impossible position and she would write a reference, if that would help. Gunvor said, "I imagine they would listen to someone like you."

On the night before the party, everyone went off to get ready and Maggie was alone in her house for the first time in a while. Maggie wandered around the rooms. It was like a stage before the show. Party tomorrow and the next day Livy would go home. She would miss her terribly. The cats trailed behind her and she pointed out to them that they would all have to do a better job of comforting each other. "Enough of this feline stuff," she said. "Now that I've got rid of most of my chickens I'm going to focus on cats. We can do this."

They both twitched their tails, but she felt they heard her. They would miss Livy too.

She'd got Walter a Valentine's Day present. It was silly. She'd signed his name up to be engraved on a flight to Mars. It hadn't cost any money, but she'd printed out the ticket and hoped he'd like it. She hadn't seen much of him the last few days, though he was faithful about calling her every night before she went to sleep. She loved that.

She'd always been a nervous sleeper and knowing he was going to call settled her. Then she could go over the day. It was a treat to look forward to. Plus he laughed at all her jokes, so she could tell her stories and he found them charming, and she found herself often falling asleep with the phone in her hands. She had not woken up for the Insomnia Club in days. But on the night before the party, she felt fidgety, even after her phone call with him. So many people were coming to her house the next day, and then Livy would be leaving and she felt restless.

She got up and sat on the little bench in her bedroom. She looked out at the stars, at the bridge. She looked over to the van Dorn house. That was when she saw Gunvor walking out of the house.

Chapter Thirty-Four

Gunvor!

What was she doing there?

Maggie didn't hesitate. She pulled on her boots, ran down the steps and out the door. She got there so quickly, she didn't stop to think about what she'd say, though when she did get there, she faltered for just a moment.

Gunvor was intimidating. She was about twice Maggie's height and she oozed contempt. Maggie could feel it coming off her like sweat.

"What are you doing at the van Dorn's house?" Maggie cried out.

"I wasn't there," Gunvor said.

"What do you mean you weren't there? I saw you walk out of it with my own two eyes."

"There's only your word for it," Gunvor said. She looked so sure of herself, so pleased, so contemptuous. Nothing got Maggie angrier than being treated as though she didn't exist, and this young woman had a talent for pushing her buttons.

"My word is pretty good," Maggie said.

Gunvor laughed. "Of course. The Sunday School teacher. Everyone's friend."

Well, it was true, Maggie thought, but that was beside the point. Anyway, that wasn't a bad thing. She'd worked hard to build up a good reputation. In a small village, it mattered.

"This isn't about me. It's about you. What were you doing there? In the van Dorn's house?"

"Why don't you tell me since you know everything?"

"Gunvor," Maggie said. "You're trespassing. Why?" Though even as the words were out of her mouth, she realized she knew exactly why. She thought of that overladen house where Gunvor worked. She thought of the smell of urine and the children screaming. She could understand why Gunvor might feel desperate to get out of there. To hide. Had she been sleeping in the van Dorn house? Had she gone there for sanctuary? But then she thought of the pile of garbage in the house, the chalice from the church. This was not sanctuary. She was looking for something else here.

The wind picked up. Maggie drew her coat around her. She couldn't talk to Gunvor in the van Dorn house and didn't want to bring her into her own.

Gunvor shrugged. "Why shouldn't someone get use out of an empty house? It's a sin, isn't it, to have all this space unused when there are people who have no place to live?"

Suddenly, it clicked into place.

"Did you stay at Hollyhock House too?" she asked.

"Sometimes," she said. She just wore a sweater with the New York City skyline, but she didn't look cold. Nordic upbringing.

"It was empty. I wasn't hurting anyone. I take pictures of these empty places and I tell people about them. On my Instagram account, so that people who need a place to stay can go there."

"And that's how Jeremy Kessler wound up at Hollyhock House. That's how he knew it was safe to go there?"

She shrugged.

"Bethany must have given you the names of the empty houses." It all made sense. Bethany was furious at Sibyl, at the bank, at Darby. She wanted revenge. She was going to be fired from the bank. She would fight it. She would probably win, but knowing Bethany she'd want to lash out and destroy, and what better way to get back at a village that prided itself on its safety than to begin feeding strangers into its midst.

"And he killed her," Maggie said.

"That's what they say. He's a convenient target."

"Do you think otherwise?" Maggie asked. Gunvor always had a way of posing as though she knew secrets no one else knew. Did she?"

"Gunvor, if you think someone else killed Bethany, speak up. You were her friend."

"You're worried about your niece?"

"I'm worried about the truth. If Jeremy's innocent, I'd like to know."

"The truth?"

"Doesn't it matter to you?"

"No. There is no truth here. No honesty. All of you living your little lives. So sure you're safe."

"But if Jeremy's innocent, wouldn't you want to help him? Why does that make you so angry? Wouldn't you want to catch the person who killed your friend?"

"So, he could be punished?"

"Yes, or contained. So he could hurt no one else."

"You think you can stop yourself from being hurt?"

"I don't think there's any way to protect yourself completely, but I think it's worth trying."

Gunvor turned to look toward the van Dorn house. Maggie followed her gaze. A piece of the gutter fell to the ground as the wind blew. The whole house looked exhausted. Half-raised blinds made it look like its eyelids were half lowered. It sagged.

"I like to watch it fall apart," Gunvor said. "Dissolution is so much more powerful than erection. Is that the word? Your culture is built on consolidation and domination. I like the smell of mice, of old Cheetohs. Of squirrels." She laughed then, a distinctive rumbling sort of laugh.

"You were the one who laughed, weren't you?" Maggie Dove asked. "At the wedding?"

Gunvor threw back her head and laughed. It was a terrible sound.

"But I didn't see you there."

Gunvor looked triumphant.

"I was downstairs, where the bride waits. There's a separate entrance. After I laughed, I ran back upstairs and out to the car. Bethany'd got me a uniform."

"You drove the Rolls Royce? You dropped her off at Hollyhock House?"

"I was supposed to stay with her," Gunvor said. "But the car was making a strange sound and I had to get it back before anyone noticed it was gone. Otherwise I would have been there. Otherwise I would be dead. Again." A girl who had narrowly survived being in the attack on the camp in Norway. Who had probably heard of horrors the likes of which Maggie couldn't imagine. Who had been damaged in unfathomable ways. And yet. She had to know.

"What did you see? Did you see Jeremy? Did you see someone else?"

For just a moment, Maggie thought Gunvor might speak. But the distance between them was too great.

"Gunvor, listen to me. If you saw something, you must tell the police. Don't keep it a secret. It's dangerous."

"The police will send me back."

"Not necessarily. They'll try to help you."

She laughed again, this time more harsh. "That's what Livy said you would say. She would say that you would trust the police."

Maggie felt like the ground shook under her feet. "Livy. You told Livy about this?"

"Of course she knows. She and I have no secrets."

She knew that Livy had spent a lot of time with Gunvor this last week. It was possible Gunvor had shared this information. But she also knew Gunvor to be a person who liked to destroy things. She suspected it would give her pleasure to cause a rift between Maggie and Livy. For the same reason she had piled up garbage in the van Dorn house. Because she had seen and lived destruction, and it seemed like know she wanted to spread it.

"Gunvor, listen to me. I understand why you're angry, but please. If you know something, tell me."

"Oh I know something," she said.

"What?"

"I know something about you, Maggie Dove," she said. "I know your secret," she said, and then she went spinning into the wind. A dervish.

Maggie stared after her stunned. Secret? She had no secret. She was as close to an open book as it was possible to be. What could she be talking about? She would have dismissed the whole thing as a lie, but Gunvor looked way too happy. She felt frightened suddenly, but of what? Herself?

Chapter Thirty-Five

Walter was first to the Valentine's Day party. Not a man who believed in being fashionably late. He wore a red sweater, a red hat, and red gloves. "Happy Valentine's Day," he said when Maggie opened the door.

"Oh I'm glad to see you," she said, and hugged him with an abandon she hadn't anticipated. "I'm just feeling a little tense," she said.

Only then did Maggie realize that she'd been so distracted she hadn't dressed up at all. She still had on her Eileen Fisher gray sweater and black pants. She should at least put on some red lipstick, but even that felt like a lot of effort. It didn't matter really because Walter beamed at her as though she'd emerged from a seashell.

"Before the party starts," he said, "I have a present for you."

"Oh," she said. "I have one for you too."

Though she couldn't remember what she'd done with it. It was in an envelope. The engraving on the flight to Mars. She hoped she hadn't thrown it out. Oh no. She had thrown it out. She was losing her mind.

Gunvor's words had unsettled her. Hard to relax and have fun when you feel like a guided missile is headed in your direction.

She brought him over to the kitchen, which he admired. He loved the silver gray and ran his hands across the walls. She was making a cherry bread pudding, her contribution to the festivities. She'd put in extra vanilla and the room smelled sweet, though the bubbling jam was disturbing. She felt like everything she saw was disturbing her.

He withdrew an envelope from his pocket. It was a plain white envelope, but he'd drawn a heart on it.

"What is this?" she asked, wondering if it could be plane tickets. An escape.

She waved it back and forth, but he held her hand still. "Open it."

She did, and withdrew a small oak leaf. It had been pressed and preserved.

She looked up into his face. It was like looking at a dog, she thought. A basset hound. His eyes were warm, his hair stood up where he'd run his hands through it.

"Do you remember the first time I met you? You were mad at me at the time, and you went storming off, but I was standing next to a tree and saw this leaf and took it home and pressed it. I sensed it would mean something to me."

"That's so lovely," she said.

She ran her hand across the leaf's soft skin. "I think that's the most romantic gift I've ever received."

She did remember that tree. She remembered how frustrated she'd been, because he was trying to prosecute someone she loved, and yet she too had felt a surge of something in her heart. Why else would she have been so angry?

"Maggie," he said. "Are you all right?"

She rested her head against his chest, listening to the strong beat of his heart. She felt calmer than she had for a day.

He smelled of laundry detergent. Fresh and clean.

She reached up to feel his smoothly shaved chin. His eyes followed her gravely, as though memorizing her. "I'm worried about Gunvor and Livy," she said. "Something weird is going on with them. Gunvor threatened me before, or I think she did. She made it sound like Livy knew a damaging secret about me, but I can't imagine what it could be. I don't have any secrets, and that's what worries me, because is there a secret about myself I don't know? I mean, could I have robbed a bank, but forgotten? I don't think so. But there's something, and it scares me."

That's when Maggie heard Gunvor laughing. It was not a humorous sound. Sounded like a machine gun. Aggressive, attention-getting. Definitely disrupted the general good will.

She heard Livy's voice as an undercurrent and walked toward it, and saw Livy pleading with Gunvor about something. Gunvor shaking her head.

Maggie felt terror settle over her. She knew Gunvor wanted to do something hurtful. She thought of her standing in front of the van Dorn house only the night before. *I love to see things fall apart.*

"Tell her," Gunvor said.

"No," Livy cried out. "No, please. I don't want to."

But Gunvor swept past her, grabbed up a bottle of wine, and went into the living room.

"Please," Livy said, running after her, but there was too much commotion. Everything seemed to happen all at once.

Agnes stormed into the kitchen. She wore a red Mickey Mouse hat, for whatever reason. "I brought the baklava," she cried out, and then there was Edgar, darting toward her. "Maggie. Maggie. Maggie." He'd made her a Valentine's Day card that had chocolate chips on it and doilies. Helen stood behind him, smiling but not making eye contact, looking a little bit to the right and above, like a marksman making a difficult shot. Music began to pound out. Mr. Cavanaugh walked in, blinking. He clutched his little dog to his chest. "*Calmate Fidelio*," he whispered. He'd made delicate doily cookies and was doing his best to keep Edgar from knocking them on to the floor.

The Faraday sisters were there, and Joe Mangione in his green jacket, and Reverend Sunday in a bright green suit and a slew of au pairs, each of them carrying a different type of alcohol. They seemed to like colorful drinks. Gunvor hugged each of them loudly, laughing and clinking glasses as she stocked up. Maggie noticed Livy putting her hand on her to slow her down, but then Graham was there. He was wearing clothes from the Banana Republic. Livy must have taken him out shopping.

Gunvor went and changed the music. "I have a better playlist," she shouted. "Listen to me. Listen to me."

She began to dance a sensuous dance, holding her arms over her head like a belly dancer and grinding against Graham, who tried to move out of her way. Most of the people from the church had congregated in the corner, next to the piano, and they were gossiping about some business to do with the piano tuner. They were not big drinkers, but had a plate of cookies in front of them. Every so often they smiled across in that myopic pleasant way that people have when they are trying not to get into trouble.

It was strange to have so many people in her house, and so many people she didn't know, and so much emotion. It was a bit like being in a Eugene O'Neill play except that at least they knew what they were arguing about. Maggie was relieved to see that Livy and Graham were swept up in each other, standing in a corner and talking intently. He looked so different than he had as a pale groom and then as a lumberjack. Now he looked professional, even professorial. She wondered if Livy would get him to enroll in a Ph.D. program. Who knew what potential someone had when someone good loved them? He was laughing, and talking with people, and it would have all been pleasant except that underlying everything was the bass sound of Gunvor's laugh.

The more Gunvor had to drink, the louder she got. She drank to a purpose. She wore tight jeans that stretched across her toned legs, high boots, and a low-cut blouse, and she had several pieces of wool twisted around her wrist. She had on large hoop earrings that had a bit of feather on the bottom. She had a bandana twisted around her neck. She was not beautiful, Maggie thought, but she was alive and vibrant and itching to get into trouble. Had she been one of her Sunday School students she would have sent her to the principal.

But there was also something haunted and needy in her gaze, something that always got Maggie in the gut. It was the same reason she'd rescued her cats. It was seeing that need. How could you not respond to it? Livy didn't have that. Whatever damage had been done to Livy she would recover from, but Gunvor had that irreparable damage. Had Bethany had that too?

She noticed Walter talking to Joe, and then she noticed everyone buzzing and looking behind her and she saw Gunvor climbing to the top of her kitchen table. The table where she read her Bible every morning. The table where all her little chickens used to sit, though now it was all clean and elegant. Livy ran up to her.

"Gunvor, what are you doing?"

"A toast," she said. "I'm making a toast."

"No, don't do this now."

"Why? You said it yourself. There's no need to keep secrets."

"Please."

Maggie stepped forward and put her arm around Livy. "That's enough Gunvor," she said. "You can see Livy doesn't want you to do this."

Gunvor reared back in a snake-like move. She'd had a lot to drink. Her eyes sparkled. Her teeth were bright white and Maggie noticed then she had on fairly elaborate eye make-up. She wondered if Amber was here somewhere. Her house was crowded with people she didn't know, though she noticed Walter moving toward her.

"Livy does want to talk about this," Gunvor proclaimed. "Why else did she tell me? Because she wanted to talk about it."

Livy looked over to Maggie. "I had too much to drink, Aunt Dove. I should never have told her."

"There's nothing better than truth," Gunvor shouted.

Livy looked like she was going to cry. Maggie'd had enough. "Gunvor, you're being a bully and you're threatening. Please leave my house."

Walter strode toward Gunvor and she started to laugh, but then a balloon popped, and she held up her hands to her face. Edgar knocked something over and she heard Helen yell. "Now you'll have to clean that whole thing up."

"I will leave your house," Gunvor said. "I will leave this terrible little town, but first I will say what I have to say. Or you should tell her. She said to Livy, "You tell her what her husband really was."

"What?" Maggie said. It was the last thing in the world she expected her to say. Stuart Dove? The most innocuous man alive? What was she talking about?

"No. You promised," Livy cried out. "No," she cried out and went running out of the room, up the stairs.

Walter started to tug Gunvor out the door, but for just a moment she stood and looked directly at Maggie. "Ask her about your husband's first wife. His real wife."

Chapter Thirty-Six

Stuart's first wife? There was no first wife. Maggie was his first wife, and his last. Gunvor might as well have said Stuart was an alien from outer space. It was unbelievable, except that Livy'd looked stricken at her words and had gone running up the steps.

Maggie started toward the stairs, toward Livy's room. One of the photographs on the landing was crooked. A photo from a trip they'd taken to Scotland when she and Stuart were just married. Maggie stopped to straighten it out. Then she started walking up the stairs, to Livy's door, tapped on it. It swung open.

"I'm so sorry," Livy said, when Maggie walked into the room. "I'm so sorry Aunt Dove."

She was curled up at the edge of her bed. Maggie hadn't been into the room in a while, and was surprised to see how she'd made it her own. Everything neatly made. The garish bed spread carefully folded. A bouquet of flowers on her bureau. A stack of books. Two of them about wood-working.

"I don't understand," Maggie said. She went over to the desk chair and sat on it. "What is Gunvor talking about?"

Stuart had been a confirmed old bachelor when she met him. Part of what had charmed her was the challenge of seducing him. She'd always had competitive instincts. She enjoyed deploying her power. Back when she was young, a woman's power to persuade a man to marry her was one of the strongest powers a woman could wield, and if you could persuade a powerful man, an authority figure, a professor, to marry you, so much the better.

"I got drunk," Livy said. "I promised not to tell anyone about it but I got drunk and Gunvor has a way of getting you to talk. I never meant to hurt you. I promised dad I wouldn't tell you."

She clutched her blanket around her. All her sophistication had dropped away. She looked as young as she had back when she came to visit Maggie the first time, when they went to the M&M store.

Someone knocked on the door. Walter. "Maggie, are you all right?" he asked.

"Yes," she said. "I'm fine."

"I'm going to wind down the party."

"Okay."

She heard him go back down the steps. Then the door downstairs opening and closing. All the guests leaving. The sound of dishes being put away and she knew that the Deacons from the church would be down there, tidying up, and that was a comfort.

"He was married before," Livy said. "Uncle Stuart. He and his wife weren't happy or anything.

But she was Catholic and they agreed to live apart. Then he met you and he was crazy about you, and you wanted so badly to get married. You wouldn't live with him. He didn't want to lose you. He didn't know what to do."

Maggie blushed, because it was true. She had wanted to get married. That was the prize, wasn't it? It was the 1980s and she was a traditional sort of person. She wouldn't have gone and lived with him without a ring. Automatically she felt for her ring, which she'd never taken off. Of course, she had plenty of friends who were living with their boyfriends, but she didn't feel right doing it and Stuart never pressed her. She didn't know what she would have done had she thought she might lose him, but part of what she loved about him was that he was traditional too.

"So how did he persuade her to get divorced then?" Maggie asked.

"He didn't," Livy mumbled. "She couldn't. She was very religious."

Maggie felt like her brain was clouding up. It was a sensation she got when she was hungry, or hot, or frightened.

"He got an annulment then?"

Livy shook her head. She pressed one strand of hair behind her ear. She kept her eyes focused on the tidy little rug at her feet.

"But then how did he marry me?" Maggie asked, as calmly as possible.

"He didn't have the heart to tell you. He was so sure that as the wedding went forward, Rowena would agree to the divorce. He kept hoping and hoping and then came the day of the wedding, and the thing was that your wedding was in Darby. No one here knew him. No one knew his history. Except for my dad, and all."

"You mean to say that he was a bigamist?"

"I'm sorry Aunt Dove."

A bigamist.

It sounded so dirty. Like something you'd see on Netflix. She felt tarnished. Whatever else had happened in her life, she'd always kept her reputation clean. It mattered to her. Now she felt like a laughing stock. Maggie Dove. Sunday School teacher. Bigamist.

"When did she die?"

"She didn't," Livy mumbled. "She's still alive."

"Where is she?" Maggie cried out.

"In New York City."

"Here, in New York. She lives near me?"

Maggie felt something boiling inside her that covered up shock, grief, betrayal. It was anger. An anger so sharp that she felt she could slice someone with it. She rose to her feet. "She lives near me," she repeated and stalked out of Livy's room and into her bedroom and there she took out her phone and called Linus, who immediately began to sputter.

"Oh, Maggie, I never wanted you to find out. Stuart would never have wanted to hurt you. He adored you, you know that."

"He married me while he was married to another woman."

She stared at their bedroom set. She remembered how pleased she'd been when her parents had given it to her. It was a family heirloom. The bed had been in her family for generations. Solid, mahogany. Generations of Leighs had been born in that bed. Honorable women married to honorable men.

Twenty years she'd slept on that bed with her husband. She knew every part of his body, had loved every part of it. How many nights had she fallen asleep holding his hand and woken up with his hand still clasped in hers? She found herself thinking of one of the trees she often walked by in the woods, a grand old thing that had been knocked over by a storm, branches forever now reaching upward, shocked into position, now covered with fungus. Calcified into rage.

"He was desperate for you," Linus said. "He knew you wouldn't be with him if he wasn't free. He couldn't live without you."

Desperate? Stuart. A courtly, slightly dry man who was devoted to his daughter and spent most of his life reading a book. The worst argument she could remember having with him was over whether to see *Saturday Night Fever*. She wanted to see it and he thought it foolishness, which of course it was, but everyone was talking about it. He'd sat through the whole movie looking disapproving, and yet years later, he'd surprised her by dancing like John Travolta. How she'd laughed then. Desperate?

"No one ever thought to tell me?" she hissed.

"We always thought Rowena would die. She was older than him, and not well."

"So the two of you sat around hoping his wife would die of old age or disease. That was the plan." It would have been ridiculous, had it not been so painful. "That means Nora knew about it," she said, as she realized. "And Livy knew. How many people knew?" She felt so embarrassed.

"For what it's worth, Maggie, I didn't think it was right for him to do. We argued about it, but you know how willful he could be."

Willful, Maggie thought. Not a word she would have associated with Stuart Dove. She wondered if she knew him at all. How could you be married to a man for twenty years and not know the most elemental thing about him? How could that be a real marriage then? Everything he said to her would have hummed with the undercurrent of that lie.

"Did she know? This Rowena. Did she know he went ahead and got married?"

He was quiet. The house was quiet, except for the soft sounds of Livy sobbing in her bedroom.

"Yes, but she held up to her end of the bargain. She never made problems for him. Never contacted you. He gave her what she wanted. She had no quarrel with him. Her life has not been easy."

"You're in touch with her," she whispered. Little blue notes. Suddenly something terrifying occurred to her.

"She didn't have a child, did she?" Maggie cried out, suddenly hit with the full ramifications of it all. She could have had five children. All of them part Juliet. But Linus all but shouted the answer. "No, no, no. They didn't have any children."

"Wait," Maggie said, her mind tumbling into a whole other direction. She was tired and yet couldn't bring herself to sink onto the bed. She would never lie on it again. "That means that Juliet was illegitimate. She was a bastard."

"Maggie, how can you say that?"

"But it's the truth."

"It hardly matters now."

"Of course, it matters. It's all that matters. All I have left are my memories of him and they're shattered. Everything I thought I knew was a lie."

"He loved you," Linus snapped. "He loved you and that was not a lie."

"Of course, it's a lie," she said. "How can you have love based on a lie? Love is about telling the truth." She thought she heard Livy's door close, Livy's footsteps. She needed to talk to her. She needed to end this conversation and yet she couldn't.

"What's Rowena's address?"

"What are you going to do?"

"I want to see her."

"I don't think that's wise."

"Damn it, Linus. I'm tired of both of you treating me like a child. I can find her address and I can do it with you or without you, but it will save me time if you simply give it to me."

"305 W. 72nd Street. Apt. 15D."

"Thank you," she said, and clicked off the phone.

She stood there, staggered. This was always the way with shock. It came out of nowhere. This wasn't even on the radar, wasn't something she'd even worried about. Who would think your husband was a bigamist? Of all the things to worry about. And yet it was the one thing that cut to her core. It broke her heart. Twenty years with a man, another twenty years remembering him, and it was all a lie.

She went out onto the landing and saw Livy's door open. She would have to talk to her. Livy must be distraught, but when she went inside, she saw Livy had written out a note.

"I'm so sorry, Aunt Dove. I thought you'd like privacy tonight so I've gone over to Graham's. I love you."

Maggie was tempted to text her, and to tell her it didn't matter, but it did matter. She could feel her heart harden. All those years of reading the Bible and finally she understood what the expression meant. Her normal, warm beating heart seemed to solidify. She fumed.

All those years people had known about her and whispered. They'd loved her, but when people know a secret about you that always puts you in a lower position. It was past eleven o'clock. She knew it was too late to call Rowena and yet she did. She found the number and Rowena answered quickly, as though she was expecting her. Maybe she was.

Probably Linus had called her the moment they hung up.

"This is Maggie Dove. I'd like to see you tomorrow morning."

"I'll be here," she said. Croaked. She sounded old.

"Ten o'clock," Maggie said.

She went downstairs. Everything from the party was cleaned up. All the plates put away, but she heard water running and she knew it would be Walter. Which it was. He'd stacked up a big pile of plates and was almost to the end. He didn't move to hold her, which she appreciated. She felt too raw to be touched.

"You heard all that."

"Tell me," he said. He turned off the water and sat down at the table. At his elbow was the Bible she read through every morning, the one that had all the dates of deaths and births. Everything in there was a lie.

"I can't," she said. She felt dirty. Bigamist. She knew it wasn't her fault. Nothing seemed to be her fault, and yet it was, wasn't it? Had she pushed him too hard to get married? How toxic was she? She felt angry, venomous.

"I just can't," she said. "I'm sorry, but I can't deal with this."

She knew he would offer her comfort. That he would hug her and make it all right. But she didn't want to find consolation. She felt too angry. It was boiling inside her, taking her over. Just for a moment she thought of Bethany and the anger that had roared through her and destroyed her. She hated the feeling and tried to tamp it down but she couldn't.

"Go home," she said.

"I don't want to."

"I'm sorry," she said, "but you have to."

He paused at the front door as though he had something more to say, but he thought better of it and left, for which she was glad. She was in the sort of mood where she might have said something unforgiveable, and she didn't want to do that.

She sat down at the kitchen counter and the cats came over and lay at her feet. Of course, she thought. They waited until she was completely broken and then they came over and offered her affection. Their eyes seemed to click. Her two survivor cats. One who'd survived the loss of his mistress, the other who'd survived God knows what hardships. Now you are one of us, they seemed to say, but she was not moved. She didn't want their pity. Didn't want anyone's pity.

She opened up the Bible and turned to the opening flap, which was where the family tree was. How many hours had she spent weeping over that family tree? Now she looked at Stuart's name, written in the marriage section. She'd been twenty-one years old when she wrote in his name. She'd been so young, so beautiful.

Now she took a marker and crossed out his name. Alongside it she wrote, *Bigamist.*

Chapter Thirty-Seven

Agnes called first thing in the morning, but Maggie didn't pick up. She knew Agnes would be outraged and on her side, but she couldn't face it. Helen called, but she didn't answer her either because she knew she was calling out of pity and she hated pity more than all other emotions. Walter called and she didn't pick up because next to pity she felt she couldn't stand love. He would hold her in his arms and protect her. She couldn't stand it. She was tired of being a victim. She'd rather be alone.

It was so dark out.

Almost 7 a.m. and the sky was black. Saturday morning. Most of Darby asleep. Even from her window she could see few lights on. Some reverberation from the bridge.

A text came through from Livy. *Are you okay?*

Yes, she answered, and left it like that.

She turned off her phone. That was another thing she didn't want to do. Think about Livy with Graham. Think about Livy going home. Thinking about Livy telling Gunvor the secret before she told Maggie. She felt so hurt. Angry too. Betrayed, and surprised. That was the worst of it. To feel so completely blindsided. It was as though the foundation on which she walked shifted. In fact, she kept stumbling. She saw obstacles swim out of the corner of her eye.

Maggie was tempted to go see Rowena without any make-up, but vanity prevailed. She dressed carefully in a dress, then undressed. What did it matter? What was the point? Then she dressed again. It did matter. She needed to arm herself and feeling well dressed would make her feel better. She wanted to look young. All right, that was shallow, but under the circumstances she felt she could forgive herself. She put on a knee length black dress, tights, and high boots, and some dangly earrings that one of her Sunday school students had given her when he got into divinity school. She didn't normally wear a lot of make-up, but now she pulled out the mascara, put on some liner, and some pink lipstick.

She went downstairs, fed the cats, and made some coffee. Then she opened the front door and just about tripped over a casserole dish. Then there was another one. It was like mushrooms popping up after storm. She knew they were tokens of love from her friends, but she couldn't deal with them right now. She left them outside. It was so cold there was no danger of them spoiling.

Then she got into her TT and drove south. She drove fast down the Saw Mill. There were not many advantages to being blind with anger, but one of them had to be that she felt more alive. She felt vivid. She tore down the West Side highway and over to the 72nd

Street exit. She was not far from Sarabeth's bakery, which was one of Maggie's favorite places in the world. She always remembered a friend of hers who had left the Towers after 9/11 and had walked north all the way to Sarabeth's, and when she walked in she wept, because she knew she would be safe there.

Though of course that was ridiculous. Sarabeth's could be bombed as easily as anywhere else. There were no safe places.

She drove east. Fortunately, early on a Saturday morning, the city was not too crowded and she was able to find a parking spot not far from Rowena's apartment. It was a building she knew. She'd often walked by it on her way to Lincoln Center. She tried to remember if Stuart had ever purposely walked by there on the way to the opera.

"Bigamist," she whispered to herself. All those years of teaching morals to Sunday school students and it turned out she was the worst offender of them all. All of a sudden, she remembered a quiet Sunday afternoon. Maggie and Stuart and Juliet working on a puzzle. Juliet, then around ten years old, transfixed by the puzzle, and Stuart smoking his pipe and sipping on brandy and Maggie busy separating the edges from the center and trying to find order in the puzzle pieces. Back then she had believed it was possible to impose order.

She remembered how the phone rang and Stuart answered it, which was unusual, because he didn't get many calls at home.

"Not here," he said, and he looked so guilty that she laughed, because she trusted him so much that it didn't occur to her he might have been up to no good. "Your mistress?" she asked, and for just a moment she saw something she'd never seen on her husband's face. A look of embarrassment. And then he laughed and began reciting from Robert Browning's "To His Coy Mistress." Only now did she wonder if Rowena had been on the phone.

"I'll call you back," he'd said.

"I'm here to see Ms. Dove," Maggie said to the doorman at the apartment building. She was damned if she would call her Mrs.

"Yes, she's expecting you," he said. "Ms. Dove."

"Mrs.," she replied.

He picked up a gold telephone and spoke into it, and then he nodded and pointed her to the elevator. "16D," he said.

The elevator smelled like every elevator Maggie had ever been in, which was to say of sweat and chicken soup. The walls were mirrored. She stared at her reflection and stood up straighter. Quickly she applied some more lipstick. Then she stepped out into the hallway, and walked to 16D.

Some classical music came from within the apartment. She rang the bell, though honestly, you'd think she'd know she was coming since the doorman had just called to tell her so. Maggie heard someone tapping a cane. Coming closer and closer like something out of a horror movie. Then Rowena opened the door.

She was severe. Commanding. She wore black and had a large crucifix around her neck.

"What do you want from me?" she asked.

"I want to understand why Stuart did this," Maggie said. "I thought him an honorable man."

Rowena took a step back. Maggie thought she might fall, automatically held out her arm to catch her, but Rowena smacked her with her cane.

"What did you expect him to do? You pursued him, you threw yourself at him."

"I was a young woman," Maggie said. "He could have said no. He could have told me he was married. I would have backed off."

Rowena shook her head. Her lip curled. She put her hand to her cross, rubbing it like a talisman.

"You would never have backed off," she snapped. "You were determined to ensnare him."

Maggie walked around her, into the main part of the apartment, thinking to position her where she could sit down. Also curious about the space.

It was an elegant room, carefully tended, although old-fashioned. The curtains were heavy gold damask, drawn closed against the sun. The furniture was heavy cherry wood. A tapestry hung on the wall. Maggie wondered if she'd made it herself. A heavy book shelf occupied most of the far wall, and Maggie noticed some of the same books as were in her study. He had lived here, she realized. He had put his imprint on this place.

She noticed a wedding portrait on one of the end tables. She walked toward it. There he was. Stuart was 40 when he married Maggie. He must have been 25 in this photo. She wouldn't have recognized him. His face unlined, his hair dark and curly. He'd had white hair for the whole time she'd known him. Rowena was beautiful, dark- haired, elegant. Imposing. They made a compelling pair.

"Don't touch that," she said, surging past Maggie and grabbing up the photo. Maggie noticed then that she still wore her wedding ring. Hers a heavy gold band, Maggie's platinum. She'd loved it, gone to Tiffany's to pick it out. Remembered the way it felt when it slid on her finger and how she'd sworn never to take it off. Which she hadn't. She felt the floor rumble slightly, though that was just the subway from down below.

"I met him in Cambridge," Rowena said. "I was working on my Ph.D. in Physics, though I gave it up for him. He needed a partner to manage his career. I gave up everything for him. When he told me about you I thought, of course. That's what he needed. A woman without a career. A malleable woman. A young woman."

Maggie thought there was some truth to what she said. There was no question that Stuart wanted things his way, and that she'd been happy to oblige him. For a time anyway. As she'd gotten older, she'd gotten more independent. She'd had a job. But it was true that she had put him first, and it caused her less difficulty than Rowena because she'd had less to give up.

"He expected me to understand. He told me we hadn't been happy for a long time. He thought I was unreasonable." She shook her head. "I told him he could do whatever he liked, but that he would not get a divorce from me." She twisted her wedding ring, a nervous habit Maggie had as well. She wished Stuart were there. She wished she could talk to him, yell at him. She felt like in another context she would have liked this woman, agreed with her.

"He had affairs, you know."

"Not when he was married to me," Maggie snapped.

Rowena laughed softly. "Are you so sure?"

"No," Maggie said. "I suppose I'm not sure of anything anymore."

"I thought we would have children," she said, "but I couldn't. I thought it was his fault, but it must have been mine. You had a child."

"Juliet. Our daughter."

"And she died."

"Yes."

Maggie waited for her to say she was sorry, but she didn't, and Maggie began to understand the depths of hatred in which this woman lived. Cocooned in this dark place, salivating over Maggie's misfortune. She imagined her hearing about Juliet and feeling glad. Feeling perhaps like it was a judgment. This whole apartment, Maggie thought, was a monument to her hatred and anger.

"He liked to talk about you, you know. He would take me out every year for my birthday. February 17," she said. "Every year."

This woman stared at her through haunted eyes that reminded Maggie of Bethany's. Aggrieved and angry. That anger had cost Bethany her life. It wasn't even that she was wrong to be angry, but that it consumed her. She could have married Graham. She could have moved away to a pretty town in Arizona and had her surgery and started a new life, but she just couldn't do it. Her anger possessed her. As had this woman's. Stuart betrayed her. But Rowena had lived in her anger for more than forty years. It was all so seductive, because you knew you had right on your side. Standing there in that overheated room, with the ground rumbling beneath her feet, and the lightning anger bouncing against her brain, Maggie felt the seductiveness of anger. But if she succumbed to it, she would push Livy away. She would turn into Bethany. She would eat herself from the inside. Stuart was dead and had been for twenty years.

She'd been given a gift of this beautiful, mercurial, vivid and loving young woman. It would be a sin to turn her away. Did she want to turn into Rowena?

Maggie started toward the door.

"Wait, where are you going? Don't you want to know what he said about you? Don't you want to hear?"

Maggie got back into the elevator and strode past the doorman, then she left the city behind. She shook the dust from her feet. It was time to go home.

Maggie neared her beautiful town. The trees waved over her head, giant friendly druids who looked down at her benignly. She would invite Walter over for dinner. Cook something special. She'd seen a recipe in *The New York Times* for fried feta cheese. She wasn't sure she could do it, but she would try. She had the perfect plate for it. A plate she'd bought at an exhibition about the Titanic. It was lovely. She was so focused on Walter and the feta cheese that when she saw his police car in front of her house, she assumed he'd read her mind and was waiting for her to give him something to eat.

That was until she saw him stride out her front door and down the porch steps.

That was until she saw his face, and then he started to speak, and then she tried to take in what he said. But she couldn't understand his words. They were too terrible to understand.

Chapter Thirty-Eight

Gunvor was dead and Livy missing.

Walter must have said it ten times. Maggie heard it ten times, but she couldn't take it in. She started to shiver. He put his arms around her, guided her into the house. Helen was in the kitchen, boiling tea on the kettle. Edgar stared at her, alarmed, stunned into good behavior. Agnes had her phone pressed against her ear. She shouted something, but Maggie couldn't understand the words. It felt like sound reverberated off her eardrum.

"I don't understand," she finally managed to say. "Livy was at Graham's. She texted me. She told me she was there." She held out her phone for proof. "And Gunvor went storming out of the house." She stood in the doorway, shouting at Maggie the words that broke her heart, that set her off on to a fool's mission to see Rowena.

"We don't know what happened, Maggie," Reverend Sunday said. She was there too. In her neat gray suit, the same one she always wore to funerals and visitations. "Graham found Gunvor this morning. He was out looking for Livy. He found Gunvor dead."

"No, but the thing is that Livy wasn't with Gunvor. Livy was with Graham. I have the text."

Walter sat down at her kitchen table and gestured for her to sit across from him. She'd spent so much time thinking about him these last few weeks that she'd thought she'd memorized every line on his face, and yet now he looked unfamiliar. She thought of how Stuart, too, had looked unfamiliar in the photo and she wondered if this was what shock did. Did it blur your mind? And yet not Livy. She saw her in her mind as vividly as if she stood in front of her. Laughing girl with her amber eyes and her beautiful smile. Livy, who'd known how upset Maggie was last night, and had left her a note that she was going to Graham's house.

"Livy did go to Graham's house last night," Walter said, "but around 10:00, Gunvor called her. She was upset and wanted Livy to come over."

"According to Graham," Maggie said.

"Yes," Walter said slowly.

"And he let her go?"

"He drove her over to Gunvor's house. To the Windsor house. Watched her go inside. She told him she'd call him when she needed to be picked up."

"So he left her there?"

"He called her at midnight to see if she needed her, but she didn't answer."

"What did he do then?"

Walter shrugged. "He thought she might be asleep, but when he called again this morning and she didn't answer, he went over there. Kacie was there with all the kids and she was angry because she was having a slumber party. Gunvor was supposed to be there to help, but she'd gone out. So then Graham went out and drove around for a bit."

"He didn't call the police!"

"He wasn't that worried. He thought they'd gone out to breakfast or something. But then he went over to Hollyhock House."

"Why?"

"Gunvor liked to stay there sometimes. She liked staying at abandoned houses when she needed to get away from her host family." Which of course Maggie knew. Which was the very thing she'd had an argument about with Gunvor. Walter went on, "He remembered that Livy told him that and then he went over and looked and found her. Gunvor. Her body. But there was no sign of Livy."

"And what now?" she asked. "You've let him go again!"

"We are keeping watch on him, Maggie."

"Keeping watch! What good does that do now? You should have been keeping watch on him earlier." She couldn't stop herself. She wanted to run and fling herself a wall. How many times had she raised questions about Graham, but no. It was Jeremy Kessler. But now it couldn't be Jeremy because he'd be hospitalized. Instead, this man who her niece loved was on the loose. And Gunvor dead.

"How did she die?"

"She was shot."

Even worse. To survive all the violence she had, and then to be gunned down.

"I've called in extra resources, Maggie. The County Special Forces are investigating and I've got a call in to State."

"How do you know if anything Graham says is true? How do you know if he even took her over to the Windsor's house? What if he killed Gunvor because she knew what happened to Bethany? Maybe he worried she'd come between his relationship with Livy. He was always the obvious choice!"

But Walter didn't rise to the bait, didn't attack her back. That frightened her more than anything. Her mind filled with terrifying images. Livy hurt. Livy in trouble. Livy dead.

"And what about Kacie Windsor? What did she say?"

Walter shrugged. "She didn't see anything. She seemed most preoccupied about the slumber party. She wanted to know how long it would take to get a replacement for Gunvor."

"I have to call Linus," she said. "I have to let him know what's happening."

"I've called him," Walter said. "He's on his way out. Joe Mangione is meeting him at LaGuardia."

Helen brought her tea, sat alongside her. "Drink it," she said and Maggie did, but it burned. She gagged.

"Why would anyone want to hurt Livy? I can understand Bethany. She had enemies. I can even understand Gunvor. She liked causing trouble. But Livy, dear Livy. Why would anyone want to hurt her?" She'd never told her how much she loved her. She'd planned to. Had a whole speech planned out for when she dropped her off at the airport. In just a day.

Walter's phone buzzed. He took it from his pocket, looked at it, frowned. "I've got to go."

"Have you found Livy?"

"No, not yet."

"I'm coming with you," she said.

"No," he said. "I'm sorry, but you can't."

"Walter, I'm not even debating this. You can take me to the crime scene or you can arrest me. But nothing short of that is going to stop me. I have to see what happened."

She was done being polite. Done believing what everyone else had to say. She had to know.

Chapter Thirty-Nine

Before they even got to Hollyhock House, Maggie could see a ring of news vans. The police had put up a barricade to seal off the road, but the vans came right up to the line, and the reporters were leaning over it, as though even being an inch or so closer to the crime scene would make a difference. It was a frozen Saturday evening in the middle of February, yet Maggie could feel the heat coming off the reporters, the cars, the teams of police officers who prowled around the house. At the sight of Walter, they began shouting, "What do you know?" "Do you regret arresting Kessler? Will you be letting him go?"

They pulled up in front of the house. Walter came around and opened Maggie's door, put his hand under her arm and led her into the house. A woman in a blue jacket looked over to him, and he went and began talking to her. Meanwhile Maggie went over to where she saw Doc Steinberg, working on the body. In the kitchen. The same kitchen that Maggie had been in only a few days ago with Walter. Then they'd been looking to find clues about Bethany's disappearance. They'd found the money. It had all seemed empty and pristine. Now it was a horror show.

Doc Steinberg grimaced when she saw Maggie. Shook her head. Maggie wasn't sure if she was warning her off, or upset, but she stepped closer to the body.

Gunvor was wearing the same clothes she'd worn to the party. Checked shirt, boots and jeans. Her hair was still back in a pony tail. Her eyes were open, surprised. The dark make-up amplified the effect. Made her look almost doll-like. She lay on her stomach, head turned. There was a bullet hole in the center of her forehead. How different she looked than when she was alive. The body really was just a shell, Maggie thought. When the soul was gone, when the vitality was gone, the light truly went away. She whispered a quick prayer for Gunvor, but she couldn't still her mind. Where was Livy? What if she was to find Livy looking like this?

"Why are you here, Maggie?" Doc Steinberg asked. "You shouldn't be looking at this."

"I have to find my niece."

"Walter will find her."

"What can you tell me?" Maggie asked. "Please, Hannah." She knew she was presuming on their friendship, but she didn't care. She agreed that Walter would find Livy, but would it be in time? He had other responsibilities. She had this one. Her whole life had narrowed down to this one desire. All the things she loved, her friends, her church, Walter, seemed dull compared to the one desire she had, which was to find Livy and bring her home.

Doc Steinberg stood up. She was a tall woman, severe. She always made Maggie think of a warrior.

"The first murder was with an axe. Don't people tend to stick to the same method?"

"Maybe the killer didn't have any more axes. Maybe the killer used whatever weapon was handy. I can tell you this, also. She was moved."

"Moved? How can you tell?"

Doc Steinberg crossed her arms. "There are signs of livor mortis on her backside. I can't be sure until I've done the autopsy, but it looks like she fell on her back, and then at some point, someone turned her over."

"Someone shot her somewhere else and brought her here?"

"It's possible," she said.

"Why?"

Doc Steinberg shook her head. "That's all she wrote."

Then she left to go talk to Walter, who was surrounded by officers.

Maggie stood there for a moment, looking at Gunvor. She realized she had no idea if anything Gunvor said about herself was true. She kept talking about how she was supposed to go to that camp in Norway where there was a massacre, but she had no idea if it was true. For all she knew, she didn't even come from Norway. She'd said she'd worked for another host family. She'd said she'd get in trouble if she had to leave. The only things she knew for sure was that she was friends with Bethany, and that Livy liked her.

Graham said that he'd driven Livy to the Windsor house, but who knew if Graham's word could be trusted? She made her living checking up on whether people really were who they said they were, and she knew better than anyone that many people lied. What did it mean that Livy was drawn to two disreputable people? Was she trusting or gullible?

The problem was, she didn't know Livy well enough to know. She was good-hearted, brilliant, mercurial, and yet strangely innocent. She'd been raised in a rarified world, separated from so-called normal people. All her friends were geniuses. They applied for grants. They fought among themselves. She knew about envy and greed, but did she know about passion?

And so she'd come to Darby, and found what?

There was a time when Maggie would have known every single person in the village, but that had changed. Strangers were moving in, drawn by the city's schools. So many old houses were for sale because of high taxes. Houses stood empty. Or not empty. People lived in them, people hiding, whether from the law or internal demons. Then there were all the people who worked to support this way of life, the au pairs, the cleaners, the trainers and assistants. People who often passed unnoticed. There was Darby on the surface, but then also Darby underneath.

She felt frustrated with herself. Had she willfully looked away from what was, in order to create a fairy story. Her husband wasn't what he'd seemed to be and neither was her village. Perhaps neither was her daughter. Perhaps neither was she. She thought of herself as kind, but perhaps she was deluded.

Was it possible that one of those people killed Bethany? Again and again she came back to Bethany's character. Abrasive, bullying, needy. Gunvor had been much like her. But not Livy. Yet they all must have had something in common.

Maggie went out of the kitchen, back into the main part of the house. She stood in the center hallway, which was dramatic. So much money had poured into this house. Kacie Windsor said they'd put a bid on it, and Sibyl said a family named Collins owned it. Even Sibyl wasn't who she seemed.

She wanted to go upstairs and look around, but a police officer stopped her. She said they were searching the area. Maggie looked outside. She noticed a battered old oak, its tree branch dangling like a broken arm.

Suddenly Maggie had an idea for one person the three young women did have in common. Someone who also appeared out of nowhere. Someone who claimed to be one thing, but might be another. She looked over to Walter, who was deep in conversation. She didn't want to involve him with this. It would mean delay, explanations, arrangements.

She went outside and stood for a moment. Then she saw someone from the ambulance corps starting up his car and she ran over to him. "Could you give me a ride back to the village?" she asked.

"Of course, Maggie. Come in," he said.

He dropped her off in front of her house, but she didn't go inside. She waited for him to leave and then she turned and went back to Main Street.

Chapter Forty

Main Street was quiet for a Saturday night. Seeing the village so deserted brought back memories of the pandemic. Same sense of fear.

No cars racing around. No teenagers laughing. Restaurants dark. A couple walked by and peered at her. When they recognized her, they smiled. So much of Darby, she realized, was its lack of fear. That people trusted each other.

Maggie walked up the hill.

She remembered one of her Sunday School students asking her once if there was anything that could happen that would make Maggie stop believing in God. No, she'd assured her. She'd been through tough times and it had never really challenged her faith. She'd never felt separated from God's love. But now she realized that there was a possibility that she hadn't considered. Not that she might stop believing in God. But that she might stop loving Him. She felt a sob bubbling inside her that she feared might turn into a scream. She swallowed it down and kept moving up Main Street.

The sidewalk was shoveled, but there were still patches of ice. She almost plowed right into Polly Nathan, who was out pushing around her baby, who was yelling, as she had done since she was born. One of the worst cases of colic ever recorded, Polly had reported from the doctor and Maggie believed her. She was the reason the Insomnia Club got started.

"How are you, Maggie?" she asked, over the sound of the baby's tears.

"It's hard," Maggie said.

"They haven't found your niece?"

"No," she said. "I'm sorry. I can't talk about it."

Maggie kept going up the hill and then she ran into Mercy Williams, the police officer who had given her three parking tickets since moving to Darby from the Bronx. One of the very few people in the world who didn't like her, which Maggie found very appealing in that moment. People might pretend to like you, but there was no reason to pretend dislike. She looked so neat with her closely cropped hair and ironed pants. Somehow Mercy didn't have the salt and water on her that had managed to puddle on to everyone else's clothes.

At the sight of her, Mercy tucked down her chin in an expression of grim determination.

"You shouldn't be out at night by yourself."

"I want to take a walk."

"It's not safe," she hissed. "There's a murderer out here. You don't know if you're a target."

That stopped Maggie. It was the first time she'd considered it. Though she doubted it. She hadn't uncovered any information damaging enough to put her in danger, she thought. And if the person who she was on her way to see intended to kill her, she'd reached the point where it didn't matter. Not if she'd killed Livy too.

"I'm not a target," Maggie said, and pushed past her.

Mercy followed her.

"You will be no good to anyone if you get yourself killed," Mercy said.

"I do not think I'm good to anyone now."

Mercy's dark eyes flashed at her. "I'll come with you."

"I don't want your help." Maggie knew she sounded like a child. But it took all her self-control to not push this woman out of her path. Mercy had done nothing but judge her and annoy her since arrived in Darby from the Bronx, and now she was worried about her.

But arguing would not help, she knew.

Mercy was exactly the sort of person who would arrest her just out of spite. Fortunately, at that moment, Mercy's phone rang. Her whole expression changed. She went on alert. "Yes sir," she said. Straightening. It must be Walter on the phone.

She turned toward the police station. "Right away, sir."

"Is it Livy? Have they found Livy?"

Mercy shook her head, irritated.

"I'm here with Maggie Dove. You might want to talk to her."

She nodded and then held out her phone to Maggie. "I've been trying to reach you," Walter said.

Maggie realized she'd turned off the sound on her phone when she went in to see Rowena and hadn't turned it back on. She had 24 messages.

"Have you found Livy?" she asked.

"No, not yet. But we've found some tunnels under this house. They must be where Jeremy Kessler hid and where he found the axe."

"Do you think Livy's there?"

"We did a quick run-through and don't see her. But we're going to look more carefully now. We'll be here for a while. What are you doing?" he asked softly. "You holding up?"

"Yes," she said, because what was the alternative. To tell the truth, which would only distract him from doing what he needed to do.

"I'll call you as soon as I find anything out. I love you, Maggie."

Her eyes flickered closed. She was so tired she felt like she was sleeping upright. Love seemed an awful burden. Love carried so much pain with it. It was so much easier not to care.

She handed Mercy back her phone.

Mercy looked like she might actually disobey Walter's orders, and refuse to leave her alone, but Maggie knew she wouldn't. She would do what Walter wanted her to do because she was a person who obeyed the rules.

"Where are you going?" she asked Maggie.

"Walter wants you back at the police station," Maggie pointed out.

Mercy crossed her arms.

"I'll walk you home."

"You can walk me home. You won't stop me from leaving."

Mercy looked in the direction of Hollyhock House. She had to get back there. Maggie knew she was torturing her, and she felt bad. But she also didn't care.

Mercy asked for Maggie's phone "I'm putting in my private number. If you run into any trouble, call me and I'll be there right away."

"Thank you," Maggie said.

Mercy shook her head and went off, as did Maggie, and finally she was at her destination. The Amber Eyes salon.

Chapter Forty-One

Maggie knew the salon would not be open as it was past 6:00 on a Saturday night and no one looked to be in the mood to get their eyes done. But Amber had said that she lived upstairs, and Maggie hoped she would be in. She rang the bell, but didn't hear anything. Was it working? She tried it again, then knocked. Then knocked again and then she heard someone calling out, "Coming!" Then there was Amber, opening the door.

Her eyes were puffy, she wore a bathrobe.

"We met the other day. I came with my niece." Maggie's voice throbbed on that last note.

"Yes," Amber said, standing in the doorway. A spicy aroma wafted out from behind her. Candles flickered. Her eyes were swollen with tears. That startled Maggie. Had Amber killed Gunvor, would she be upset about it? Maggie supposed it was possible. Just because you killed someone didn't mean you wouldn't regret it.

"Have you heard about what happened?"

"What happened?"

"Gunvor's been murdered and Livy's missing, and I hoped you might help me find her."

"Gunvor." She clutched onto the edge of the door. She looked like she might slide right to the ground. She was barefoot, Maggie noticed. Her feet must be freezing.

"How?"

"Could I come in and talk about it?"

"No," she said. "No, I'm sorry, but I can't." Amber started to close the door, though Maggie moved quickly and put her foot in the space. The door whacked against her foot, pinching it. Amber looked down, puzzled, as though wondering how Maggie's foot had happened to grow there.

"I'm sorry to be so insistent," Maggie said, "but I really do have to ask you about my niece."

"But I don't know anything."

"That's okay," Maggie said. "I just want to ask you some questions, that's all."

Amber poked her head out and looked up and down Main Street. Maggie looked too, there was nothing much to see. A police car went by. Amber kept on thinking. There was something slow-moving about her, Maggie thought, as though she were under water.

She was frightened, that much was clear. But of what? Not of Maggie. She'd been part of that inner circle of Gunvor and Livy and Graham and all the assorted young people who cruised around at night. She knew their secrets. She knew Bethany. She'd done the make-up for her wedding. Now two of them were dead and one missing. Was she the murderer? But for what possible motive?

The only thing that struck Maggie was that she seemed so out-of-place in Darby. Not many single women moved here, and usually the ones who did had family relations. There wasn't a huge social scene, not compared to what went on in Manhattan. She seemed a little older than the others in her circle, in her thirties whereas Livy and Darby were in their twenties. And she was frightened. There was no question of that.

"Please," Maggie said. "Bethany's dead. So is Gunvor. Livy's missing. You all must have known something that drew this killer. Maybe you don't know what it is. But you can't just sit around waiting for a killer to show up. You have to fight back."

"I don't know if I can."

"You must. I'll help you."

She looked out the door again.

"Okay. Come upstairs," she said. Maggie followed her up. She'd been in this house before when it was a framing shop, and in it before that when it was a needlepoint shop, but she'd never been upstairs. The house was owned by Hal Carter and it looked like he'd put work into fixing it up. There were rooms to the side that it looked like he might want to rent. She followed Amber up to the top floor and into her room, which was in the attic. It was all one large loft, and there were cushions all over. One of the cushions held the imprint of her body. She gestured for Maggie to sit, but Maggie knew that once she lowered herself into those chairs she'd never get up. She'd taken Edgar to a children's art museum once and thought they'd need a crane to lift her. Now was not the moment for foolishness.

"I think I'll stand," she said.

"Okay," Amber said, and she kept standing herself, though now that Maggie could see her more closely, she realized that she looked exhausted. And frightened. For the first time it occurred to Maggie that she might be giving off a more frightening vibe than she realized. She tried to look reassuring.

"You know, I think I will sit down, if you promise to help me back up."

"Oh. Okay. Yes."

Maggie sank down into the chair, which enveloped her. From this vantage point, the room looked different. She was below window level. It was as though she were hiding.

"Have you heard what happened? Gunvor was murdered sometime last night," Maggie explained. "After she left the party. Someone shot her and moved her body to Hollyhock House, near where Bethany was killed."

"Oh," she whispered. Her eyes flickered closed. She looked like she might fall right asleep. She clutched her silk robe more tightly around her.

"You must have seen her yesterday. I noticed that her eyes were all made up for the party."

"No, I don't think so."

"Amber, your eyes are quite distinctive. Did you teach Gunvor to do it herself?"

"Was there a note?" Amber whispered.

"With her body? Would you expect there to be?"

"Did it mention me?"

"What are you talking about, Amber?"

"He's coming for me."

"Who is?"

Her eyes seemed to roll back in her head, as though she were having a vision. She gave off an aroma of illness, Maggie realized. She was off-balance. In fact, all the cushions might be thrown about in order to protect her from falling. She noticed too that all the blinds were drawn. Was that because it was night or because her eyes hurt? The walls were bare except for one portrait of an older woman that might have been Amber's mother or might have just been up on the wall before it was renovated. Maggie felt like they were having parallel conversations, that she was asking one set of questions about Gunvor and Amber was asking a different set of questions about something else.

"Amber," Maggie said, clasping her hands together, trying to fight her fluttering heart, thinking of the minutes ticking by. If Livy was in trouble. What if all these ticking seconds were costing her her life? "Could you take me back to the beginning? What is it that you think is happening?"

"He's been following me."

"Who is?"

"Peter Robineaux."

"That's someone you know? Someone you're related to?"

Amber groaned.

"I was living in an apartment in New York City. My career was thriving. Everything was going well. My neighbor was Peter Robineaux. We were friends, that was all. He'd come over every so often for a drink. One night we went to the movies. It wasn't anything serious. Then he asked me to go away with him to Bermuda. I couldn't go. I had work, and, I didn't want to go." Her accent became more pronounced as she talked. She sounded more of an upstate New Yorker.

"Around then I began going out with someone at work. I liked him. Peter began sliding notes under my door. Telling me that I was a slut. He called up my boss. He wrote things on my Facebook page. I tried blocking him, but he kept reappearing. Whenever I would go out, he would time it so that he was going out at the same time."

"Did you tell the police?"

"Yes," she said. "But there was nothing they could do. He hadn't harmed me."

A train went by, its shriek making them both jump. Amber fingered a necklace that had slipped beneath her robe. It was a large hand-made looking piece. Heavy. A reminder of something?

"It got so bad I was afraid to go out. Afraid to go to work, to see my lover. I could hear Robineaux next door. I could hear him breathing. Watching me all the time. One night, I couldn't take it anymore. I packed up a few things and I left. I'd read the article about

Darby and it sounded like a safe place to live. I thought maybe with a small community I'd be safe. I changed my name. I changed my job. I figured I wouldn't work with the theater anymore. I canceled all my social media accounts. I don't use credit cards anymore. I don't even have a phone. I tried to go off the grid, but I always knew he'd find me somehow."

She'd done exactly what Bethany had done, but in reverse, Maggie thought. She thought of what Walter had said about how people disappear when they need to leave unbearable situations. Here was one young woman fleeing a terrible situation and connecting with a young woman who had come to Darby fleeing hers. She wondered if Amber had told Bethany her story, and if that's what had inspired her to run. But then how did Gunvor come into it? She too was fleeing a terrible situation, though in her case she was running from violence and grief. And Livy? Running from a broken heart. And did they all wind up coming together with someone who wanted to harm them?

"Have you seen him? What does he look like?"

"I have his picture," she said. She got up and walked over to the picture on the wall, and then she reached behind it and pulled out a photo. She handed it over to Maggie, who examined it. He was an exceptionally good-looking man. Could have been a model. Dark, curly hair. Strong. She thought his eyes seemed intense, but that could be because of what Amber had just told her. Maggie didn't recognize him at all.

"Three week ago, I had a message. He said he found me. He was coming for me. Bethany got everyone together to protect me. Like a Neighborhood Watch. They took turns patrolling around my house. Gunvor helped, and then Livy joined in too. And Graham. But we haven't seen him.

"Why didn't you tell the police? They would have helped you."

"I did tell the police, but there's nothing they can do if he hasn't made an explicit threat."

"But didn't he?"

"Not explicit enough."

Would something like this have given him a reason to kill Bethany and Gunvor, Maggie wondered. Angered over being thwarted in his efforts to get to Amber, would he then have gone after her friends? Did he have Livy?

She called Walter and told him what Amber had said. Was this man on his radar? Could he be the killer? A few minutes later Walter called back. Peter Robineaux was in jail. Had been there for a month.

So not him. Not Peter Robineaux. Livy almost 24 hours gone and no closer to an answer. There was nowhere for Maggie to go but back home.

Chapter Forty-Two

By now it was early Sunday morning. Maggie went into Livy's bedroom and looked around, not sure what sort of clue she could find. Livy had gone storming out of the house when she upset Maggie. Over something that seemed so meaningless now. Maggie's pride had been hurt, her husband had behaved stupidly. And for that she had let this girl go storming out of her life and into what?

Linus's plane had been delayed, thank heavens. She didn't think she could bear to see his frightened face. She must resolve this before he got there.

The room was tidy. All the little pineapples in order. No secrets here. No stolen notebooks. No secret clusters, that Maggie could see. No secrets. The one secret Livy had known she'd told to the wrong person.

She'd added a few pictures to the wall. One of her and Graham in the forest, arm and arm. They were standing outside of Lockwood Lumber. He must have taken her there to show off his office. That reminded Maggie of the picture Edgar found in the 1934 newspaper of all the various Lockwoods lined up holding their axes. All the faces on the front page looking somewhat familiar, all of them ancestors of people who still walked on Main Street. There were a lot of new people in Darby, but a lot of them had been here for generations. She wondered if you walked down Main Street one hundred years ago if everyone would look more or less the same. Certainly, she suspected, the Colemans would. All of them with their chins.

That reminded her of all the Coleman pictures in Bethany's bank office and how proudly she showed them off to everyone who came to her office.

The oddest idea began to come into her head.

Shadow jumped on the bed in front of her, like inspiration taken flight. White Kosi tumbled alongside her. They both stared at her as though to say, don't wait. Act.

It was 6:00 in the morning, early to be calling on someone. Waking him up. But he just might know the answer. He might be the only one obsessive enough to do the research.

She got in her car and drove to his house.

Chapter Forty-Three

The thing about Edgar and Helen was that neither one of them slept. Ever. So when Maggie showed up at their door a little after six in the morning, they both greeted her with their pale faces, holding onto books. A similar expression of wariness and welcome.

"Is everything okay?" Helen asked. She looked as though she might have been crying. "Do you want some coffee?"

"I need to talk to Edgar," Maggie said.

Helen's face, twisted, pinched a bit and in that moment, she looked exactly like her son. Maggie wondered if Helen realized, or ever would realize, that it was she Edgar resembled, and not his father.

"What's he done?" Helen asked.

"I need his help," Maggie said, and then she looked at Edgar and said, "I need to see something you've been researching."

Helen shrugged and walked away. Edgar nodded solemnly and led Maggie to a small room at the back of the house.

It was a little library. There was an old stone fireplace and he had been sprawled in front of it, laptop before him. He lived and breathed Wikipedia.

"You know how I told you to stop researching that family? That whole thing with the degenerate?

"Yes."

"Did you stop? Did you listen to me?"

He looked mournful and shook his head.

"I knew you wouldn't," she said. "Would you tell me what else you found out?"

He looked at her wonderingly and then his whole face dimpled into a grin. He went behind the computer and drew out a stack of papers. There were lists of names and dates. Birthdays. Descendants. He'd mapped the whole thing out.

"You know, I think you're a genius," she said to him.

It was all so obvious. She'd been so preoccupied with the outsiders in Darby that she'd lost track of the history of the community itself. The way grievances could twine their way through generations.

"Can I come with you?" he said. "I know where she is."

"No, this is not safe. You stay here."

She just prayed she wasn't too late.

Chapter Forty-Four

Maggie heard screaming coming from Kacie Windsor's house. Children's screams. She remembered Walter saying something about a sleepover.

She knew she should call Walter right now. She knew what she was about to do was foolhardy and yet she believed that only she had the power to take care of this. So much rested on a sympathetic persona. So much depended on Maggie's ability to connect with people. Guns would not save Livy. Neither would force. What had set all of this in motion was grievance, and only sympathy would resolve it.

As she started to make her way to the house, the front door slammed open and a woman ran out. She held two children by the hands and she called behind her, "Thank you, Kacie. Thanks so much. I'll call tomorrow to set up a playdate."

"Thanks Holly," Kacie called back.

She stood in the doorway, holding her baby with one hand and clutching her toddler with another. The baby howled. Kacie had on a smock and sweat pants.

Her glasses were off-kilter. She caught sight of Maggie and waved. "Hey," she said.

"Hiya," Maggie said. "I've come by to talk."

"Come on in," she said, beckoning Maggie inside. If she found it remarkable that Maggie had shown up just after seven in the morning, she didn't say so.

Up close Maggie could see how exhausted she was. Her eyes had pillows under them, her face had a gray pallor.

Maggie stepped inside and almost immediately skid on one of the Legos. She bent down to pick it up, but soon realized the impossibility of the task. The floor was littered with Legos. In fact, the baby had a Lego in her hand, but Maggie pried it out.

"I should have canceled the party after the whole Gunvor thing, but I just couldn't do it. Elizabeth has been looking forward to it so much, and I couldn't bring myself to disappoint her. And after all it wasn't as though she and Gunvor were so close. I know, that's unsympathetic, but you only turn seven once."

Maggie nodded, aimed herself toward a chair, but noticed a bowl of pancake batter on it.

"That's where it went to," Kacie cried out. "I meant to make pancakes for dinner and then I couldn't find it."

Maggie picked up the bowl and started toward the kitchen. "How many kids did you have sleep over?"

"Twelve," Kacie said, sinking onto the chair. "Plus my own five."

"You didn't have anyone to help?"

"No, well it sort of runs itself doesn't it. I know I'm a control freak, but I do like to do things my own way."

"Your husband?" Maggie asked. She set the bowl in a sink crowded with dishes. Under other circumstances she would have started washing them, but now was not the time. She headed back into the living room, where Kacie seemed to be sinking into the chair. Maggie began to wonder if what she suspected was true. Could this exhausted woman represent a danger to anyone?

"He's in Houston on a business trip. He'd hoped to be back in time, but there was bad weather, so he got stuck." So too had Linus been caught. Poor Linus, who was on his way to Darby to find out what happened to Livy.

For a moment Maggie wondered if the husband could be a figment of Kacie's imagination, but there was no question that someone had fathered these children and they did all look alike. Same flushed red cheeks, blonde hair and runny noses.

"They're almost all gone, anyway. Just one mother left to pick up her kid. There's always one, right? She was supposed to be here early because indoor soccer starts at nine, but what can you do?"

Her eyes closed and Maggie automatically put out her hands to catch the baby, who might otherwise have tumbled onto the floor. She was an agreeable baby, used to being held. Not fidgety at all. Maggie looked at her and wondered what she would be like in twenty years, what memories she'd have of this period of time. What grievances she'd hoard.

Just then Kacie's phone rang and she flinched awake. "Hello. Yes. No, no problem. Get here when you can."

A door flew open and two children ran past. "Can we have the chocolate now, mommy? Do we have to wait any more?"

"No," she said, holding her hand to her head. "But make sure to ask Gillian if she still has chocolate allergies."

"Okay," they said. The kitchen filled with the sound of rustling and then the kids ran back and there was a brief moment of quiet. The baby settled into Maggie's arms. She smelled of the sweetness of babies, with a slight undercurrent of urine.

Maggie knew the moment of quiet would be brief. And she needed to use it.

"I've been thinking a lot about Bethany and how she was going to help you buy Hollyhock House," Maggie said.

"Nothing's going to come of it now," Kacie said. "Now that she's gone, there's no one to help us. Though I suppose with Gunvor's body there, that will probably depress the value. Oh, I know," she said, looking up at Maggie. "I know that seems cold-hearted, but we so desperately need more space. You can see that, can't you?"

"You must have gone to Bethany's office to fill out all the paperwork."

"Yes. We wanted to go to a bigger bank, but their rates were good. And she was so aggressive."

The baby began squirming a bit, but Maggie held on to her.

"Did you happen to notice the pictures on Bethany's walls? She was very proud of her heritage."

"All the police officers, you mean?"

"It must have been a shock to you," Maggie said.

"Why's that?" Kacie smiled at her politely, but something shifted in her eyes. She'd seen those eyes before. In a photograph. In the newspaper. "Oh, I'll take her back," she said, holding out her hands for the baby, but Maggie held on to her. She rocked her back and forth. Some instinct compelled her to hang on.

"Because her great-grandfather arrested Franz Stanger, and he was your great-grandfather, wasn't he?"

"Why would you say that?"

"Everything kept coming back to that house and it finally hit me that there must be a reason for it, but I couldn't figure out what that was, and then I began to think about grievances, and why someone might hate that house and the people associated with it, and I asked an associate of mine to investigate." A seven-year-old associate, she thought. "He traced Stanger's genealogy. Franz had six children. His wife had a breakdown after he was executed and all the kids were taken away, except for the oldest daughter, Inga. She had a child in 1936 and her name was Francie. Then she grew up and had a child, but Francie died young, and so her mother raised the little girl. That child was you. Katherine Cindy Raines. Kacie."

"You know, this is not a good place to talk," Kacie said. "I think we should go to another room. Why don't you give me Elizabeth and I'll put her down?"

"No," Maggie said. "I think I'll hold on to her for now."

"You can't keep my baby from me. I'll call the police."

"Will you?" Maggie asked. She fought to keep her voice calm. She suspected that what this woman needed more than anything was calm. She must be exhausted. Maggie remembered an article she'd read once about how most people want to confess. That holding a secret inside you can be torturous, and if they feel safe enough, they can be persuaded to reveal everything. From somewhere in the house a dog began to bark, a serious sounding dog that she must have put away while the children were here.

Could Livy be in that room, she wondered. Could she be with that dog?

"What do you want?"

"I want my niece."

"I don't know your niece."

"Her name is Livy. I believe she came here last night, looking for Gunvor. I don't think you knew that Gunvor called her when she got home last night. From the party."

Kacie shook her head and walked toward Maggie, holding out her arms for the baby. Her top was unbuttoned, she wore no bra. Everything about her sank and drooped. Her nails were ragged, unmanicured. Maggie realized that the smell of urine she thought was coming from the baby actually came from Kacie. She couldn't believe that she was there, holding a child as a weapon, but it was the only weapon she had. Forgive me, she whispered, speaking to God for the first time in more than a day.

Kacie didn't have much fight in her. She folded easily.

"Bethany was so proud of her great-grandfather. Started talking about him the minute I walked into her office. She had no idea who I was. She started talking about how he was famous for capturing Franz Stanger. She talked about my great-grandfather as though he were an animal. How he'd hunted him down. How he'd trapped him and brought him to justice. How he'd been executed, and then, when I asked her if she was so sure Stanger was guilty, she just looked at me like I was insane. I told her that there was a wave of anti-German feeling at the time. My grandmother told me all about that. Look at Bruno Richard Hauptman. They arrested him for the Lindbergh kidnapping, but they never really had proof. They arrested him because he was a German immigrant. My grandmother told me all about it."

She warmed to her story, the grievance taking over. As Maggie had suspected and hoped, once she started talking, she would tell it all. "Their lives were ruined. Do you know what they did to them?" she hissed.

"They put the younger brothers and sisters in an orphanage. Two of them died within the year of tuberculosis. The others died early, they didn't stand a chance. My grandmother herself was forced into marriage with a terrible man. She had no choice. She needed protection. He hurt her terribly." She started to cry, wiped her nose. One of the smaller children wandered in, but she shushed her. "I'm talking about grannie," she said.

"Grannie," the little girl said, and leaned her head on her mother's knees, putting a sticky finger in her mouth.

"They destroyed my family. And all Bethany did was talk talk talk about the Coleman family. What great police officers they all were."

Maggie thought about all the ways history could come back to haunt you. How things that were thirty or forty years old could still hurt. You think it will go away, and it does fade. But it's possible to keep picking at a hurt. She had done it to herself. She had been unwilling to let her grief fade away until Livy came. Livy. She groaned and Kacie looked at her. Startled.

"And you knew that she was going to leave her wedding because you heard Gunvor talking about it?"

"Yes," she said. "Bethany would come over here. She had such a loud voice. They had no idea that I was listening. They would go into Gunvor's room and she'd be shouting about all her plans. How she intended to walk out on the wedding. How mad she was at her parents.

On and on she went and she never thought about me, and how I might be listening. She didn't care about me at all, or the children. I was nothing to them except a mother. They thought they were being so clever."

"So you knew she would be going to Hollyhock House?"

"Yes, they talked about it. She would go there and wait until it was time for her surgery. Then Gunvor would come and pick her up. She even talked about the money. I didn't take it. I didn't care about the money, though I could have used it. I didn't want them calling me a thief. No, I waited for her. It was perfect. She was so surprised when she saw me. The look on her face. She couldn't figure it out, until I raised the axe."

Poor Bethany. So caught up in her victory. So happy with her vengeance. So blind. Anger blinded you to life.

Meanwhile Kacie stroked her daughter's hair. She imagined her passing down these stories to her children just as her grandmother had passed them down to her.

"It was your grandfather's axe?"

"Oh yes. My grandmother had managed to find it. She saved it. In case I should need it."

"Bethany must have run?"

"Yes, but she didn't have a chance. Running in the woods. In that dress. I let her run a little ways. I didn't want blood in the house. It's going to cost enough money to buy it and renovate it. That's why I shot Gunvor. I could have used an axe, but at the end of the day, it's so messy."

Only now did Maggie fully realize how strong she was. Kacie had always seemed so bowed down by her children, sagging under the weight of them, but her arms were strong. She'd been carrying around weights for seven years.

"Where were your kids? You didn't take them with you?"

"No, my husband was home that day. I told him I was going out to the grocery store. I doubt he noticed."

Another child came in right then and said she'd like some Juicy Juice. As though on auto pilot, Kacie crossed to the kitchen and got the little box. She must have had 100 of them carefully stacked inside a pantry. Someone had made an effort to create order here, perhaps the husband. Or Gunvor?

"Make sure not to drop it on the couch," she said. "I don't want to get that cleaned again."

Then she came back again and sank down onto the chair.

"And Gunvor?" she said softly.

For the first time Kacie looked disturbed. "I didn't know she was coming home that night. She never came home early on a Friday night. If I asked her to stay home on a Friday, she got mad at me. I thought I had the house to myself."

But Gunvor had gone storming out of the party. She'd been crazy that night, drinking herself into oblivion. She'd just jettisoned her friend, her life. She would have to leave Darby behind after that tantrum.

She must have known that she'd made an enemy out of Maggie.

"She interrupted you?" Maggie asked.

Kacie began wringing her hands. That was a good sign, wasn't it? So she was not yet irredeemable. She did feel guilt. "I was looking at family photos. I'd just put the kids to sleep. Of course, it fell to me because Gunvor couldn't work on Friday nights. It was my quiet moment and I was looking at a picture of my great-grandparents and Gunvor walked in.

"She was talking on the phone. Looked like she was crying over something." Talking to Livy, Maggie thought. Asking her to come over. Needing a friend to talk to. "She almost walked right on top of me, and then she looked down at all the photos. She looked right at the portrait of my great-grandfather and I knew she recognized him. I don't know how."

Because of Edgar, Maggie thought. Because he'd been walking around with the newspaper clippings.

"She was going to report me. I could see her putting it all together. I had no choice." She reached over to a small table next to the couch and pulled out a gun. Little and black and unmistakably what it was, and yet so like a toy. Did she always carry one with her? With the children around? "I had to shoot her," Kacie said. "You can see that. She didn't leave me any option. Now, please give me back my daughter."

"No," Maggie said, clutching the little one more tightly to her, though her action horrified her. Was she truly using a baby as a shield? But then she thought of Gunvor, with whom she'd argued. Poor Gunvor with her freckles and her loud laugh. Who she'd been so mad at because of the chalice. And Livy, who must have shown up soon after, completely innocent.

"What was I going to do? You tell me. Give me an alternative scenario and I'd take it, but I didn't have any choice. Was I going to let her destroy my family? I couldn't do that. Let it happen all over again. Let my children be taken away. Put into foster care. It would destroy their lives. I couldn't let that happen. I didn't want to kill her, but I didn't have a choice."

"Why did you move her then?"

"I couldn't leave her here, could I? Not with all the kids coming to the slumber party the next day. You think that would be appropriate?"

"No," Maggie said, since she seemed to want an answer. The baby was making her dizzy, all the aromas coming off her, the stress of having a gun pointed at her, her worry over Livy and this woman's crazy eyes.

"Of course not. You didn't factor that in, did you? I needed to get her out of the house, but I had to quick get a blanket and wrap her up. It wasn't easy, and then I had to get her into the car, and get all the kids in the car."

"You brought them with you?"

"What's wrong with you? You think I was just going to leave them alone. I had to wake them up and get them dressed and put on their winter coats, and then I drove her over to the house and I quick got her inside and then I dashed back to my house because I still had a lot to do to get ready for the party, and then I'm darned if I don't get back and another one comes along."

"Livy," Maggie said.

"I don't know. I didn't know her."

"She's my niece," Maggie whispered.

"Oh," Kacie said. "Oh. Well, I had no way to know that, did I? She was ringing the bell, ringing the bell, telling me she'd spoken to Gunvor and she was supposed to come over and see her. I told her Gunvor wasn't there. I thought she'd go away, but she wouldn't let it drop. Had to come in. Forced her way in."

"Then what?"

"I didn't know what to do. I couldn't take the kids out all over again, and my husband would be coming home soon and he doesn't like any bother."

Maggie felt like there wasn't enough air in the room. She smelled maple syrup and thought she'd never eat a pancake again.

Just then one of the parents burst through the front door, the mother of the last child remaining. Quickly Kacie put the gun in her pocket, only the edge of it sticking out. "I'm so so sorry, Kacie. Am I the last one? Always am, aren't I? You must hate me, but it's pandemonium out there. The traffic light was down on Broadway and the line of people was surreal and oh, poor little Elizabeth. What's wrong?" she said, and she held out her arm to the baby.

"I've got her," Maggie said. That baby was her only leverage. The only hope she had of getting Kacie to tell her where Livy was. Now this woman was coming toward her, huge diamond ring flashing in the air like a strobe light.

"No, give her to me. She loves Auntie Tiffany, doesn't she?"

Little Elizabeth began to wave her arms. Maggie clutched her even more tightly. "I've just got her calmed down," she said.

What if Livy was bleeding somewhere? What if she only had minutes? This woman had to go. She would do anything.

But Kacie swooped up just then and plucked the baby out of her arms and before Maggie could grab her back, her arms were empty. "Poor little one," Kacie crooned. "Have you been wanting your mommy?"

Little Gillian came running out then, surrounded by a clattering posse of Windsors, all of them screaming and yelling and laughing and Tiffany put her arms around her own daughter. "Did you have a fabulous time?" she crooned.

Gillian had frosting all over her lips.

Tiffany laughed. "She always has the best time at your house. Oh. Look. You let your kids play with guns too. My mother-in-law doesn't like it, but I feel like better to play with toy guns and get it all out of your system."

Kacie's eyes narrowed. At this point, what would stop her from killing all of them? She wanted to signal to Tiffany that she should leave, but she was one of those women who couldn't bring herself to step out the door. She was going on and on about a second-grade teacher who didn't give enough homework and Maggie watched Kacie's hands roaming over the gun and meanwhile her mind was fermenting with images of her niece with a gunshot wound. Had she spoken about Livy in past or present tense?

Finally, it looked as though Tiffany was truly going to leave.

She grabbed up little Gillian and they waved at Kacie. "I'll call you this week. It's my time to host. We'll set something up."

Kacie waved good bye and as soon as the door closed, she turned to Maggie. She held her baby in one arm, the gun in her right hand.

Slowly she backed into the kitchen and settled the baby onto a little rocking seat propped against the dishwasher. Then she yelled for Anne. "Come get your sister," she said.

Immediately a young girl ran in who looked exactly like all the other kids. Without asking she scooped up the baby and started out.

"Stay in the playroom for a bit," Kacie said to her. "Put on *Frozen*."

"Okay mom."

She dashed out and finally it was just Maggie and Kacie, though Kacie was the one with the gun. Now, Maggie thought, she was seeing the face that Bethany had seen before she died, and that Gunvor had seen, before she was shot. It was a frozen sort of face. Focused, as though all her concentration was focused on something just past Maggie's shoulder. It was an inhuman face, devoid of compassion.

She was going to die, Maggie thought.

It seemed so cruel after all she'd gone through. She thought of Livy. She thought of Walter and how much she wanted to get to know him better. How brief this happiness was. She felt her eyes wet with tears. She hoped it didn't hurt too much. She whispered a quick prayer to God, and at that moment the front door slammed open. She and Kacie jumped and Edgar raced through, and barreled into Maggie. "Are you all right?" he asked. "I thought you might have come here."

He pressed his head against her stomach and Maggie turned to face Kacie, hoping to see pity or some acknowledgement that this had all gone too far, but all she saw was implacable hate.

Chapter Forty-Five

There was no point to asking how or why. There never was with Edgar. He had figured Maggie was there, he had come to rescue her. Now his life was in danger as well.

"Why do people keep coming through that door," Kacie snarled. She began gnawing at her lip.

Maggie forced herself to keep her voice calm. Peace was the only weapon she had with this woman. Clearly, she was trapped in a vortex of emotion, and if Maggie could but offer her a safe haven, perhaps she could help her.

"You don't need to do this. There are people who can help you. People who can help your family."

Kacie barked a laugh. "You are telling me they will let me keep my children."

"They will take care of your children. They will help them."

"The way they cared about children when they took my aunts and uncles and put them into foster care. It's a hard truth but children are pawns." She eyed Maggie shrewdly then. "You know that. You held on to my baby."

"That was wrong of me," Maggie said. "But you could let him go."

"No, I have to do this now. My husband's coming back soon. I can't wait."

Edgar didn't whimper. Didn't seem afraid at all. He clutched Maggie's hand as though he had a plan. Maggie considered pushing him toward the door. If she did, Kacie might well shoot, but maybe she could draw her fire. But what if she didn't? What if she shot Edgar instead? She was descended from a man who did terrible things to children. A degenerate, as Edgar had put it.

"Follow me," Kacie said.

She nodded toward a door in the corner.

"This way."

Maggie looked around. There was no place to run. Plus, she had to know if Livy was down there. She walked toward the door.

It led to the basement.

Kacie gestured for them to go down the steps. Maggie held out her hand, Edgar put his little warm one in hers and they proceeded down the steps.

It was an unfinished basement filled with toys. There were chalk drawings on the walls. One of those yellow cars that populated the nursery school. Dinosaurs all over. Soccer balls, two hockey pucks, one hockey stick and a net. A doll with her head ripped off.

And on a tattered couch was Livy, stretched out. Pale. A bruise on her face. Hands and feet tied together.

But she was alive. Maggie could see her chest going up and down. She was alive.

They were in a terrible position. They were trapped by a crazy person. Who held a gun. Things were about as bad as they could be and yet Maggie felt joy bubbling inside her. She felt like laughing, that was how giddy she felt. Livy was alive. When someone was dead, they were gone, but when they were alive, you could hope.

Edgar let go of Maggie's hand and flung himself on top of Livy.

Kacie just shook her head. She looked around the room, working out her plan. Upstairs she could hear something slamming.

"Get off that La-Z-Boy," Kacie yelled. "Someone's going to get hurt."

She must intend to shoot them and get rid of their bodies, but dragging three bodies to a car was a whole other level of magnitude than dragging one. She was insane. But no one was paying any attention. Her husband was gone at work. Her kids didn't know any better.

Maggie had her phone in her pocketbook, but there was no way to get at it, and even if she did, she couldn't press in the number without looking at it.

She noticed then that Edgar had clambered on top of Livy. Trust him to be inappropriate even in the worst possible situation, she thought, but then she realized what he was doing. He was untying the ropes. Livy was lying still, but Maggie felt sure she saw her eyes flicker. She was pretending to be unconscious.

All Maggie had to do was keep Kacie occupied. Distract her until Edgar freed Livy. Together they ought to be able to fight back.

"Please God," she prayed. "You have not made me strong and you have not made me brave, but you have made me very chatty. Let me put that to good work now."

"So," she said to Kacie. "Those La-Z-Boys are impossible, aren't they? I used to have one and then one time my daughter jumped on it and she broke her arm. So frightening the sound her arm made. Like a snap, and I was so frustrated because I'd told her a thousand times not to climb on that thing." She whispered a quick apology to her daughter, who'd never done any such thing, who spent most of her childhood sitting in a chair and reading a book.

"They don't listen," Kacie said. She put her hand to her head.

"I know. I remember I used to say that when I gave birth to my daughter, I pushed out my brain too."

"Yes," Kacie said, burping up a laugh. She eyed Maggie thoughtfully. How lonely she must be, Maggie thought. How isolated.

"No one tells you how time consuming it all is."

It was probably wrong to use compassion as a weapon, and yet it was the only weapon she had.

"My grandmother used to tell me how wonderful it was to be one of eight children. She used to tell me stories. How they loved each other. How they ate dinner together every night. That's why I wanted to have so many children. I wanted them to have that experience, but it doesn't seem the same, and then, when I think about having three more, I don't know. What would you do?" she asked Maggie.

"What would I do?" Maggie said. "Well, I only had one child, so I'm probably the wrong one to ask."

Edgar must have the rope off by now. Maggie forced her eyes not to flick in that direction. She didn't want to give them away. "I do wish I'd had more. Though not seven more. Quite honestly, I had my hands full with one. I worried about her all the time. You try to protect them but you can only do so much."

"I heard about your daughter," Kacie said. "I'm sorry."

Maggie looked at her carefully. This woman who had killed two young women that she knew of, and who planned to kill three more, seemed quite genuinely saddened at Maggie's own loss. Was that what evil did, did it twist itself around you like a vine so that you couldn't tell what was good or bad? She felt the strangest sense of connection with this woman who planned to shoot her, though it seemed to her forgiveness could take you only so far.

She noticed some movement. The ropes were untied. She had seconds. She hurled herself at Kacie, who was so startled she fell over, the gun falling out of her hand. Maggie Dove hurling herself on it. Damn knees. Kacie hitting her on the head. Livy and Edgar there, fighting her, and then the sound of the door upstairs opening.

A man's voice calling out. "I'm home!"

Footsteps upstairs. The basement door flung open and a man called down, "Honey, I'm home. Is there anything for dinner?"

Chapter Forty-Six

Livy was all right. She had a concussion and a fractured rib and needed to spend the night in the hospital, but those were small things. She was alive. She would recover. Maggie felt filled with gratitude.

All that night she sat by Livy's bed. Doc Steinberg was adamant that no one else could visit. Livy needed rest, and so Maggie's phone buzzed with texts all night. Walter texted from the jail. He was there with Kacie. Linus texted from the airport. They were having the worst flight imaginable. The Insomnia Club texted. Reverend Sunday texted. Agnes texted. Helen texted. Graham texted. She felt buoyed by their words, but she was content to sit in silence, to listen to the steady beat of the heart monitor and all the murmuring of a hospital at night. She needed stillness. She needed time to restore.

It could have gone so differently.

She saw the image so clearly. Livy lying on the couch. Unmoving. Had she got there too late. That pale face of hers frozen. The smile never to appear again. That honking laugh. The utter immobility of death.

Livy groaned in her sleep. Maggie leaned forward, held her hand.

She was here. She had to push the nightmares away. The past was out of her control, but this was the present. She had to embrace it.

It was the middle of the night when Livy woke up. She looked around frightened for a moment but then Maggie squeezed her hand.

"Aunt Dove. You rescued me."

"A miracle."

"You looked so angry." Livy smiled. "You looked like the wrath of God."

"I have a suspicion thunderbolts could have come out of my fingers."

"How did you find me?"

"Pure panic," Maggie said. "I think I forced my mind into a sort of seizure."

A technician ran by, holding a chart. Someone's fate in an envelope.

"It all seems so obvious now, but ever since Bethany disappeared my mind has been swirling around the idea of grievance. She was so bitter about everything that had happened, and then it seemed to me that everyone I spoke to was aggrieved about something. Her parents were angry that she wasn't the sort of daughter they wanted. Gunvor was aggrieved about her host parents. Well, she was right about that. Helen aggrieved. Sybil aggrieved and angry at Bethany and the bank, but that's what made me think about it.

"I realized that 1934 isn't as long ago as you would think. I mean, I know people who lived then. Memories cast long shadows. Things happened twenty or thirty years ago that seem as vivid as if they'd happened yesterday. And I thought then how some forms of anger, or grief, don't go away. Neither does love, come to that.

"I'd felt all along that this had to do with some form of grievance, because of the person Bethany was. I realized that Bethany was aggrieved, but she was also proud. I don't know. It all jumbled together, and I was thinking about daughters, probably because I was thinking about you and Juliet and then all of a sudden, I remembered something that Edgar had told me about how Stanger had eight children. I thought about how many children that is and wondered if maybe one of them was angry. I don't even know where that came from except that it seemed possible to me that maybe one of them wouldn't want Hollyhock House sold. Well, I got that wrong. But I also thought that maybe one of them would know about the axe. Fortunately, I knew that Edgar has certain compulsive qualities and I felt confident that once he got intrigued with a story, he'd never let it ago. So I thought it likely that he'd checked out those eight children. Which he had."

Livy sighed.

"Maybe you should go back to sleep," Maggie said. "You must be exhausted."

But Livy wanted to speak. "Gunvor called me," she said. "I was with Graham, and I was so angry about everything, but she wanted me to come over. She was really upset. She didn't mean to cause so much trouble. She really liked you, admired you."

Poor thing looked dazed with the bandage wrapped around her head. Her blue eyes were bloodshot and her hair, which had been so perfectly cut, was now all wet where the nurses had cleaned her off. She looked wounded. "Did she kill her?"

"I'm sorry," Maggie said. "It must have happened just before you got there. It's just a miracle Kacie didn't kill you." It was only because there was a slumber party. Maggie didn't say it. It seemed cruel to tell someone that the whole trajectory of her life depended on something so foolish.

"Oh," Livy said and curled into herself. "That hurts. But that's so wrong. She was so sure she would be killed. She thought she was cursed, because she was supposed to die in the massacre in Norway, and she should have been there, but then she got sick.

"She felt cursed. Do you think she was?"

"I can't believe that," Maggie said. "But I don't understand. I wish I did. I wish I could have helped her." She thought of that laughing, provocative girl with the freckles and her plaid shirt and the way she was always kicking a soccer ball. Livy closed her eyes and drifted off, but Maggie stayed awake all night. She couldn't sleep. She felt herself blend in with the rhythms of the hospital, with the nurses and doctors who checked in with Livy throughout the night.

It was early in the morning when Linus burst into the room, looking slightly harassed and rumpled. Nora strode around him, pushing ahead. Maggie was startled by how assertive she seemed.

"Livy," she cried out, and hugged her daughter.

"*Salvato erupto si,*" Linus said to Livy.

Maggie had forgotten that they spoke to each other in a made-up language.

"*Salvato erupto si,*" she replied.

"*Tonta tu?*" Nora said. She'd been crying.

"*Mahara si.*"

"Very well then," he said and turned to Maggie. He looked like Stuart, but so much older. Smelled like him too. A musty sort of smell that came from reading old books and smoking pipes. "You have saved my daughter's life," he said. "For that I can never repay you."

Then he wrapped her in his arms and he began to cry.

Nora nudged him then.

"I'm sorry," he said.

"For what?"

"For not telling you about Stuart and Rowena."

"Good Lord," she said, because she'd completely forgotten. She'd forgotten about her meeting with that horrible woman. "You have nothing to apologize for. Or anyway you do, but it doesn't matter. It's in the past," she said. Possibly the best words in the world, Maggie thought. It's in the past.

The nurse came in and said, "There's a young man who's been waiting all night. Would you mind if he comes in now? His name is Graham Lockwood."

"Graham?" Linus said.

"Oh daddy, you're going to love him," Livy said, and turned the full wattage of her smile on him, so that Linus, who was normally the most snobbish of men, gave Graham a great handshake and said welcome.

Graham looked dumbfounded to be welcomed so warmly.

He looked exhausted. Maggie hadn't seen him, knew he'd been in jail for a bit, and he must have been out with Walter last night, looking for Livy. He clasped her hand gently, asked her if it hurt.

A reporter popped in just then, talking fast. Hotly pursued by a nurse, she suspected.

"Are you Maggie Dove? Did you really save that girl's life?"

She looked into his earnest face. He wasn't mocking her. He was asking a serious question. She savored his words. She'd spent the last two decades feeling like her daughter's death was her fault. She was The Mother Who Lost Her Daughter. What matter that she knew it wasn't true? There was a part of her that believed it was true, and as long as you believed that to be the case, it didn't really matter what you knew intellectually.

She had been the mother who lost her daughter and now she was the woman who saved a girl's life. She'd changed her definition. She'd changed who she was.

"Yes," she said. "I believe I did."

Chapter Forty-Seven

onday afternoon Livy was released from the hospital. She went to a hotel with her parents and Maggie went home and took the world's longest shower. Never had hot water felt so good. Then she went into her kitchen and the cats followed her down. They seemed sort of pleased to see her. She decided to get them some milk, and when she opened the refrigerator, she was astounded to see that it was full of casseroles.

The Deacons had been working like fiends. Dolly had made her special veal and bean casserole that was restaurant quality. Chris had made the best chocolate chip cookies in the world. The Faraday sisters were not great cooks, but they'd dropped off a hunk of cheese and some bread. Agnes dropped off an uncooked filet mignon that Maggie suspected she'd retrieved from Bethany's wedding. Barbara made a carrot cake frosted with buttercream icing. The Insomnia Club sent some coffee cake.

Shadow started licking her tail. She hinged her leg over her head and looked like a paper clip gone wrong.

Maggie called Helen.

"I have a ton of food. Would you and Edgar like to come over?"

"I don't know." She heard the guilt in Helen's voice, knew her to be a good and wounded person. Where there was love there was a solution. They would find it.

"Please," Maggie said. "I want to help. I can help. There has to be a way we can do this together."

"I feel so ashamed," Helen whispered.

"That is not a helpful word," Maggie replied.

"I know. I owe him more. He did good, didn't he?"

"He did very good. He saved my life. That's your boy. Now come. Please."

She'd just started to set the table when Livy and Nora and Linus and Graham showed up. "We were planning on going out to dinner," Linus said, but Maggie showed him her refrigerator and suggested that he stay. Having gone that far, she figured she should ask Walter as well. She hadn't seen him in a day, which felt like a while. Then Agnes called and said she'd heard that Maggie was having a dinner party. She'd bring a chicken.

Loaves and fishes, she thought.

She didn't have an official dining room, but by rearranging the furniture in her living room she could jerry-rig a sort of arrangement. She put out all the plates and then she saw Mr. Cavanaugh go by with his dog and invited him in as well.

"I'll play the piano," he said.

"How delightful."

Then Reverend Sunday came with her special ambrosia pudding, and they all assembled around the table and she said grace and then Walter tapped his wine glass and said he'd brought a special badge for Edgar. Would he come up and receive it? Edgar went to the head of the table with a posture that called up the ancient knights, and he shivered with excitement as Walter pinned the silver badge to his shirt.

"In recognition of extreme heroism," Walter said.

Then everyone wanted to know how Edgar had managed to untie Livy's knots and he went into a lengthy explanation and it seemed that he would be happy to act it out, but fortunately decided not to. He looked calmer, Maggie thought, and Helen looked calmer.

"You must be so proud of him," Agnes said, and Helen beamed and said, "I am."

She stroked his cheek. He leaned against her. His eyes drooped slightly, the way the cats did when she scratched their backs. "I didn't realize how special he was."

Maggie knew Helen had a hard road in front of her. Problems did not resolve themselves so quickly, generally, but perhaps this would give Helen the push she needed to go to the therapist. Sometimes people just needed a push in the right direction.

Then they ate and drank and at one point Livy stood up and said, "I'd like to make a toast to my Aunt Dove."

She stood there with her glass raised, eyes shining. She'd put on some make-up and she looked dramatic and slightly foreign. She was pale from the weekend's drama, but the spark in her eye showed she'd recovered.

"What can I say about my Aunt Dove? She took me in. She introduced me to Graham. She introduced me to adventure. Oh, and she saved my life."

Everyone cheered at that, and Maggie felt like she would soar through the roof. For just a moment she was sure she felt Juliet standing alongside her, clapping along with all the others.

Then Livy giggled and looked Maggie right in the eye. "I hope you won't mind, Aunt Dove, but I've been thinking I would love to come and stay in Darby for longer. I can get my Ph.D. at Columbia, and Graham is thinking of getting a degree in tree surgery."

That night, after everyone had gone, Maggie went into her kitchen and pulled out the family Bible. She took a moment to breathe in its familiar musty scent. Her mother had tended to this Bible, her grandmother, her great-grandmother. It went back in her family for generations and one of the most heart-breaking parts of losing Juliet was thinking that this whole line came to an end.

Now Maggie opened it to the genealogy page. There was Stuart's name, which she'd crossed out. She wrote his name again over that. She was going to cross out the word bigamist, but figured she'd let future generations figure out what had happened there. She looked at Juliet's name, which was stained with old tears. Then, alongside her name, where there was space for other children, she wrote Livy's name. She looked at it and it seemed so right. Why had she ever thought that love had to follow neat lines? Love overflowed, sometimes in uncomfortable ways. But love never stopped. That was the important thing.

Her doorbell rang. It was Walter. He would stay and watch *Jeopardy*. He would stay. She felt excited as she went to open the door.

THE END

Acknowledgements

Turns out it takes a couple of villages to write and publish a novel, and I'm very grateful to the people who populate mine.

Especially:

Keri Barnum of New Shelves Books, for her creativity and hard-work. Anna Gray, also of New Shelves, for her work on social media graphics and Maggie Dove trailers.

Mila (milagraphicartist.com) for the stunning book cover and Amit Dey for interior design.

Paula Munier, Amy Collins, Gina Panettieri and the rest of the fabulous team at Talcott Notch Literary. I could not ask for better advocates.

Dana Isaacson, for believing in Maggie Dove.

Alex Steele and Gotham Writers and all my friends/students. There's no better resource (or joy) for a writer than spending hours talking with other writers.

The mystery-writing world, which has been so much cozier than you would think. Special shout out to the kind souls at Mystery Writers of America, Malice Domestic and Miss Demeanors (missdemeanors.com) Also to Linda Landrigan and Jackie Sherbow, who've given Maggie Dove a chance to tell her stories at *Alfred Hitchcock's Mystery Magazine*. Thanks also to Dru Ann Love, for her kindness and wisdom.

My beautiful little village of Irvington-on-Hudson, which is not exactly Darby, but shares certain trees.

The Irvington Presbyterian Church, which has been a place of grace and hope for me. Special shout out to the IPC book club, which has shown me what readers look for when reading a book. Hugs to Chris and Rhett Omark, who have been Maggie Dove superfans from the start. And many, many thanks to Marge Hone, who was a huge help to me in getting this ready for publication.

Chris Canning and Patricia van Essche designed a magnificent website for me. www.susanjbreen.com

My circle of friends, most especially Melinda Feinstein, Terry Gillen, Leslie Mack & Robin Freedman, and Kay O'Keefe.

My family of Breens, Brennans, Bucks, Lujans, Murcotts, Turchettes and Zelonys (with a special hug for my brother, Rob). Much love to Rosey Singh and my friends at the Good Shepherd Agricultural Mission in India.

My treasures: Tom Breen and Lucy Gellman, Kathy, Alex and Savannah Brennan, and Chris Breen. My loved one, Will.

And my dear husband, Brad. Who is everything.

About the Author

Susan Breen is the author of the Maggie Dove mystery series, originally published by the Alibi digital imprint of Penguin Random House and now rereleased by Under the Oak Press. Her first novel, *The Fiction Class*, also published by Penguin Random House, won a Westchester Library Association Washington Irving Award for "readability, literary quality, and wide general appeal." Her short stories have been published in *Best American Nonrequired Reading*, as well as an assortment of magazines ranging from *American Literary Review* and *The Chattahoochee Review* to *Alfred Hitchcock's Mystery Magazine* and *Ellery Queen's Mystery Magazine*. She has a story forthcoming in the anthology *Murder Most Diabolical*. Susan teaches novel-writing and does editing work with Gotham Writers in Manhattan. She lives in the Hudson Valley with her husband, two sweet dogs (cockapoos) and two slightly opinionated cats. Her three children are flourishing elsewhere. You can find more information about her at www.susanjbreen.com.